BAY OF *Refuge*

BAY OF *Refuge*

Restored

Part 3

Mary E. Hanks

www.maryehanks.com

Suzanne D. Williams Cover Design:

www.feelgoodromance.com/

Cover photos: micromonkey @ iStock; vernonwiley @ iStock

Author photo: Ron Quinn

Visit Mary's website:

www.maryehanks.com

You can write Mary at

maryhanks@maryehanks.com.

For Charles,

aka Dad or Lanny,

Thank you for accepting my brothers

and me as your own and loving us.

For Jason,

You are still the one.

God is our refuge and strength, an ever-present help in trouble.

Psalm 94:19

Basalt Bay Residents

Paisley Grant – Daughter of Paul and Penny Cedars

Judah Grant – Son of Edward and Bess Grant

Paige Cedars – Paisley's younger sister/mom to Piper

Peter Cedars – Paisley' older brother/fishing in Alaska

Paul Cedars – Paisley's dad/widower

Edward Grant – Mayor of Basalt Bay/Judah's dad

Bess Grant – Judah's mom/Edward's wife

Aunt Callie – Paisley's aunt/Paul's sister

Maggie Thomas – owner of Beachside Inn

Bert Jensen – owner of Bert's Fish Shack

Mia Till – receptionist at C-MER

Craig Masters – Judah's supervisor at C-MER

Mike Linfield – Judah's boss at C-MER

Lucy Carmichael – Paisley's high school friend

Brian Corbin – Sheriff's deputy

Kathleen Baker – newcomer to Basalt Bay

Bill Sagle – pastor

Geoffrey Carnegie – postmaster/local historian

Casey Clemons – floral shop owner

Patty Lawton – hardware store owner

Brad Keifer – fisherman/school chum of Peter's

James Weston – Paul's neighbor

Penny Cedars – Paisley's mom/deceased

One

Paisley Grant clutched Judah's hand as she watched her sister, Paige, and Craig Masters standing across the street acting like a happy couple, or a family for that matter, until she couldn't bear to watch them anymore. She'd rather have saltwater poured into her eyes or be imprisoned in the pantry staring at her mother's ghastly abstract paintings than to see Paige with *that* man.

But what if they were married? What if Craig was the father of Paige's two-year-old daughter, Piper?

A bitter taste filled Paisley's mouth. She pivoted away from the scene in front of City Hall and glanced at Judah, her previously estranged husband with whom she was reconciling. Could he comprehend the horror she felt at the thought of Craig being her brother-in-law? How could she cope with the cad showing up at family gatherings? Christmas dinners? Ugh. Of course, Judah had his own grievances with the guy.

She glanced back as Craig tossed Piper into the air, then caught her. Piper squealed. Paige smiled up at Craig with such a sweet, loving expression that Paisley wanted to gag.

Even though it wasn't hot, her forehead dripped with sweat. Her lungs seemed to shrink into themselves, starving her of air. Why did her respiratory system rebel against her? Why couldn't she breathe while under duress the way normal people did?

Maybe she should leave Basalt instead of staying here. Why torment herself? If she kept living in this small town like she originally planned, how could she avoid Paige and Craig? How could she ignore the gossip that would circulate about them? Everyone knew everyone's business.

Exactly. Didn't her sister hear the rumors about Craig and Paisley running away together, three years ago? Hadn't the town's gossipmongers prattled about it within Paige's hearing? The tales were lies, but her sister should have recognized Craig as a man not to be trusted. Someone to avoid in the co-parenting department.

Although, anyone could be blindsided by kindness, right? Even Paisley had been taken off guard when Craig jumped in and helped with Dad's high blood sugar incident four days ago. He may have even saved Dad's life and, in doing so, almost convinced her of his sincerity. *Almost.*

Just thinking of how she had to coexist with Craig during that dreadful time caused tension to strangle her airway. Her inhalation became raspy. A burning sensation crawled up her breastbone. A familiar weight of anxiety pressed down on her chest. She snagged Judah's gaze. *"Help!"* she tried to communicate.

"You okay?" He slid his arm over her shoulder and pulled her to his side.

His closeness, his caring attitude, should have reassured her that everything would be okay. That they could face whatever life threw their way together. Instead, she gritted her teeth and fought the urge to call for a Lyft to transport her away from Basalt. Maybe go to Florence or Coos Bay. But turning her back on him a second time? Hurting him when they just reconnected, when only today she promised to marry him again? He didn't deserve that. She wasn't heartless, either, no matter what her dad said about her being good at running.

In fact, his accusation from earlier made her want to stay and prove him wrong. That's right! New resolve coursed through her. No way was she leaving. She'd stand her ground and show Dad, Judah, and everyone else in this small-minded town that she came back to make things right.

Inhale. Exhale.

As if he sensed her panic, Judah wrapped both of his arms around her and pulled her against his chest. She pressed her cheek next to his sweatshirt, closing her eyes to the scene she was appalled and mesmerized by. She breathed in his warmth and pleasant male scent. He held her to him, not saying anything, just stroking her back. Mumbling something, maybe praying.

Was it only an hour ago when he dropped to his knee in the mud and asked her to marry him again? And she joined him on the sidewalk, kissing him like a woman wildly in love. Her world felt righted. God smiled on her. She and Judah were better together than they ever would be apart—that's what he told her, right?

But then *this* happened. Paige and Craig and Piper. But wouldn't there always be a *this*? Life was a sea of turbulence with trials, problems, and regrets hitting her like waves crashing into the rocks. While she succumbed to fear and panic, how did everyone else cope? She took a deep breath, trying to rein in her focus and her crazy, mixed-up emotions.

She leaned back and noticed a troubled expression on Judah's face. Was he avoiding her gaze? Why? He didn't know about Paige and Craig before today, did he? What if he knew all along and didn't tell her? No, surely not. But what if—?

She staggered backward. Her skin felt on fire. She set her palm on her chest, unable to draw in a full breath.

"Paisley?" His face contorted. "What is it? What can I do?" He tugged on her arms as if to draw her closer to him again. Like that would solve everything. *If only.*

She shook her head, holding out her free hand for him to stay back.

"Paisley? Do you hear me?" His words sounded tinny and far away.

She glanced toward City Hall again. Paige took the little girl from Craig's arms and pointed in their direction.

"Unca Dzuda!" Piper pulsed her hand, lunging her body up and down while somehow managing to remain in her mother's arms.

Judah waved and smiled. He seemed so accepting and nonjudgmental. Far from how she felt.

The engagement ring slid down her finger, and she twisted it back and forth. She fell for Judah again so quickly during the chaos of the hurricane and Dad's illness. Was she too hasty? She swallowed hard. No, she wasn't having second thoughts. She wanted to marry him. Loved him.

It was just …

A tightness in her stomach raced headlong into her chest, strangling her throat, pinching her esophagus like seaweed caught around the prop of an outboard. She sucked in dry, useless air, needing more oxygen. Maybe if she went to the beach, got away from Craig and Paige—Judah, too, if only for a few minutes—and breathed in the sea air, she'd feel better.

"I'm sorry. I just—" She turned away and rushed down the muddy sidewalk, dodging debris left over from Hurricane Blaine, hoping Judah didn't hate her for running from him. Her boots slipped in the few inches of dirty water lingering on the street from the storm surge. She didn't acknowledge any of the utility workers who were laboring over electrical wires and mending telephone poles.

"Paisley!"

Judah wouldn't be able to keep up with her with his bum leg. Although, even she couldn't run as fast as normal with her struggling oxygen intake. She nearly tripped going down the boulders to the beach below street level.

Once she reached the sand, she trudged along at a steady pace. To her left, the waves pounded the beach, crashing against the rocks. Beyond the cove, a fishing boat chugged past. On the peninsula, sea-foam exploded in pulsating repetitions and, as if they had a homing instinct, her boots turned in that direction.

"Paisley! Wait up."

She pushed herself to stay ahead of him, leaping over and around the surf dancing up and down the seashore. The closer she got to *Peter's Land*, the rocky point she dubbed in honor of her brother as a kid, the easier she breathed. Her lungs expanded naturally. The sea air was healthy for her. Another reason to stay in Basalt, right?

A few hours ago, Judah suggested that they come down to the peninsula and check on it. Although he said they wouldn't walk on it, nothing was stopping her from reaching her destination now. Not Judah's voice. Not even her own inner warning system telling her that it might be dangerous.

Sitting on the tip of the peninsula with seawater bursting over her might be exactly what she needed. Maybe then she could figure out how to live around her sister and Craig without going mad.

The idyllic beauty of the ocean usually filled her with peace. Would that happen today?

Two

Judah stomped down the beach after Paisley, but he couldn't keep up, thanks to his limp. Not that his reaching her any sooner would stop her from doing what she seemed determined to do. But he wanted to be with her in case something bad happened. Like her fainting, again, or slipping on the wet rocks.

In her haste to reach the point of the peninsula, she probably wasn't considering that the long, narrow land mass was unstable after Hurricane Blaine. No one should charge past the gaping holes left by the storm six days ago. Yet, he witnessed her panic. He knew she'd seek sanctuary on the unsafe boulders. And even if he yelled her name until his face turned as gray as a sea lion's, she wouldn't listen to him.

How they went from kissing, talking about a vow renewal ceremony, to her running from him as if he were at fault for the situation back there with Craig and Paige, he didn't get. *Women.* He tromped around a tidal pool, chewing on his agitation.

If only she ran to him instead of away from him. If only she could find refuge in their love. What husband didn't want to be an anchor for his wife to depend on? Sure, being her North Star, her everything, would feed his ego. Might make him feel better about himself after their three-year separation, and all that may or may not have happened in Chicago that they still hadn't discussed.

He groaned.

But she needed far more than his inflated male ego and his desire for her to want him. She needed healing and restoration and a peace only God could give. She needed a Savior. Something Judah could never be. Never wanted to be. But that didn't stop him from wishing he was the one she leaned on, the one she desired as a husband, and not the one she ran from.

He stepped over a chunk of driftwood, not breaking his stride, and watched his wife scurrying down the beach. Maybe his father-in-law was correct about his daughter being good at running. At the time, he sounded heartless. Now Judah wondered. Thinking of Paisley being a runaway bride was torture. Would she keep doing this? His footfall stumbled. Should he keep chasing after her?

Ugh.

Of course, he would. He was her husband, legally and at heart. He loved her. Hadn't he asked her to marry him again? He'd follow her to the ends of the earth or Chicago or wherever she might run until she sprinted back into his arms. But how long would it be until she embraced him as her husband?

A pain burned in his chest that had more to do with his emotions than the way he pushed himself to trudge through the sand on his sore leg. He stepped wide to avoid crushing a crab scuttling for shelter. Running from him too? Did he have that effect on everyone? He groaned again.

Not far ahead, Paisley reached the cluster of boulders extending into the cove and climbed upward. If something happened, it would take him precious minutes to get out to the point.

She'd tell him he was being silly for worrying. That after living here for twenty-five years, she knew her way around the coastal rocks. Still, the boulders were slick from saltwater pouring over them. Although, not any slicker than last time. *Last time?* A breath caught in his throat. That day she fainted, and he barely got to her in time. He pushed himself to go faster.

There, she reached the top and seemed steady. A surge of waves barreled against the peninsula, bursting water and froth into the air. For the slightest second, she glanced back, a hint of a smile on her lips. He held his breath as she skirted the gaping places where large boulders that he labeled Samples C and D for his reports had been before the hurricane. Just as she reached the farthest point, where narrow rocks extended into the sea, white spray erupted into the air and fell over her like a waterfall. The scene looked magical, but he knew the dangers.

He reached the pile of boulders and clambered up. Since he'd been climbing these rocks for a couple of decades, he instinctively knew where to place the soles of his boots.

Out on the point, Paisley dropped down onto what he knew to be her favorite perch on a chunk of basalt. Even from here, he saw the waves rolling up, splashing onto her lap.

He braced himself as he climbed, battling wind gusts that nearly knocked him backwards. He stretched his hands out, balancing himself. Once he reached the top of the peninsula, he headed toward the point. "Paisley!" He yelled so she'd hear him over the sound of the surf.

She glanced back, met his gaze for a half-second. A foaming, powerful wave crashed against the rock she sat on. Water splashed over her, arcing and cascading downward. She lifted both hands into the spray of saltwater, laughing. A dazzling array of droplets shimmered in the sunlight around her. The beautiful, mesmerizing sight made him pause.

With her hands uplifted, water pouring over her, he felt drawn to her like steel to a magnet. She was the woman he wanted to be with for the rest of his life. He'd do anything to bridge the gap between them, to make her feel safe, and to help her life be better. Starting with staying by her side. Mentally, he fortified himself for getting soaking wet and freezing cold in the next few steps.

"I'm going to sit by you now." He warned her so she didn't get startled when he dropped down beside her on the narrow place.

Another blast of water showered over her as Judah came closer, soaking him too. He gasped, even though he told himself to be ready for it. He lowered himself next to her as another icy spray cascaded over them. He inhaled sharply.

Paisley swiped seawater off her face. "Isn't this amazing?"

"Uh-huh." Judah blinked hard to rid his eyeballs of the sting of saltwater. He shuffled closer to her, making sure he didn't slip and pull her into the drink with him. "How are you?" he asked when the waves receded.

"Better now."

"Glad to hear it." He took a risk and draped his arm over her shoulder. He wanted to keep her safe, but he also needed ballast for his precarious position. They sat for a few minutes with the sea dancing about them. Each rush of water felt a little less frigid and invasive. Either he was adapting to the chill of waves splashing over him, or his body had become numb to the jarring cold.

Paisley leaned against him as if drawing warmth from him and into herself. Water droplets running down her face, she met his gaze. Her deep dark eyes sparkling in his direction made him want to lean in and kiss her. He didn't, but he wanted to.

"I'm sorry for running from you."

Her words soothed the ache in his chest. "You're with me now. That's all that matters." Even if it meant getting drenched and shivering with ridiculous tremors. He clenched his teeth to stop them from chattering. Hardly effective.

"Did you know about Paige and Craig? Before, I mean."

It was difficult to hear her over the sounds of the surf.

"What? No. Of course not. Paisley, I couldn't believe they were together."

She stared at him for several heartbeats. He held her gaze, hoping she knew she could trust him. Another wave hit them. They both gasped and sputtered.

"I thought maybe you knew and kept it from me."

"Why would I do that? I thought Craig and Mia might be together."

"Why?"

"The way she giggles when she talks about him." Although, the receptionist for Coastal Management and Emergency Responders—called C-MER—acted flirtatious toward Judah, too. Good thing he already told Paisley about that.

"I couldn't stand it." She gazed toward open waters. "Seeing my sister with the man who—" She coughed then buried her face in his sweatshirt. She trembled in his arms. He held her but, due to his soaked condition, couldn't offer her much warmth.

Another spray arched over them and he closed his eyes. Lifting his face, droplets fell on his cheeks. When he opened his eyelids and brushed the moisture away, Paisley watched him.

"Thank you."

"For what?"

"For following me. Even when I thought I didn't want you to. Even when I pushed you away."

At least she realized she did that. If only she grasped how much he wanted them to be together, sharing their lives. Yet, her propensity to run was disconcerting. Something for him to pray about in the coming days.

Three

After another saltwater shower, Paisley shook her head to clear her ears and face of water. She met Judah's gaze, feeling calmer now. Drenched, but calmer. "Thanks for staying with me. For not pummeling me with advice. I get enough of that from Aunt Callie."

"And Maggie Thomas." He wiped his left hand over his wet dripping hair. "What advice would I have? I don't know what you're going through."

"Exactly."

"But—"

"No, don't ruin it!" But her curiosity got the better of her. "Okay. But what?"

He gave her one of his sweet smiles. The kind that curled her toes in her boots. He stroked his cool palm down her wet cheek, his gaze holding hers captive. She didn't move.

"I wish—" Water dripped from Judah's hair, rolling down his face and landing in his six-day-old beard. His pale cheeks looked concave from the cold. He licked his bluish lips, which made her think back to when they kissed such a short time ago. "Okay."

"Okay?" Did she miss something?

"I wish … when you felt the urge to run … you'd find strength and courage in me, your husband. The man who loves you more than any person in the world." He swallowed like doing so hurt. "I'm here for you, Pais. Honest, I am. But I'm no superhero. I'll make mistakes." More water crashed over them. "But I promise you … I'm going to be by your side, doing the best I can for you as long as we both shall live." His words sounded like vows.

A spray of water hit them, splashing into their faces. They both spat and sputtered.

His words replayed in her mind. Wait. Did he think she expected him to mend their past? To fix them. Of course, he couldn't. Even she couldn't do that. Hadn't she tried? At least, he was being honest and real about their flaws. About her need for more than he could offer.

He said he wanted her to run to him, but was he strong enough to hear her heart? Her struggles? What if the doubts and failings she wrestled with drove them further apart? Maybe she could show him that she was trying to reach out to him, too, by sharing something honest and being vulnerable. That's what he wanted, right?

She cleared her throat. "When I saw Paige with Craig, I wanted to get away from them, away from my thoughts and anxieties. I'm sorry, but part of me still wants to run."

He let out a long sigh. Perhaps, an accepting sigh.

"I thought of heading south and going somewhere on the coast." She wiped seawater off her face. "I never want to be far from the Pacific again. Maybe Coos Bay."

"Paisley." He groaned.

She clenched her jaw. How could she be honest with him if she couldn't talk about the deepest parts of her soul? Her fears, grief, and even her urge to run.

She imagined a set in a movie with a closet so crammed full of junk that when the actor opened it, the items exploded into the room. Just like what her hidden emotions might do if they were ever exposed. Maybe that's why she ran three years ago and why she wanted to run now—to escape the truths and lies she stuffed away for so long.

Could she remarry Judah and jump back into the same existence she ran from? She found such joy in falling in love with him again. In reveling in his kisses. Imagining their honeymoon. But in her honest-to-goodness life, could a Cedars and a Grant have a forever kind of happiness? It didn't work before. Were they making a terrible mistake again? Anxiety twisted knots in her stomach. She had to move, or run, or—

"I have to go." She jumped up.

"Paisley?" Her name sounded wrenched from his lips. Raw pain zagged across his face. "You're not … not going to leave me again, are you?"

She told herself she wouldn't. "I was a horrible wife to you before." She shuddered at the picture of her midnight escape. "You don't deserve the same fate." She yanked off the diamond ring and held it out between her trembling thumb and index finger. The shock and agony on his face made her ashamed. "I'm so sorry." Why did she agree to his proposal? She could have saved him this misery. Her too. "You're a good man. I'm the one who's messed up. I can't drag you through another marriage. Through another possible failed r-romance."

"You are n-not a horrible w-wife. Never." He clasped her free hand. "W-we went through a crisis. We both lost our footing. I want you back. You!"

His humility, his not blaming her, his still wanting her, was tender and beautiful. Yet her fingers continued to extend the engagement ring.

He wobbled to a standing position on the rocks beside her. "I want you as you are, Paisley. We still love each other." He laid his palms on her cheeks, staring into her eyes.

Oh, Judah. Love wasn't the issue. How to live as husband and wife, talking heart to heart, exposing the deepest parts of themselves without judgment or rejection, that's what they failed at.

He dropped his hands, closing them around her fingers clutching the ring. He probably feared it might fall into the ocean. She didn't want that, either.

"Please, keep it. Give us time. Everything's going to work out, you'll see." His facial expression relaxed.

She almost agreed, but then another round of waves burst over them. She slid the ring back onto her finger. Better safe than falling into Davy Jones's Locker.

"Don't make a hasty decision and break up with me because you're upset with Paige." He shouted over the noise of the wind and waves.

His words felt like a slap. He assumed she was ending their engagement because of her sister's stupid decisions? Her core heated up. Inner fumes raced to her temples.

She jerked backwards. Too late she realized what she did.

Four

Judah watched in horror as Paisley tripped over a rock and fell backwards into the sea. "Paisley!" He lunged for her flailing hands but missed her fingers. In seconds she disappeared beneath the churning waves.

He screamed her name again and fought to remove his boots. His frozen hands made his movements clumsy. Where was she? When she didn't bob to the surface, he took a deep breath and executed a shallow dive into the waves. Frigid water encapsulated him like an icy tomb, leeching the warmth from his body. He froze, rebelling against the cold. But he forced himself to swim, begging his limbs to obey, and fought the current. He surfaced and gasped, drawing in gulps of air. Not seeing her, he plunged into the darkness again.

He couldn't recognize anything beneath the surface. Only blurry, nonhuman shadows. How far did the undertow take her? He kicked and flailed his arms, thrusting his hands outward, desperate to touch her hair or clothing. He didn't feel anything but churning water rushing past him. In desperate need of air, he lunged for the surface again. Gasping in great gulps of air, he bobbed in circles, searching the troughs of waves where a person might be hidden. He floated on a crest, then got thrown backward by the powerful tug of the surf.

He ignored the freezing, gnawing cold and kept thrashing about in the sea, constantly moving as he hunted for her. "Paisley!" A mouthful of saltwater gagged him. He coughed and nearly choked. He shouted again. Just about to dive beneath the roiling waves, he heard a sound. A voice.

"J-u-u-d-d-a-ah."

He turned around 180 degrees, following the direction where he thought he heard her. A swell crashed over him, submerging him, blinding him. Was that his one chance to find her? No! He couldn't lose her. He kicked frantically, begging God in silent pleas. *Save her. Help me find her.*

Some twenty feet away, her hand bobbed into the air. But then, the bubbling sea swallowed her. He swam the breaststroke harder than he ever had, his breathing raspy as his arms and legs sliced through the water. With each arm rotation he combatted the waves, the frigid cold, and his fears. *I will find her. She will be safe. God, help us!* He repeated the phrases in time to the throbbing of his heart. As he swam, his weighted clothes pulled him downward as if dragging him to the ocean floor. He wouldn't succumb. Would battle to reach his wife and save her.

Was that—? Yes, blue fabric. Her sweatshirt. It disappeared. A mirage? An optical trick? No, he saw something. "Paisley! Hold on!"

Despite his exhaustion, he swam toward her, hammering the surface with his arms and kicking his legs until his limbs felt numb. Useless.

He raised his head and took a breath. There she was! Not far away, she floated on her back, her arms crossed over her chest. Hallelujah! It was a good thing she knew the basics of survival in the sea. That it didn't take extreme cold to get hypothermia—just colder than normal body temperature. If Judah felt the sluggish weight in his limbs, she had to feel it worse since she had been underwater longer than him.

The next time he glanced up, she jerked, her hands flailing, then she vanished into a wretched whirlpool like a monster yanked her feet straight down beneath her.

"Paaaaaaissssssleeeey!"

With the peninsula jutting into the bay, opposing currents sometimes created a dangerous powerhouse of swirling water capable of dragging a victim into its vortex. How would he pull her out? He didn't have lifesaving gear. No one lined the beach to help with forming a human chain.

Paisley's life depended on his quick action. And God's intervention. *Please.*

He swam straight into the churning waters. At the outer boundary of the bubbling cylindrical shape, the downward pull nearly tore off his pants. The swirling whirlpool jerked him, yanking and twisting him, a prisoner in its clutches. Terror pressed in on him, squeezing him, as the sea yanked him downward. Could he even survive? Was he too late to rescue Paisley?

Fighting the crushing forces, he flung his hands outward, searching for her. But the monstrous ocean hurled him in circles, trouncing him like a broken toy. Down he went, deeper into the dregs of the whirlpool, a mountain of water almost overpowering him. Soon he wouldn't be able to hold the breath in his mouth. His air gone. *Lord Jesus.*

Then thud. He rammed into something. Someone. Before

he could grab hold of hair or limbs, she was snatched away—it had to be her. *Paisley! My love.* He flailed his hands and kicked his feet. There. Hair. Face. Fingers. He wanted to sob but couldn't. He grabbed hold of her body, none too gently, clenching his limbs around her limp form like an octopus.

He tried to feel her neck for a pulse. An impossibility. He must get her to the surface. But going straight up into the whirlpool would be deadly. They had to go even deeper, which could also be fatal. He let go of her with one hand, then shoved his palm upward against the sea, repeating the motion, pressing against the waters, forcing them lower into the ocean.

His head felt like it might explode from the pressure. Then, sensing a reprieve from the whirling oppressive monster, he lurched sideways, still holding Paisley and kicking with all his might. He prayed he wouldn't let go of her, begging God to save them and for his air to last.

Once they were far enough out from the whirlpool's grasp, he kicked hard to the surface. *Hold on. We're almost there.* He broke free of the water, coughing and gasping, drawing in ragged breaths. Air never tasted so sweet.

"Paisley!" Still limp. He pressed his fingers against her neck, kicking to keep them afloat. There, a pulse, maybe. He had to get her to shore. The waves were too rough to perform lifesaving procedures. He rolled onto his back, drawing her with him, as water splashed over them. He swam as hard as he could with one hand and held onto her with the other. His energy failing, he let his body ride the waves toward the peninsula.

Suddenly, she jerked and gasped, shoving against his chest. *Thank God!* She was alive! She coughed and vomited, but he held her and kept swimming toward shore. When she swung her elbows, fighting him as if he were the enemy dragging her to her death, he called out to her. "It's m-me, P-Paisley. I've got you."

"I c-can swim on my own. Let go." She glared back at him. "Let go of me."

She looked so pale. Every protective fiber within him balked at the idea of releasing her. If she swam on her own, she might get dragged back into the whirlpool.

"L-let g-go, Judah!" She kicked him, her legs getting tangled with his.

"Okay. But I'm staying right beside you." She went unconscious before. It might happen again. Did she have hypothermia? He'd watch her closely. "If you feel too weak, hold onto me."

She gave him a slight nod.

Together, side by side, they swam toward the northwest side of the peninsula. The pounding waves propelled them forward, almost too fast. At the last second, he wrapped his arms around her to shield her from getting dashed against the rocks. She crawled onto the shore on her hands and knees, the water pounding over her. She collapsed on the rocks, panting. Her dark eyes stared at him dully as he climbed up beside her.

"You okay?" His legs shook. So did his shoulders and arms. He collapsed beside her, gasping and spitting and breathing hard.

She closed her eyes.

"Paisley, stay awake!" He smoothed his hand over her face, feeling her cold clammy skin against his fingers. "Paisley, stay with me, please." His insides felt ragged, his lungs burning from the physical strain he endured, and his heart aching from the emotional turmoil of nearly losing her. "Pais?" He rubbed her shoulder gently.

"I'm okay."

"Thank God. I'm so glad you're okay."

"M-me t-too."

Now to get her warm and dry. Where were his boots? He needed his boots. He checked around the rocks. Didn't see them. The waves must have dragged them out to sea. Great. Now he had to walk to Paige's, carrying Paisley, in his drenched socks. Or barefooted. He was exhausted too. But he'd do whatever was necessary to get her to warmth and safety.

She still lay on the rocks, her body shivering. Placing his hand on her back, he felt it rise and fall slowly. Even with shallow breaths, hearing her inhaling and exhaling comforted him. "Pais? Can you hear me?"

She didn't answer.

He ran through the list of hypothermia markers. Shivering. Slurred speech. She had stuttered. Shallow breathing. Yep. Weak pulse. He touched two fingers to her neck. Slow. She was drowsy and energy-less. Lost consciousness in the water. Confusion? Maybe. To be on the safe side, he'd move her gently so as not to trigger irregular heartbeats that could bring on cardiac arrest.

"Paisley, we have to find warmth. You need to get dry."

She squinted like the sun was too bright, instead of seeing the gray overcast sky above them.

"D-did you f-fall in?" She pointed at his socks leaving a trail of wetness.

Didn't she remember? Confusion. Memory loss. Check. Check. He needed to get her to Paige's fast. Maybe take her to the ER. "C'mon, Pais, stand up. No sudden movements."

She lifted her head in increments. As her torso came off the rock, he wrapped his arms around her, pulling her against his chest.

"You're cold and w-wet." She shivered.

"Both of us are." He gritted his teeth to stop them from chattering. A wind gust hit them, and he held onto her.

"*Thatssss fuuunny.*"

"What is?"

"The air *blowwwing upmynossse.*" She slurred the words together.

"Can you walk?" If not, how would he carry her across the rocky peninsula without tripping in his socks? Hefting her over his shoulder might endanger her more. "If you can't walk, I'll carry you. But you should try walking on your own."

"I can w-walk, *silllly.*" She snorted.

"You're wet and freezing. You might have—" No use alarming her. Taking her right hand with his right hand, he led her forward while he kept his left arm braced across her back.

Fortunately, he took a proactive stance. She stumbled a couple of times. Once, she would have landed back in the water if he wasn't guiding her. They trudged slowly across the rocks. He shook so hard he couldn't walk straight, but she trembled even worse. Something fierce gripped him inside his chest. He had to protect her, keep her safe.

Just as they reached the parking lot, she went limp, almost sinking to the ground. He caught her and scooped her up. His footfall somewhat unsteady, he kept his stride aimed toward the subdivision where blankets and dry clothes awaited.

"W-where you t-taking m-me?" She squinted at him.

"Paige's."

"No." She swayed in his arms, fighting his hold. "*Pleeeeassssse,* no."

"We have to get to Paige's. Our stuff is there."

"I *donnntwanna* go there." She made a moaning sound. She

slid from his arms, pushing her palms against him. She wobbled, nearly falling over, but he held onto her. "That way to m-my d-dad's." She pointed a shaking finger toward town.

"We have to change our clothes at your sister's." He tugged on her hand, leading her with him. He felt the stitches in his leg pinch. His limbs must be getting more sensation into them now.

"I w-want t-to go to my dad's." Teeth chattering, she clutched the fabric of his sweatshirt. "Please, Judah?"

How could he refuse her anything after what they'd just experienced? "Fine. But it will be a longer walk." During the storm, the stairs exploded at Paul's. How would he get up to the second story to get clothes and blankets?

He scooped her up again.

"Judah—"

"Just stay quiet." He heard the gruff tone of his voice, but it couldn't be helped. He was fatigued and worried. Carrying her was the safest way to get her to Paul's.

His wet pant legs rubbed against each other as he passed the community church. His dripping socks hung off his toes by a couple of inches. In his arms, Paisley's frame shook. She hadn't spoken in a while. "Paisley." He jostled her in his arms. "You awake?"

She groaned. At least she was conscious enough to respond.

Tonight, he'd monitor her breathing and make sure she warmed up slowly. The old method of using a naked body to warm up a victim with low body temperature crept through his mind. From his C-MER training, he knew a patient with mild hypothermia should warm up with passive rewarming, not with direct heat. He would search for thick blankets. Borrow some from James Weston, Paul's neighbor, if he had to.

If her condition worsened, he'd drive her to the ER in Florence. Or, now that the road was accessible, he could call for an emergency vehicle. Since they still didn't have electricity, he'd plug his cell phone into the truck's lighter ASAP.

When they reached the house, he would have to do something Paisley might not like—might even be mad about. His first task was getting her out of her wet clothes.

Then he'd start warming her up.

Five

Paisley was stuck in a horrible dream. The ocean kept grabbing her, twisting her, sucking her down into a dark whirling tunnel. Then it hurled her body along the waves like a bouncing ball. The nightmare played over and over until she awoke with a start. Breathing heavily, she thrashed her arms, fighting whatever held her down. She clawed at the fabric around her body but couldn't free herself. Where was she? She stared wide-eyed at the ceiling. Dad's?

What pinned her arms? Did the sea mummify her? She glanced downward at what appeared to be swaddling blankets. Even her head was wrapped in a cocoon of some sort. The only exposed part was her face. The blanket brushed against her bare skin on her legs and stomach. She drew in a breath. Bare skin? Where were her clothes? Who took them off?

Inside the blankets, she skimmed her palms down her torso. Warm skin. Damp underwear. Whew. At least she still wore her panties and bra. She rotated her shoulders in the cramped space. Just barely able to wiggle her fingers and toes, it appeared everything worked. Why was she in her dad's living room? She couldn't remember anything after—

Oh. She fell into the sea. Was drowning. Swallowing water. Judah rescued her. Brought her here because she didn't want to go to Paige's. Then what?

The mattress rocked beneath her like a rowboat adrift on the ocean. Must be an air mattress. She turned her head to the left and found Judah's blue eyes staring back at her. All but his face was covered up, too.

"How are you?" His voice sounded scratchy.

Why were they sharing the same bed? "Are we married?" Did they have their vow renewal ceremony and she forgot? They planned to wait—she knew that much.

"Of course, we're married." He smiled in a lazy way. "I married you seven years ago, remember? You're still my wife."

"But, um, not again? We didn't—"

"Not yet." His grin infuriated her.

She huffed. "Then why are you in bed with me?"

"Would you have me sleep on the floor?"

"Maybe."

He snickered. The air mattress swayed up and down as he rotated onto his side. "How are you this morning, other than inquisitive?"

"Grumpy. Tired." And, yes, curious. She eased her hands upward until they reached beyond the blankets. "I feel like a mummy."

"Me too." His cheek rested on his pillow. The way his gaze danced, she half expected him to lean in and kiss her good morning. "Do you remember anything about yesterday?" He stared at her intently. Maybe checking her pupils.

"Um, you asked me to marry you."

"Yes, I did." His smile grew wider.

"I … I kissed you." The words caught in her throat. If their kissing only happened in her dreams, she'd be so embarrassed for mentioning it.

"Yes"—the word came out breathy—"you did. And?"

"Paige and Craig …" The thoughts she tried to escape yesterday flooded back. "I ran from them. From you." She scrunched up her shoulders. "I had a bad dream about the ocean trying to kill me." She attempted to sit up, but the blankets pinned her down. Then she remembered her lack of clothing. "Did you undress me?"

"I had to." He explained about the rescue and his borrowing the air mattress from James. "Can you wiggle your toes?"

"Yes, I tested them."

"Fingers?" He wiggled his.

"Yep."

"Good. We survived another crisis." He sighed. "The Lord rescued you again."

"Apparently, He used you."

Judah's face hued red.

"I don't remember you taking off my things. What about your clothes?"

"Came off too."

So they were lying side by side, both nearly naked, and she hadn't even known?

"I was a complete gentleman."

"Hmm. Any plans for getting our dry stuff?"

"James will bring over a ladder." Judah nodded toward the ceiling. "Then I'll go up and dig around for some warm things."

"Good." She tried sitting up again but fell back on the mattress. "Can you help me?" This was ridiculous not being able to move on her own steam.

"Sure." He bobbed to a sitting position, wiggling the whole mattress as he freed himself. The blankets fell away from his bare chest.

She stared at the dark hair on his upper torso before tearing her gaze away. Goodness. She saw him without a shirt before. However, by her sudden heart palpitations, she might be more ready for their vow renewal ceremony than she realized. Or maybe that dip in the sea and Judah's rescue made her a little lovesick.

Sliding his hand beneath her back, he lifted her upper body with his arm. She folded in half like a taco. "Ugh."

He unwound some of the blankets, stopping before she became too exposed. She weakly clutched the blue fabric about herself, lacking energy. Lying back down seemed the smartest thing to do.

"You okay?"

His concerned expression brought back a memory. Real or a dream? She glanced at her hand, relieved to see the engagement ring. Why did she think it might be gone?

"I wondered if I lost your ring." She thought of it as his ring. Not necessarily hers. She gave up her ring a few years ago to pay the rent in Chicago. He was a sweetheart to give her another one.

"I asked you to put it back on." He stared at the wall across from them.

"Back on?"

He wrapped a blanket around his shoulders, covering his chest. "You wanted to give it back. End things between us."

"No way. Why would I do that?"

"You panicked again." His eyebrows dipped. "You thought we wouldn't work a second time when things ended badly the first time."

"Oh, Judah." Some hazy part of her memory lined up with his rendition of yesterday's troubles.

He scooted to the edge of the mattress with the blanket wrapped around him. "You asked why I'm beside you in bed. I watched and made sure you breathed okay through the night."

"You watched over me all night?" Her face flushed.

"Off and on. I checked your pulse. Made sure the blankets were snug." He stretched his eyes, squinting, then blinking. "Around four, I dozed off." He yawned.

And she planned to break things off with this man who dove into the water to save her? The same one who risked his life to find her. What if he hadn't been willing to do that? She could be dead. Might be if not for the guy sitting in her bed with blankets draped about him.

"You are something, Judah Grant." Heaven forgive her selfishness. Ever since she came back to Basalt, this man had loved her, shown her grace and goodness. How could she consider walking away? Return his ring? What a crazy notion. "I'm sorry for trying to give you back the ring."

His eyes filled with moisture. "I just want us." His hand left his blanket and found hers. He drew the ring on her finger toward his mouth and kissed it. "Forever." His vow?

Whatever she contemplated about breaking up with him was petty and stupid and far from how she felt now. "I want that too."

He didn't cross the small distance between them to kiss her. His shining gaze said he wanted to. Was he waiting for

38

a signal from her? Permission? Or was he still acting like the perfect gentleman?

Fatigue and confusion made her thoughts fuzzy. She laid back down, wrapping herself up in the comforter. He snuggled one of his blankets over her. She closed her eyes. Must have dozed.

The last thought on her mind was of herself sashaying down an aisle dressed in a pretty white gown. Maybe that dream could still come true.

Six

When Judah reached the back door to Paige's, he didn't bother wringing out his socks. Earlier, when he got James's ladder and climbed up into his father-in-law's bedroom, he found a flannel shirt and a pair of pants that were too short. He still wore them, and left Paisley jeans and a shirt too. Since she was asleep, he hustled over here to grab their things and get back before she woke up.

He knocked, then entered. "Hello? Judah, here."

"I'm in the living room."

He followed Paul's voice. The older man sat in the recliner with his feet propped up. "Where's Paisley?" Paul adjusted his glasses, squinting. "Where did you two stay last night?"

An unexpected rush of guilt hit Judah. Was his father-in-law accusing him of doing something wrong? He and Paisley were married even though they had been separated. Besides, they only slept on the same air mattress. Even when he took off her clothes, he did it with the utmost care and in fear for her life. The same way he would have performed a cold-water emergency rescue for anyone. Well, maybe not *the same* as for anyone. He took extreme care of her. His Paisley. His wife.

Lying next to her this morning, he disciplined himself not to kiss her. Not to scoot close. Not to want more. Yet, he couldn't deny his eagerness for them to exchange vows and renew their commitment to their marriage. Then loving her completely would be the greatest gift imaginable.

For now, he'd be patient. Wooing her. Waiting for her to want to be with him as much as he wanted to be with her. However, that day couldn't come fast enough.

Paul stared at him with a stern expression, apparently still awaiting his answer.

"Oh, um, er, we stayed at your house. James lent us an air mattress. I set it up in the living room."

"Oh?" Another frown.

"Paisley may have had a mild case of hypothermia."

Paul shoved himself off the chair. "Is she okay?"

"She's sleeping now. If she shows any signs of distress, I'll take her to the ER."

"What happened? How did she get so cold?" Paul ran his palms over both his arms as if he felt a sudden chill, too.

"We went out on the peninsula." Judah shrugged. It wasn't his place to tell Paul about the anger Paisley felt over Paige being with Craig. However, there wasn't any harm in explaining about the accident. "We were talking. She stepped backwards. Lost her balance and fell in the water. She got sucked into one of those whirlpools."

"No." Paul wiped his nose. "I never would have expected such a thing. She's been near the sea for most of her life. Knows the current. Swims good." He shook his head.

41

"It happened fast."

"You saved her?"

Judah nodded, shrugged, downplaying his part. "The good news is she's doing better. I warmed her up with plenty of blankets."

"Good, good." Paul rocked his thumb toward the hall. "You here for your bags? They're by the bathroom."

"Thanks." Judah took several steps, then paused. "I asked her to marry me again."

"You did?" A wide smile crinkled Paul's face. "Why, Son, that's the best news I've heard in years." He lumbered toward Judah, then embraced him and patted his back. "How did my daughter take your proposal?"

"She said yes." Judah's face stretched into a huge grin. No reason to mention that she almost gave him back the ring.

"Maybe I'll get more grandchildren now, hmm?"

Um, well, did Paisley even want kids? After a couple of first trimester miscarriages, then losing Misty Gale at six months into the pregnancy, would she be brave enough to try again? Would he? A knot formed in his stomach.

He excused himself to locate his and Paisley's bags. Right next to their stuff, someone had placed his shoes. Perfect. He dug through his belongings for a pair of dry socks, then slipped into the footwear. What a relief after trudging around in soaking wet, filthy socks.

He grabbed the wet clothes they threw over the shower rod during their stay. Then he returned to the kitchen with his arms full of damp things and their luggage. Paul stood by the back door in his coat and rainhat.

"Going somewhere?"

"Thought I'd go back to my own house."

"Oh, okay." Was Paisley ready for that? Paul's and her last conversation ended badly. Judah didn't want her getting upset in her condition.

"Besides, you two might need a chaperone."

His cheeks heated up. "We are married, sir."

"Oh, right." Paul nodded but didn't step away from the door. "Paige and the little one will be awake soon. They must be beat. Sleeping in this late."

"I can imagine." Judah took a couple more steps. "I have my truck. You want to ride along?"

"I'll drive my car."

"There's a lot of mud and debris in the streets. Might be hard for a low-riding vehicle." He readjusted his load.

"Maybe I should ride with you, then."

"Yep. Maybe we can start fixing up your place."

"My thoughts exactly. Let me help." Paul clasped Paisley's pack.

Judah trudged out to his truck and tossed the wet items in the back, followed by both bags. He remembered his father-in-law's medical situation. "Did you grab your insulin?"

"I'll get it later. Don't worry about it."

"Where is it? I'll run back and grab it." His hand on the passenger door, Judah waited for the man's answer.

Paul huffed. "I don't need anyone bossing me around, playing nursemaid."

"Uh-huh. And I don't want Paisley running back over to gather things you could take care of now."

Paul harrumphed and crossed his arms.

A car pulled into the driveway next door. Evacuees returning home by the looks of their dazed faces as they exited the vehicle. Judah waved. The older neighbor shook his head as if he couldn't believe how bad things were. A lot of citizens probably felt that way about Basalt Bay.

"Where did you say it was?" Judah persisted.

"On the end table in the living room." Paul grumbled. "In a black grooming bag."

"Be right back." Judah shut the truck door. He hustled into the house, trying to be quiet.

Paige entered from the hallway. Her messy hair looked like she just woke up. "Oh, I didn't expect to see you here."

"Hey, Paige." He felt awkward after what happened yesterday when Paisley saw Paige and Craig together. "Welcome home."

"Thanks." She wiped her hands over her face. "Did you get all your stuff?"

"I did. I need to grab something of your dad's." He continued toward the end table. Was she aware of her father's illness? Should he mention something? As Paisley's husband, he was a member of this family. But he should stay out of it. Let the two sisters figure out their father's medical needs.

"Where is he?" She squinted toward the kitchen.

"He's going back to his house where Paisley and I are staying." He picked up the black bag.

"Oh, right." Her eyes widened. "I saw you two holding hands. That surprised me."

No more than the shock he and Paisley experienced about her and Craig. "Yeah, it's kind of a miracle. I asked her to marry me again."

"You did?" Her voice rose high.

"She said yes."

"That's amazing." Paige smiled. "Welcome to the family, again, Judah." She gave him a quick hug, rubbing her hand over his shoulder.

"Thanks." If only he could explain about Paisley's reaction yesterday. "I should go. Paul's waiting."

"Right. Go ahead."

He strode outside and jogged down the steps. His leg didn't feel too badly after yesterday's difficult swim and all the weight he put on it carrying Paisley.

"Judah?"

He paused.

"I wish—" Paige stood on the porch, glancing up at the sky. "Just tell Paisley hi for me, okay?" She met his gaze with a teary smile.

"Will do." Part of him wanted to close the distance and give her a brotherly hug. Maybe tell her everything would be all right. Sisters unable to talk to each other had to be one of the saddest things. But how could he judge when he barely spoke to his father? The Cedars and Grant families both needed interpersonal healing. Something else for him to pray about in the coming days.

As he slid behind the steering wheel, dropping the bag between them, Paul grumbled like he was upset about Judah interfering and bringing the insulin. No one could force him to take the required dosage. But if Judah didn't bring it along, Paisley would stomp over here and grab the meds herself, whether she was physically up to it or not. He couldn't let that happen.

He put the truck in reverse, contemplating how she might react to her dad after their previous argument. Heaven help them all.

Seven

Paisley blinked several times, gazing around the room. Still at Dad's. Still wrapped in toasty blankets. She moved and felt the hard floor beneath her back. The mattress must have lost some of its air. She wiggled her toes and fingers. Her muscles felt stiff. She rocked back and forth, trying to sit up on the sagging air mattress. After several attempts, she freed herself of the blanket straitjacket.

"Judah?"

No response.

A red checkered flannel shirt and a pair of men's jeans lay folded at the foot of the mattress. Her dad's? Judah must have gathered them. She slid her feet onto the damp floor and stood slowly. At least, the room didn't sway. She picked up the jeans. She barely got into the men's clothing when she heard a thump-thump on the porch. A loud knock.

"Judah?" Why would he knock?

"Paisley?"

That voice. Why was *he* here?

She buttoned the shirt fast, but her fingers fumbled with the task.

Another round of banging came at the door. Should she pretend she wasn't home? Last time that didn't work well. Craig just found a way to barge in.

She heard footsteps again. He peered through the plastic covering the living room window. She gulped. Her heart pounded rapidly. If he tried breaking in, the thin sheet wouldn't hold. What would she do then? He waved, but she didn't reciprocate.

Her mind still felt fuzzy from sleep, and maybe from being so cold and going unconscious yesterday.

Judah, where are you?

"I just want to talk to you." Craig's muffled voice came through the plastic. "Please, open up." He pointed toward the door.

Did he know she was alone? That Judah wasn't here to oppose him. What choice did she have other than to see what he wanted? She unlocked the door and held it open about four inches. "What do you want?" Her voice sounded low and scratchy. She cleared her throat and glared at him through the narrow space.

"What's wrong? Are you sick?"

"Never mind." She started shutting the door. Opening it was a mistake.

He thrust his shoe into the gap. "Wait. We need to talk."

"No, we don't. Not when you were peeking in my window. You should leave." She clutched her father's baggy shirt tighter at the neckline while leaning against the door. Craig's clodhopper remained stuck.

"You wouldn't answer the door." He gritted his teeth. "I'll leave as soon as I get something off my chest—if you'll let me have my shoe back." He glanced downward.

She was tempted to shove harder on the door. But remembering the way he helped her dad, convincing him to take his insulin, she eased back. "Haven't you caused enough trouble?" A snapshot of him and Paige flashed through her thoughts.

"You saw me with Paige." He exhaled. "You were probably shocked to see—"

"So what? You and Paige. Big deal." She pretended it didn't matter.

"Would you mind stepping out onto the porch so we can talk? Or shall I come inside?" He lifted his hands, palms out. "I don't mean you any harm. I promise."

She heard that before. "Why should I believe anything you say?"

"I helped with your father, didn't I?"

Yes, he was kind to her dad, but that didn't mean she trusted him. Even villains had moments of compassion and humanity.

She stared into his dark eyes, loathing the fear he caused her in the past. But then, a wave of fatigue and weariness came over her. "I have to sit down." She swayed. Hated appearing weak.

"Something is wrong."

She held out her hand. "Don't touch me." She shuffled toward one of the decrepit rockers that had been on the porch for as long as she could remember.

"Do you have the flu?"

"No." She dropped onto the chair, bracing herself lest it give suddenly. One of these days it would have to be replaced. Craig sat down on the other rocker, even though she didn't invite him to do so. She remained tense, wary, ready to jump up and go inside at the slightest provocation. She didn't forget the night he stomped through this house, yelling out her name, petrifying her. How she clutched a Mason jar in her hand, ready to strike him.

"If you're too sick—"

"Whatever you came here to say, say it. Then go." She sighed. Even talking was exhausting. "Just stay out of my life, would you?" She took a couple of breaths. "Judah will be back any second." *Hopefully.*

"I can't do that." His mouth formed a grim line.

"Because of Paige?" A rock of bitterness thudded in her gut. "Are you two married?" She clutched the wooden handrails of the rocker, her fingernails digging into the soft wood.

"Married?" He chortled. "Why would you think that?"

Relief shot through her. "You're not married?"

"Definitely not."

Oh, good. "Are you … romantically involved with my sister?"

"That's for her to say." He stared back at her with a scowl.

At least they weren't married!

"Okay. So, what did you want to say? Just say it, then go."

Judah's mantra about grace and mercy skipped through her muddled thoughts, but she stuffed them away. Even he would be angry if he saw Craig sitting on her father's porch talking to her.

"You still consider me the enemy after all I did to help you and your dad?" Craig thrust his fingers through his dark unkempt hair.

"You're still here when I told you to leave. Is that helping me?" She gritted her teeth to keep from saying something mean. Didn't work. "Why come around me at all when you know I can't stand you?"

He winced. "I came by to explain something. Although, I can't tell you everything." He ran his palm over his face. Then sighed like whatever was on his mind weighed too much. Guilty thoughts, perhaps.

"How about just being honest?"

"Look, there's more at stake here than you know."

"What do you mean?"

He leaned over the broken railing and spat. "Starting with the mayor."

"What about him?" Her heart rate skipped a beat.

"He knows about us." He clenched his lips together. "He'll use the information for his own purposes."

"Us?" She snorted. "There's no us. Never has been."

"Not according to Mayor Grant. He orchestrated the fiasco between—"

"Between whom?"

"The night that I—the night you and I—" He huffed. "I shouldn't say anything. It's just, I care about—"

Judah's truck roared across the lawn, coming to a brake-squealing stop below the porch.

Craig shot to his feet. "He's not going to like my being here."

"No kidding. Neither do I." Although, now, she wanted to hear his explanation. What did her father-in-law orchestrate that night?

Judah leapt out of his truck, his face red. "What are *you* doing here?" He charged up onto the porch and stood in front of Craig.

"Judah. Don't—" She leaned forward then sank back into the chair.

The two men stood like enemies in a battle, glaring at each other.

Another door opened. Dad slid out of the vehicle and stared at the trio with wide eyes.

"I said, what are you doing here?" Judah's voice rose.

"Talking with Paisley. That a crime?"

"Possibly. What were you discussing?"

Craig's chin lifted. His look haughty. He thrust back his shoulders.

Judah took another step forward, fists clenched.

Two hotheads in a faceoff.

"Let's all calm down, huh?" Paisley tugged on one of the belt loops of Judah's jeans that appeared too short. Dad's probably.

He glanced at her. "You okay?"

"Been better. Just tired."

"What happened to you?" Craig squinted at her.

"It's not your concern." Judah spoke gruffly. "You shouldn't be here."

Craig smirked. "Lord of the castle throwing out usurpers, huh?"

"At least you admit that you're a usurper."

"Guys, hey, stop." She shoved herself off the rocker, swaying, and stepped between them.

Judah grabbed her arms. She almost toppled backward and he helped her sit down again. "Just rest, will you? You're still weak."

"Then don't start a fight I have to referee."

"I'm not." He nodded toward Craig. "I didn't invite him here."

"Neither did I." She wiped her forehead. "I'm so tired."

"You okay?" Dad strode across the wet grass, staring up at her.

She was warmed by his concern, even though the last thing he said to her wasn't very nice. "I stumbled into the water. No biggie."

Craig's shoulders sagged. "Something did happen. Paisley?"

"Hypothermia," Dad supplied.

"What?"

"Possibly," Judah corrected.

Craig dropped on his haunches beside her and took her wrist to check her pulse.

She jerked away from his touch. "Like Judah said, it's not your concern."

He stared at her, then stood. "Are you taking her to the doctor?"

"Yes."

"No."

Judah and Paisley both spoke at once.

"I'm fine. Stop worrying."

"You don't look fine," Craig muttered.

"Thanks a lot."

"I should go." He stepped off the edge of the porch, landing on the grass. Then paused. "Just take care of her." He marched down the sidewalk, heading toward Paige's.

"Good riddance." Judah winced. "What did he want?"

She sighed. "Can we just let it go?" She was too fatigued. And with her father standing here listening, she didn't want to get into a conversation over the cryptic things Craig mentioned.

Judah's eyebrows raised. "So, you feel any better?" He scuffed his shoe against the warped porch.

"Sleeping helped."

"You're both wearing my clothes, I see." Dad chuckled.

"Yeah. Thanks." What he said about her being good at

running replayed in her thoughts. Something else for her to forgive and get over.

"I brought our bags." Judah nodded toward the truck.

"It'll be nice to have my own things."

"Me too." He lifted his leg, exposing his bare ankle between the edge of the pants and his shoes.

"You took a dunk in the bay, huh?" Dad spoke. "Not like you to be so careless."

She stiffened.

"She tripped. Just an accident." Judah defended her.

"Maybe she was upset. Not thinking straight." Dad squinted at Judah like he might be to blame.

"I saw Paige and Craig together, okay?" She glared at her father. "So, yeah, I was upset."

He shrugged. "Paige and Piper came home, but I didn't see Craig until just now." He nodded at Judah. "Ready to get started on the house?" He trudged inside.

She groaned, annoyed by his lack of understanding.

"I'll be in shortly." Judah leaned closer to her. "You sure you don't want to go to the doctor?"

"I'm just going to rest." She rocked the chair, listening to the creaking sounds.

"I told your dad I asked you to marry me." He rocked his eyebrows.

"What did he say?"

"That it's the best news he's heard."

"Doesn't surprise me." She ran her hands over the worn arms of the rocking chair. "He may like you more than me." A strange melancholy filled her.

"Even if I'm a Grant?"

"Even then."

"Judah!" Dad called from inside.

"Guess I should help him get started on the renovations." He stroked his fingers over her hand. "If you change your mind about going to Florence—"

"I won't. But thanks."

He brushed his lips against her cheek, making her heart rate pick up, then he strolled into the house.

She sighed and closed her eyes, wishing she could shut out the frustrations she'd dealt with since waking up.

A few minutes later, she heard loud thuds—wood chunks being thrown or piled up. Then hammering. No luck shutting out the racket.

She rocked the chair, letting herself melt against the frayed backing. But despite her determination to relax and possibly fall asleep, Craig's visit replayed in her thoughts. What did he mean about Mayor Grant knowing about him and her? As if they were a couple? Ridiculous!

Was Edward somehow involved in her attack three years ago? If so, how could she discover the truth?

Eight

Before they started working on the stairway, Judah took pictures of the flood-damaged house with his newly charged cell phone. Later, he'd send them to Paul's insurance adjuster. He would do the same thing at the cottage when he got the chance to drive out there.

He pounded a hammer against the wall in the stairwell, listening for a dull thud to confirm the location of the next stud. He and Paul were building temporary, interior stairs resembling a ship's ladder, so they wouldn't have to climb in through the second-story windows. The materials were a hodge-podge of remnants left over from when the previous stairs exploded.

They'd asked James for any large pieces of wood he might have. At first, he said he needed all his spare materials. Who knew when the next disaster might hit? But after they pleaded and cajoled, he showed them two long planks—leftovers from a decking project—that were a perfect size for bracing the stairway at a shallow angle. The stairs would be a far cry from passing inspection but would be stable and usable.

Judah heard something. Was someone shouting? Paisley? He stopped pounding nails. More yelling. He dropped his hammer and sprinted for the front door.

"I did not!" Paisley coughed as if she struggled to catch her breath. "You're small-minded and mean and just plain wrong about this."

Judah reached the porch and saw her standing on the muddy sidewalk in front of the house, wagging her finger at Patty Lawton, the hardware store owner. The older woman's face was a burgundy hue, and her clenched teeth made her look rabid. His first instinct was to sprint to his wife and protect her. He leaped from the porch, wincing, then charged across the lawn.

He knew Miss Patty was part of a group of businessowners who accused Paisley of breaking into their stores and stealing, or doing damage, on the night of her graduation. Although years had passed, some still held it against her.

"Who else would kick in my door and steal lumber and nails?" Miss Patty planted her fists on her hips and scowled.

"Someone steals and you automatically think it's me?" Paisley tossed up her hands. "How bizarre is that?"

"As soon as I heard you were in town, I knew there'd be trouble!" Miss Patty shouted.

Judah dodged between the two women, facing the store owner. "What's going on here?"

"She thinks I stole something." Paisley grabbed his arm and nudged him out of the way. "It wasn't me!" She glowered at the other woman, seeming capable of fending for herself.

Still, Judah stepped to her side, ready to intervene if necessary.

"All that hammering." Miss Patty jabbed her finger toward

Paul's house. "I know where those nails and boards came from. You can't fool me."

"No, you don't know where they came from." Judah didn't appreciate being accused of thievery, either. "We didn't take anything from your store!"

"This doesn't concern you." Miss Patty scowled at him.

"You're accusing us of deeds we didn't commit." He wouldn't touch her, but he took a nonthreatening step forward. "That concerns me plenty."

She avoided his gaze and glared at Paisley. "Are you going to be honest now?"

"I have been honest." Paisley crossed her arms. "Since returning to Basalt, I haven't entered your store. Miss Patty, I couldn't break down your door if I tried."

"I remember your wily ways, Paisley Cedars."

"Grant"—Paisley and Judah spoke at once, correcting her on Paisley's last name.

Judah had heard enough. Maybe he should escort the woman back to her business establishment. But first, "What's this about? Why are you accusing my family?"

"Now she's your *family* after being gone for years?" Miss Patty cackled.

A fire burned in his throat. About to tell the woman off, he felt Paisley's hand link softly into the crook of his elbow. Was she telling him to calm down? *Lord, help me.*

He took a breath and redirected his thoughts. "Think about it. Our neighbors are in a crisis. Someone may have needed emergency supplies."

"Someone like you?" She gave him an icy stare. Her intensity could elicit a confession from an innocent bystander.

"Not me, and not Paisley. Now, if your store carried food,

things might be different." He glanced down the street. "I might do anything to provide for my family."

Miss Patty gasped.

"But your store doesn't have food. However, everyone in Basalt Bay needs supplies. Some don't have money." He kept his tone calm. "I'm not saying it's right, but you can't blame folks for trying to get their lives back."

Miss Patty jabbed her finger toward him. "I'm telling Mayor Grant what you said. Bad communications do corrupt good manners." She glared at Paisley before whirling around and trudging down the sidewalk.

Paisley tugged on his arm. "Let it go."

But he couldn't. "Miss Patty, hold up." He jogged after her. "A little compassion would go a long way toward being neighborly."

She spun around so fast she nearly slapped him. "How dare you lecture me. All I need is another Grant giving me orders!"

Her vehemence surprised him, and yet he pushed on. "You call yourself a Christian, right?"

"Do *you*? Last I checked, Grants weren't notorious for having a high morality rating."

What did she mean? Was she referring to the mayor's public opinion polls? "My father doesn't have anything to do with this situation, or how we should be treating each other."

"Okay, fine. But I'm not swinging wide my doors for people like you and Paisley to take what they want." Her glare insinuated he did just that.

"For goodness' sake, we didn't break into your business."

"I say it was *her*"—she jabbed her finger beyond him—"and you're covering for her."

Paisley stepped next to him. "Then you'd be wrong." She

faced her accuser with a calmer manner than Judah had. "I would never steal from you or anyone else."

"With your past misdeeds, how can I trust you? How can anyone?"

"Because I've changed." Her voice went soft.

Judah was so proud of her. She *had* changed. They both had. That's what would make their marriage stronger this time around.

"And because I'm sorry."

Her humble words seemed to take the starch out of Miss Patty. "You admit to doing the wrong?"

"I'm not admitting to this break-in." Paisley wiped the back of her hand across her forehead. She looked pale. Had she overexerted herself?

Judah wanted to scoop her up and carry her back to the porch where she should have stayed. To demand that she rest for the remainder of the day. He doubted she'd approve of such an action, especially in front of Miss Patty, one of the town's formidable gossips.

"Then what are you saying?" The older woman's tone ratcheted higher.

"That I'm sorry for my past mistakes." Paisley gulped. "I apologize for throwing mud at your windows when I was a teenager."

Miss Patty's jaw dropped open.

"For stealing … batteries … gum … and trinkets. That was wrong."

Judah put his hand at the small of her back, amazed by her honesty and contriteness.

"I knew it!" Miss Patty hooted. "You're a thief and a reprobate! How could you not be with a mother—"

"Don't you say a word about my mother!" Paisley thrust her index finger toward the store owner. "This has nothing to do with her. I take responsibility for *my* actions." She sighed. "And, just so you know, I wasn't the only one who stole from you on graduation night. But what I did was wrong, and I'm sorry."

One of Miss Patty's eyebrows rose. "Is this a trick to get me to remember past mischief, instead of focusing on what you did this week?"

"I didn't break into your store recently." Paisley groaned. "But if it would help … I'm willing to do some … community service hours … for the mistakes I made in the past."

Judah's admiration for her jumped a few notches.

"I came back to Basalt to make amends." She shrugged. "That's what I plan to do."

"It's about time." Miss Patty thrust her shoulders back. "Meet me at the hardware store in the morning. You can wash windows and clean up the flood damage."

"I'll be there first thing."

"Good." The woman eyed her for a good thirty seconds before shuffling down the street. "I'll lock up anything of value too."

Judah gritted his teeth.

"That went well." Paisley must not have heard Miss Patty's parting jab.

"You were fabulous." He squeezed her hand. "You okay?"

"Tired. But, yeah. Thanks for standing up for me."

"Of course." He linked his fingers with hers as they headed back toward Paul's.

"What's next on your agenda?"

The soft way her dark eyes stared into his gaze made his

footsteps lighter. What did she ask? "Oh, right. Removing the tree from the roof. Getting the bathroom door unstuck."

"Wish I could help."

"You're going to rest and only rest for the remainder of the day."

"Yes, sir." She gave him a mock salute.

He chuckled, doubting she'd do what he said.

Nine

Five hours of work had never seemed so long. Between Miss Patty's snippy attitude over everything Paisley did, and how tired she was, she had to keep reminding herself that making amends was worth it. For each task she completed, the woman gave her another. How many more chores would the store owner expect her to do?

"Have you finished cleaning the windows?"

"Yes."

Miss Patty squinted toward the front of the store. "You call that clean?"

"I tried."

"Try again."

"Yes, ma'am." Feeling like a teenager working off a grounding, she grabbed the glass cleaner. Her shoulders ached from all the reaching. Plus, her crisis in the sea made her especially tired. Even so, she was determined to give this her best effort.

"Have you swept the floors?"

"Uh-huh."

Miss Patty peered at the linoleum. She bent over at the waist, adjusting her glasses. "Aha!" She stabbed her finger toward something. "Sweep that again!"

"Okay." An hour later, Paisley felt wilted. Still, she asked, "Anything else you need me to do before I go?"

"Before you go?" Miss Patty gaped at her. "Grab the duster off the counter and dust all the shelves."

"All?" The woman was a tyrant!

"Are you here to work, or not?"

"Yes, but—" Paisley groaned. "Fine. I'll take care of it." She gave Miss Patty a halfhearted smile. How did Dad put up with the woman's demanding attitude for all those years while he worked for her?

"Well? We don't have all day."

"Right." She grabbed the brown feather dusting tool and whisked it across shelf after shelf. Needing a distraction, something to keep herself from bolting for the door, she let her mind wander to thoughts about Paige and Craig. Not a healthy diversion, but effective. How long were they dating? How did they meet? What would Paige say if Paisley told her that she thought she was dating a creep?

Inhaling dust, she coughed and waved her hand through the air filled with floating particles.

"What's wrong? Are you lollygagging again?" Miss Patty harped as if Paisley took a ten-minute break instead of spending ten seconds coughing.

"The dust irritates my lungs." She swallowed back another urge to cough. "Would you mind if I left? I'm so tired and still recovering." That probably sounded like a lame excuse.

"Look at all the work we still have to do." Miss Patty swayed her hands toward a pile of items they removed from the shelves earlier.

"Couldn't we finish tomorrow?" No, wait. She didn't want to return tomorrow. She wasn't under any obligation to work for Miss Patty. She did volunteer hours out of the goodness of her heart, in hopes that the woman might forgive past mistakes. So far, that didn't happen. The store owner seemed as grouchy and vindictive as ever.

"If the electricity comes back on, the store will be open tomorrow." Miss Patty adjusted the edge of her baggy shirt. "I had hoped you would accomplish more. I should have known better about a Cedars."

Paisley gritted her teeth and dusted faster, stirring up more dirt, using the motions to work off her annoyance. See if she ever came into this store again.

Someone entered the front door, causing the little bell to chime.

"I'm not open," Miss Patty hollered.

"Paisley here?"

Judah! Hearing his voice thrilled her. Did he come here to take her home? Beautiful man.

"She's busy. Come back later," Miss Patty barked.

"Paisley?" Judah called out.

Good. He didn't follow the woman's command.

"Over here." She dropped the duster on a shelf, then met him halfway up the aisle. She charged into his arms, hugging him. Her lifesaver.

"Hey, sweetheart. What's wrong?"

She shook her head, not trusting herself to speak within Miss Patty's hearing. She smelled the scent of wood on his clothes and clung to him a little longer.

"You okay?" He pulled back.

She tried to communicate "*I need to get out of here!*" with her gaze.

"We've got a serious problem at your dad's."

"We do? Is something wrong with him?" Was Judah going along with her wanting to leave, or was he serious about there being a problem? "Is Dad okay?"

"Can you step outside so we can talk?"

"Oh, sure." Good idea. Get her outside, then make a run for it. She made the mistake of glancing at the stern-faced shop owner.

Miss Patty tapped her wristwatch. "Time's wasting."

"I'll, um, be back in a second." Now, why did she say that? Judah clasped her hand and led her out the door.

"What's happened? Or was that a fake warning to get me out of there? If so, good going." She sighed, relieved to breathe fresh air.

"It's Callie. She's back in town and mad as a hornet."

"At whom?" Paisley pictured her aunt's angry face. Red blotchy skin. Double chin jutting out. Her scowl could make spiders flip over and die.

"She's mad at the world. You. Paige. Your dad. He's the one who sent me to get you." He nodded toward the street. "Ready to leave? Paul and Callie already exchanged heated words."

"Did she demand that he make her sweet tea?"

"How'd you guess?"

"It's her MO. She plops down on the rocker and expects instant service."

"Yep. Sounds right. Paul ordered her to go home and make her own tea." Judah held his palms together in a pleading gesture. "Can you come back and pacify her? It's World War III over there."

She snickered at the familiar ritual between Aunt Callie and Dad. "If I go, Miss Patty will be irate." She glanced back toward the windows she cleaned earlier. "But I've done enough here."

"Excellent." His arms came around her in a squeeze. "How are you doing?"

"Exhausted."

His eyes widened. Before he could comment on how she shouldn't be overdoing, she tapped his chest with her finger. "Wait here." Taking a fortifying breath, she trudged back into the store. "I'm sorry but I have to return to my dad's."

"But you aren't finished. You promised—"

"I know, but"—Paisley swallowed—"I could ... come back later." Ugh.

"Why can't you follow through on what you promised?" Miss Patty harrumphed. "Maybe your word isn't—"

"My wife's word is gold." Judah followed her. "If you can't see that, you're blind."

His sticking up for her was sweet.

"Aunt Callie needs me. She's at Dad's."

"Callie's back?" The older woman peered around the room, probably seeing all the work left to be done. "She'll have plenty to say about her rebellious niece disappearing for three years."

Judah groaned.

Paisley tugged on his arm. "Don't worry. I talked with her before the storm. Sorry to leave you in a lurch."

"Promise to come back later?" Miss Patty called as they exited the door.

When Paisley and Judah arrived at Dad's, Aunt Callie sat on one of the dilapidated rocking chairs on the porch. The chair's lower rails thudded unevenly against the water-damaged floorboards.

"Hi, Aunt Callie," Paisley called as she crossed the still soggy yard.

Her aunt's brow furrowed. "Paisley Rose, where have you been? I've been sitting here forever waiting to talk to you. No one would bring me tea, either." She glared at Judah.

"Sorry. I didn't know you were back. I've been helping at Miss Patty's store." She trudged up the wooden porch steps that someone, probably Judah, built today. No wonder he smelled of wood. One step was longer than the other two, but they felt sturdy beneath her shoes.

"Last I knew you and Patty Lawton didn't get along." Aunt Callie sniffed.

"We don't."

"Yet, you're helping her when you haven't offered your aunt any help."

Aunt Callie sure could be a pill sometimes.

"Do you need something, Auntie? Are you having trouble?"

"I could hardly get up those stairs." She jabbed her chubby index finger toward the new construction. "Why make such irregular steps? A body could fall off the side and no one would care." She was in fine form today. Full of complaints. She made a gurgling sound as she glared at Judah.

"The stairs are fine and functional. You should have seen us before, hopping up and down off the porch." Paisley glanced back and winked at Judah. Then she stepped closer to her aunt and patted her hand. "What's the problem, Auntie?"

"Ask my hardheaded brother." She muttered something about stubborn men.

Apparently, siblings never outgrew some squabbling.

"What has he done now?" Paisley peered through the plastic

covering the front window. Where was Dad hiding? What did he say that got Aunt Callie all riled this time?

"He wouldn't listen to me. Never listens to me!" Aunt Callie pelted another squinty-eyed glare at Judah. "This is a private matter, young man. Cedars family only."

"He's family too, Auntie."

"He's a Grant."

"So am I." Paisley sighed, tired of the interaction. "What's this about?"

"Maybe I should go inside." Judah trudged up the steps, met her gaze for a second, then disappeared into the house.

"Tell my brother I'm still waiting for refreshments!" Aunt Callie rocked the chair more fervently. "Paige is back. There are rumors, again."

Again? From when Paisley left town? Or from her teenage years?

"There are always rumors. Besides, aren't you one of the instigators of some of Basalt's finest tales?" She said it jokingly but knew it was true.

Aunt Callie gasped and sputtered. "H-how dare you s-say s-such a thing? Accuse me of being a gossip? Why, I never."

Paisley played along. "So this is real news? What have you heard?"

"She's together with *him*."

"Him?"

"Her love interest—that Masters fellow. Everyone's talking about it." Aunt Callie yanked a tissue from her baggy shirt's wristband, then dabbed at her nose.

"What's the problem?" Paisley had her own beef with Craig. Judah did too. Why was her aunt concerned?

"Have you spoken to her?" Aunt Callie stared at her.

"No."

"Why not? Isn't it about time you two buried the hatchet?"

"Why don't you and my dad bury the hatchet?" She was being bold, but turnabout was fair play.

Aunt Callie snorted. "Why, Paisley Rose, your father and I get along fine until he gets his stubborn streak all in a dither. Then he hides like a five-year-old kid. Won't talk. Same as when he married your mother." She clapped her hand over her mouth. Her face turned red and splotchy. "Forget I said that."

"What about when Dad married Mom?"

Her aunt wiped her hanky beneath her eyes. "We don't speak about it, so don't ask."

That made Paisley even more curious.

"Your sister having a child outside of marriage"—Aunt Callie rushed her words as if trying to change the subject—"and hanging around that man. It's not right. Something needs to be done."

"What Paige does is her own business." Paisley wouldn't contribute to the local gossip wheel.

"Fiddlesticks." Aunt Callie harrumphed. "What she does affects the whole family, especially in a small town like ours. Your father should do something. Say something. I told him so!"

Oh. No wonder he was hiding. "I'm tired. Do you mind if we finish this conversation another time? About the tea … we don't have any to offer you until the electricity resumes."

Aunt Callie moaned. "Whose fool idea was it to say we could return to town when the power wasn't back on?"

"Mayor Grant's."

"Figures."

"Everything takes more time than planned." At her aunt's glare, Paisley tried to appease her. "Miss Patty says the lights will come back on any second. Then you can go by and visit her."

"Hmph."

Sinking onto the porch floor, too tired to stand for another minute, Paisley leaned against the bare wall where shingles were torn off by fierce winds during the hurricane. She closed her eyes and sighed.

"Something wrong with you, child?" Aunt Callie's rocking stopped.

"Just tired." Dead tired.

"Pauly said you had an accident. Didn't tell me what kind."

"I fell into the sea."

"Didn't your mother tell you to stay off that treacherous peninsula?"

"About fifty times." But Mom had been afraid of even wading in the ocean.

"What are we going to do about Paige?" The rocking resumed.

"Nothing."

"Nothing?" the woman yelped. "I'll have you know—"

Paisley blocked out her aunt's rambling. The last thing she heard was something about another person ruining the Cedars name.

Someone else besides Paisley.

Ten

Judah laid down on the air mattress next to Paisley, staying so close to the edge he nearly rolled off. Earlier he found the slow leak and put duct tape over the hole. Best case scenario—come morning they wouldn't be lying on the hard floor.

Exhausted, yet wide awake, he tried not to move. He didn't want to awaken his wife who had to be as beat as he was, since she went back to work for another hour at Miss Patty's. He was proud of her for trying to do the right thing for others, but he wished she'd take it easy for a few days.

Trying to fall asleep, he counted imaginary orcas leaping in the sound. Quoted Psalm twenty-three. Yawned a couple times.

His mind wandered over the day's events. They finished the crude interior stairs. Then, while he worked on the outdoor steps, a front-end loader came by and scooped up debris from the street and dropped it into a dump truck. Not a perfect fix, as some trash still littered the road, but most of the garbage piles on the block were cleared away.

Later, a logging truck stopped in front of the house, and one of the workers said they were doing salvage logging. The guy volunteered to bring down the tree leaning against the roof in exchange for the wood. A great trade as far as Judah was concerned. Using a crane called a cherry picker, attached to the rig, they safely brought the tree to the ground. Another guy used a chainsaw to cut it in half, and they loaded the pieces onto the logging truck—all without Judah and Paul having to do anything.

The lights flashed on and off in the kitchen. Yes! Judah sat up, trying to stop the air mattress from rocking.

Outside, a cheer rang out. Clapping and whistling sounds followed. Folks were celebrating the return of electricity. Lights, heat, and power for tools would be a huge step in getting their lives back to normal after the hurricane.

Paisley moaned. "What's the ruckus?"

"Electricity's on. We survived!" He felt lighthearted just saying it. They ought to kiss like on New Year's, or hug, or something.

Her eyelids closed. A peaceful expression crossed her face. He listened to her steady breathing and thanked God for His goodness in keeping her alive.

After ten minutes of sitting on the edge of the mattress, and still not feeling sleepy, he stood and shuffled to the front window. He gazed through the plastic—another thing in need of repair—and saw lights shining from the houses across the street. Throughout the day, voices and hammers rang out in the neighborhood. Now, with the return of power, the noises might keep going through the night.

He shuffled back to the mattress and grabbed the blanket he'd been using. He wrapped himself in it, making sure Paisley was covered in her blanket, then he sat on the floor near the window. He'd stay here until he got good and sleepy. He had plenty to think about. Pray about too.

At some point things quieted down. Hammers were put to rest. Without even realizing it, he dozed off leaning against the wall. Hours later, he awoke to noises coming from the kitchen. Eggs cracking? Who had eggs? What a delicious smell! Dare he hope for coffee?

He stood and shoved the blanket off. A kink in his neck made him cringe. Sleeping while sitting on the floor was a bad idea. As he ambled toward the kitchen, he stretched the tightness out of his shoulder muscles. He sniffed some wonderful scents and grinned at the domestic scene of Paisley standing in the kitchen, cooking breakfast.

"Mornin'."

"Good morning." She raised her mug. "Coffee?"

"You bet."

With her back to him, she worked with the coffee machine. He strolled closer and peeked over her shoulder. Scrambled eggs steamed in a large frying pan. "Where'd you find eggs? Everything smells great, by the way." He sniffed her neck. "Mmm. You too."

"I have mysterious ways for getting what I want."

"I don't doubt that." He chuckled, happy to hear a cheerful tone back in her voice. "It's hard to imagine anyone having fresh eggs in Basalt Bay."

"Who said anything about fresh?" She winked.

Kissing her sassy mouth splashed through his thoughts. "You must have slept well."

"Yep. I feel more rested." She handed him a cup of black steaming coffee.

Their fingers touched in the exchange. He felt a little zing. Did she feel it too?

"No creamer. Sorry. Can't have everything."

No, he guessed he couldn't. "That's okay." He sipped the drink. The heat nearly burned his throat, but it hit the spot. He sighed in pleasure. "I've been waiting for this."

"Me too. I'm on my second cup."

Paul thudded down the steps in his boots. "Something smells good."

"Coffee and eggs, if you want them." Paisley even smiled at her father.

"I'll have both." He moved stiffly, finally reaching the main floor. "You two sleep okay on the camping mattress?"

"I did." She messed with the coffee machine and gave Judah a pointed glance.

Did she wonder why he slept on the floor? Might she assume he slept away from her for some reason other than insomnia? Avoiding temptation, perhaps?

He almost laughed. What red-blooded male didn't have *that* on his mind when he slept next to the woman he loved? But with all the work, his injury, her falling into the sea and nearly drowning, then having potential hypothermia, he was dealing with a lot of things other than contemplating their next step. And as far as he knew, they were waiting to share a bedroom until they exchanged vows.

Still, he would take flirting with her as far as he could. He stepped behind her while she scooped eggs onto three plates. He leaned in to plant a kiss on her neck. Instead, he got an elbow in his gut. He groaned.

She made a wry face at him and nodded once toward her dad.

"What? I was just going to kiss you."

"Mmhmm." She passed him a blue lunch-sized plate piled with eggs.

What got into her this morning? Yesterday, she was lethargic, and worked for Miss Patty when she shouldn't have. Of course, he was just as preoccupied with getting this house livable. Now she seemed feisty. Happy, even.

He liked it. Loved her. And he'd watch for his chance to kiss her good morning. Maybe talk about whatever she thought was the reason for him not sleeping in the same bed as her. Might be an interesting conversation. For now, let her think what she wanted.

Paisley handed her dad a cup of coffee and a plate like Judah's. "Compliments of your neighbor, James."

"James?" Paul's eyes widened. He guzzled about half the cup in one swallow.

"Says he has connections to the outside world."

"Well, glory be." Paul set his cup on the counter, then stuffed eggs in his mouth. "I'll go by later and tell him thanks."

"Want to sit on the porch?" Judah snagged Paisley's gaze and nodded toward the front of the house.

"Sure."

They carried their plates and coffee cups outside and dropped into the old rockers. The silence was comfortable while they ate. Life felt good.

"Thanks for fixing this."

"I heard some bad news this morning." She sipped her coffee. "James says there's a community meeting at eleven." She rolled her eyes. "What do you suppose that's about?"

"Maybe the mayor has a restoration plan for the city. About time, nine days after the storm." He took the last couple bites of his eggs. With his mouth cleared, he spoke again. "Might be a good idea to pool resources. Think the grocery store will open today?"

She shrugged. "If so, there'll be a rush on it. Same as Miss Patty's. Yesterday, she expressed concern about that."

"Nice of you to help her, even when she didn't exhibit the kindest nature."

"She never warmed up to me." Paisley chuckled. "That woman doesn't have a chip on her shoulder. She has a massive chunk of basalt."

"She needs the Lord's grace in her life, like we all do." He sipped his coffee. "Did you want to go to the town meeting?"

"Hardly. I hate City Hall."

"I figured." He took her empty plate and piled it on top of his. "Plenty of stuff to be done here. Not that you should do anything. I mean, you can rest while your dad and I work."

She wrinkled her nose at him. "I'm not afraid of hard work."

"I meant, after your near miss, you should take it easy. You worked too hard yesterday."

"So did you." Her gaze scolded him. "You have an injury too. And you got as wet and cold as I did in the ocean."

"There's so much to do." The responsibilities and tasks weighed on him. He still had repairs to do at the cottage, and he needed to find a job to provide for them and pay the mortgage.

"That's why you need my help." She gave him another sassy grin.

He could get used to these flirty expressions. Her mischievous side had always been alluring to him.

Now probably wasn't the time to talk about the air mattress, what she thought of their sleeping arrangements, and when they'd say their vows. The diamond ring sparkled on her left hand in the morning sunlight. At least she still wore it. *Focus on that, Grant.*

"So, did you want to go together?"

"Where?" He was distracted by her dark eyes shining back at him. The way she licked her lips.

"To the community meeting." One of her eyebrows arched. "Maybe you didn't get enough sleep last night, huh?"

Aha. She *was* thinking about that. He hid his grin. Then he stood, bent over with the plates in his hands, and kissed her cheek. His bearded chin nuzzled her face an extra second before he stood back up. "You still smell nice."

She snickered.

"We can go to the meeting together, if you want." His turn to wink. "If we dare."

"Dare?" A wide smile crossed her mouth and her eyes twinkled. "I have a dare for you, Mister Grant."

Mister? "Oh, yeah?"

Her impish grin made him a little nervous.

She jumped up, giggling. The plates rattled in the space between them. At her intense gaze, his breath caught. He'd go along with anything she said to keep a warm glow in her gaze and a sweet smile on her lips.

"So, here's the deal." She tipped her head, still grinning. "If I leave City Hall before the meeting is over, I'll do one thing you want me to do."

He gripped the plates tightly. "One thing, huh?"

"And if you leave the meeting before it's over, for any reason, you have to do one thing that I want you to do." Her wink and grin made his heart flip-flop.

His thoughts leapt to kissing her. "I'm game."

"Good." She skipped around him and reentered the house.

He blew out his breath. *Tone down your thoughts, Romeo.* He shook his head and chuckled. Not a chance.

One thing was for certain. He would not leave the town meeting before she did for any reason.

Eleven

Paisley dropped into a chair a few rows from the back of the community room in the basement of City Hall. Judah sat beside her. Challenging him to a dare was fun and exciting to consider, even if she might not be able to force herself to sit through Mayor Grant's speech.

Judah's gaze met hers. Was he thinking about the dare, too? If she left the meeting first, what might he ask her to do? Move out to the cottage with him? Yikes. She may have opened a can of worms. But if she won …

He still hadn't shaved his beard, which made him look rugged and sexy. She grinned at him as her thoughts leapt back to when he kissed her face on the porch. How he stayed close, their cheeks touching, a few extra seconds. His beard felt ticklish, and she was tempted to shuffle and turn his brief kiss into a real toe-curling one.

Regrettably, she didn't. They agreed to focus on getting the remodeling work accomplished before they moved forward with their vow renewal. Yet, when they were being flirty and romantic, she had a hard time remembering why they made such an agreement.

This morning, when she woke up and discovered he didn't sleep beside her, she was a tad disappointed. Even though they were wrapped in separate bedding the night before, she liked sleeping next to him. Waking up beside him. Not being alone. Sigh.

Mayor Grant entered the room and paused by their row. Decked out in a three-piece suit, his designer attire seemed like overkill, insulting even. Most attendees were dressed in work clothes, jeans and sweatshirts. Dirty clothes at that, since there had been little time for catching up on laundry. Was this another case of the mayor not being empathetic to the people in his jurisdiction?

He reached out and shook Judah's hand, ignoring her. "Son, glad you could join us." His voice boomed as if including the rest of the group. "I'm pleased to hear you didn't end up in the pokey." He guffawed.

Yeah, real funny. He referred to their fear of Deputy Brian throwing them in jail for staying in town against the evacuation order. Fortunately, that didn't happen.

"Thanks, Dad." Judah slid his arm over the back of her chair. Was he trying to include her?

Edward grimaced in her direction, then walked on, greeting people loudly as he strode toward the podium.

The interaction made her stomach turn. Heat rose up her neck. Her throat tightened. She tugged on her neckband. If she needed air, she'd go outside. Forget the dare. But she didn't want to forget about it. She'd rather tune out Mayor Grant and imagine what one thing she might ask of Judah.

Just then, Craig and Paige strolled down the aisle. Paige carried Piper. Craig grinned like he owned the world. Wasn't this what Paisley feared? That nowhere in Basalt would there be a safe place not to see them.

Paige glanced at her and smiled. Paisley returned a nod but pivoted away when she found Craig's gaze on her. She fiddled with a hangnail on her thumb to preoccupy herself.

A white-haired woman scooted past Judah's knees, past Paisley's, and dropped into the next seat. "Why hello there, dear."

"Oh, Kathleen, I didn't recognize you. It's great to see you!" Paisley smiled at the woman who gave her a jar of peppermint oil to sniff during her panic attack on the night of the hurricane. "How are you?" She settled back in her chair.

"I survived the evacuation." The older woman chuckled. "My house is okay. A little damaged. Others fared far worse, so I can't complain."

Paisley nudged Judah. "Judah, this is Kathleen. Sorry, I don't remember your last name."

"Baker." She extended her hand.

"Hello." He lowered his arm from behind Paisley and shook the woman's hand. "It's nice to meet you."

"My pleasure."

"Kathleen's new to Basalt. I met her during the storm of all storms that none of us will ever forget."

"Isn't that the truth?" Kathleen chuckled.

Judah leaned forward. "Where did you stay during the evacuation?"

"Inland with friends." The woman shuddered. "What a terrible drive in the storm. Oh, my, I was thankful to reach safety. You two?"

"I stayed here." Paisley rocked her thumb between them. "We both did for part of it."

"Here in town?"

"We did. Foolishly, perhaps."

"I'm so glad you're safe." Kathleen smiled. "Maybe we can get back to normal living, huh?"

"Definitely." Paisley glanced at Judah, and he winked. What did he think "normal living" meant to them? Sharing the cottage. Waking up together. Gulp.

"Uh-oh. Don't look now. Trouble's coming." The white-haired woman nodded toward the back of the room.

Maggie Thomas, the innkeeper of the Beachside Inn and one of Paisley's most difficult people to get along with, marched up the aisle, head held high.

What did Kathleen know about Maggie Thomas's brand of trouble? Did she already have dealings with the sharp-tongued woman?

Maggie dropped into a chair in the front row with her shoulders thrust back and her chin lifted. She nodded at someone as if communicating something. What did she have up her sleeve?

"I'd like to call our post-Blaine community meeting to order. Welcome, everyone." Mayor Grant's sparkly-white grin would have made his hygienist proud. "If you can take your seats, we'll get this chat over with so we can all go home."

A few attendees agreed. Others laughed. Some shuffled to empty chairs.

"I'm glad all of you made it safely through the evacuation and your stay in various host cities." The mayor leaned one elbow on the podium. "We appreciate the shelters whose doors were open to us. Let's give it up for our safe havens." He led the group in a round of applause.

Before the clapping ended, Maggie jumped up. "Mayor,

why didn't you go to a shelter like the rest of us were required to do?"

His chuckle sounded odd. "Now, Maggie, you know my house is on the highest location in Basalt Bay. No need to leave my fortress. The missus and I were safe. Thank you for your concern."

"I thought you had to leave town, too." Her voice rose as she faced the crowd. "The town ordinance is for *all* citizens, right?"

"That's what I thought too!" Sounded like Aunt Callie.

Paisley scooted lower in her seat. She didn't mind the mayor getting put on the spot and publicly humiliated, but even Maggie Thomas returned to Basalt before the evacuation order lifted. She glanced over Judah's shoulder. A couple rows back, her aunt sat on the far left. Miss Patty sat next to her. One woman whispered in the other's ear. Both were gesticulating. What had them all worked up?

"Are you excluded from following the laws of our town?" Maggie persisted. "Maybe the mayor can do anything he wants, huh?"

"Now, Maggie, why don't you take your seat? Let's get on with our city business."

The innkeeper harrumphed but sat down.

Mayor Grant cleared his throat. "Is everyone's power back on?"

"Yes!" "Finally." "About time." People called out responses.

"Rest assured I've been urging the utility company to get your electricity back on since day one."

Leave it to Edward to pat himself on the back. Even in a post-disaster meeting, he made himself out to be the hero.

"It's true." He took a sip from a water bottle on the podium.

"If not for my diligence, many of you would still be out at the entrance of town, twiddling your thumbs, waiting for the all clear."

Maggie leapt to her feet again. "I have good reason to believe—"

"Are you leading this meeting, Maggie?" The mayor grimaced. "I'm sure we all have plenty to complain about. Big messes to fix." He lifted one boot. "My favorite cowboy boots nearly got ruined in the mud. I'm upset about that."

Some laughed at his attempt at humor.

Paisley rolled her eyes.

Maggie sat down stiffly.

"How about we dust off our grateful attitudes, hmm?" Edward grinned again. "We're back in our homes. Back in our city. Electricity's on. We're safe and alive."

"Here, here." Craig? Why would he speak up for the mayor? The two hardly got along.

Mayor Grant droned on for a while about the town's disaster and clean-up protocols, calling on the citizenry to jump in and help their neighbors. He even encouraged folks to go the extra mile and be Good Samaritans whenever possible.

Paisley nearly choked on his hypocritical words. Just four days ago, when she suggested that he take Maggie to his safe, warm home on the hill in the aftermath of the hurricane, he refused. So no one could blame her for tuning him out now. When she glanced at Judah, his attention was focused on someone other than his father. Craig?

That man stood. "I agree with you, Mayor Grant. Those who remained after the emergency evacuation caused unnecessary safety risks to themselves and to those on the rescue team. It cost valuable man hours. Fortunately, no lives were lost." Craig's voice deepened. "Those people who took risks for themselves and others should be fined or required to do community service hours as a penalty for not following the town's security protocol."

What? She gripped Judah's arm. His muscles tensed beneath her hand.

"That's right!" "Yeah." "I agree." A cacophony of voices rose.

She and Judah exchanged glances. She wanted to slink even lower on her chair, maybe melt to the floor and crawl out the door.

"People!" Mayor Grant palmed the air to quiet the group. "Mr. Masters—"

Craig was "Mr. Masters" now? What was going on with these two? Didn't Craig try to warn her about Edward?

"Can you give examples of these infractions?" The mayor crossed his arms.

"Of course." Craig turned and stared at her.

The rat. She squinted right back at him, warning him to shut up with her gaze.

"For one, Paul Cedars refused to leave town."

How dare he talk about her father!

"Even when prompted to leave by a C-MER employee, he refused."

Paisley gritted her teeth. Gnashed them together, more like.

"The man had a serious medical condition." Craig's voice rose. "He needed immediate attention. Might have even died without intervention."

Paige, sitting next to Craig, glanced up sharply.

Paisley's glare sent a hundred fire darts hurtling in his direction. If only one of them would strike him dumb.

"He should have been transported to the emergency room,"

Craig continued in an authoritative voice. "I did what I could to help him. Otherwise, things wouldn't have ended so well for Mr. Cedars."

He sounded so noble. Paisley wanted to leap out of the row, sock him in the nose, and run from the building. Dare or no dare, she had enough of this community nonsense.

A rumbling of voices grew louder.

"Then what happened?" Mayor Grant hollered over the clamor as if he wasn't apprised of the situation. He probably coerced Craig into talking. Or paid him off.

Paisley's fury toward both men quadrupled.

"I stayed in town and risked my life to help him."

Judah gripped the top of the chair in front of him with both hands. She touched the crease of his arm. No reason to come unglued over a parasite like Craig. Besides, maybe that's what he and the mayor wanted. To get the town's suspicions off themselves.

Paisley wished her sister would glance back so she could read her expression. Did she experience any of the irritation and betrayal Paisley felt? She appeared to be entertaining Piper by pointing out pictures in a book. Maybe not listening now.

"Mr. Cedars wasn't the only one who stayed behind, right?" Edward asked. Why would he publicly embarrass his son and daughter-in-law like this?

Craig coughed as if something was stuck in his throat. Guilt, probably. "That's correct, Mayor Grant."

What about the riot these two may have incited near the entrance to town? Someone should mention that. Let embarrassment fall on those most deserving.

"Paisley Cedars Grant remained in Basalt Bay also."

The louse. Her insides quaked. And not with fear.

Judah clasped her hand and held it firmly. Keeping her, or himself, from jumping up and saying something in their defense?

Kathleen patted her other hand, trying to comfort her. It didn't help. Paisley's heart pounded erratically beneath her ribcage. A fire burned in her soul.

"The woman in question has disobeyed orders before." The mayor adjusted his tie, giving the audience another toothy grin. "She's got a record a mile long for causing trouble, we all know that." Another rowdy laugh.

She wanted to jump up and call him a dirty liar. A scoundrel.

Judah leapt to his feet, beating her to it, although not the liar or scoundrel part. "Now, hold on, *Mayor.* Leave my wife out of this! I stayed here too. I'm as much to blame for *Mr. Masters* being inconvenienced and risking his personal safety as anyone."

"Here, here." Deputy Brian's voice sounded snide behind them. "I'll take them into custody, now, Mayor."

Custody?

Judah spun around. "You had your chance."

Uh-oh. Maybe he shouldn't have said that. The deputy already had conflicts with him and her.

"Any time works for me." Deputy Brian took a step forward.

A rumble of voices rang through the crowd. Might be another riot right here.

"What's this? A family feud?" Brad Keifer, the fisherman who helped Judah get back to town in a skiff, stood up behind Craig. "I thought this meeting concerned getting the town up and running. Making smooth transitions. This bickering garbage is a waste of our time."

"Yeah!" "That's right." "Get on with it." Residents shouted.

The mayor pounded a gavel. "Be quiet! Mr. Masters has the floor."

Paisley clenched her jaw. While she was tempted to get up and flee from the absurdity of this meeting, she also felt compelled to stay and hear whatever might be said. Especially with Judah standing as if he wasn't finished talking.

"I say Mr. Masters is done giving his biased account, anyway." Judah's voice grounded out. "No one wants to hear about him being such a humble *Good* Samaritan."

Paisley almost laughed at the shocked reaction on Craig's face.

"That's for sure!" Maggie called out.

"If it wasn't for me, pal"—Craig punched his finger toward Judah—"you could have gotten gangrene. Or worse."

Judah lunged into the aisle.

Oh, no. Oh, no.

"If it wasn't for you, my wife wouldn't have been scared out of her mind."

"You don't know what you're talking about." Craig scrambled past people, making his way into the aisle.

"I know about you sneaking around my father-in-law's—"

"Let's take this outside!" Craig thumped his finger against Judah's chest. "Now!"

"You'd like that wouldn't you?" Judah's hands clenched at his sides. "To fight. Cause more trouble."

Some in the crowd stood, pummeling the air with their fists, yelling out for one or the other to take the first punch.

Paisley's heart pounded fast. She remembered the last time these two fought in the ocean. She stopped them, then. Would she have to do that now?

Mayor Grant pounded his gavel. No one seemed to be listening.

Judah and Craig stood opposite each other, looking like gunslingers in an Old West duel.

Brad Keifer jumped into the middle of the possible fray, his hands extended in both directions. Deputy Brian grabbed Judah's shoulders and yanked him backwards.

"Hey!" He shouted, fighting the deputy's hold.

Brad pointed at Craig, telling him something, probably to stay put.

"Order! Order!" Mayor Grant's voice rose as he pounded his gavel.

When Paisley spun around to check on Judah, he and Deputy Brian were already gone.

Twelve

Judah sat on the edge of the cot in the jail cell, his elbows on his knees, staring at the wall an arm's length away. His first time behind bars. Hopefully, his last. The deputy told him lunch would be delivered soon—not much comfort in that. Irritation churned and gnawed in his gut. He needed to get out of here and find Paisley. To somehow forget the last hour had happened.

Why did he stand up in that meeting? And charging at Craig? He was normally a peaceable man. But he had to defend his wife. Would do the same, if given another chance.

He stared at the gray walls, feeling them closing in on him. How long would he have to stay here? Locked up. Incarcerated. Such disturbing words.

Did his father set him up with that stunt of Craig's, knowing Judah would defend Paisley? Did he prompt the police officer to be ready then laugh as Judah was dragged from City Hall?

Too farfetched even for the mayor, right? Edward Grant was a prideful man with faults, but turning on his own son? Judah groaned.

Back in the meeting, he thought they'd discuss efforts to coordinate resources, figuring out the best ways to help folks and get the town put back together. What a mockery. Instead, Mayor Grant and his puppet, Craig, pointed fingers at Paul, Paisley, and Judah. Hearing his previous coworker lambaste his wife and father-in-law had been too much.

Lord, why did it come to this? Me sitting in a cell stewing for who knows how long? Would he have to spend the night? "Why" bounced around in his brain, in his mouth, until the bitter taste made him want to gag.

What would they write in his file? Did he have a file? Would Deputy Brian note that Judah "almost" got into a fight, sticking up for his wife? Or the other thing they accused him of—remaining in Basalt contrary to evacuation orders. A record would make finding another job difficult.

He groaned and covered his face with his hands. He'd just wanted to reconnect with Paisley, help Paul fix his house, and get the cottage ready for his bride to come home. Now, this.

He should never have attended that lousy meeting. He learned his lesson—stay away from his father, and Craig. Why wasn't that man thrown in jail? He instigated the near fight.

Another thought hit him. What if Craig followed Paisley home? Continued harassing her? Especially now that he knew Judah was detained in the jail.

He moaned, hating this feeling of confinement. Had to get out! He jumped off the cot and banged his palms against the bars. "Hey, Corbin!" He yelled the deputy's last name several times. No response. Maybe Brian could check on Paisley for him. That was his job, right? To ensure citizens' safety. Not just to do the mayor's bidding.

If only Judah could wake up and discover this whole ordeal was a nightmare. He paced the six feet of floor space in front of the bars. Then retraced his steps.

He was supposed to be helping Paul fix the jammed bathroom door today. Not standing idle in this shoebox, wishing he punched Craig in the face. Why did he hesitate?

He blew out a long breath.

I'm sorry, Lord. I'm angry. Still wanting revenge. I should be contemplating what I'm thankful for, how all things work together for good. That there's something to be learned here. Maybe humility. Sigh.

He dropped back onto the cot. After a few minutes, he stretched out on his back, staring at the stark white ceiling. It seemed to get lower and lower. An optical illusion? He shuffled on the stiff mattress. What a miserable, uncomfortable bed. How long would he have to sleep on this? How could he sleep on it? How could anyone?

He tried to pray. To accept and make sense of what happened. *Our Father…* Ugh. He couldn't stir up the humbleness he should have. He felt lacking and irritated.

His thoughts traveled back over the last couple of days, and he recalled some of the good parts. Paisley and him reconnecting—an answer to prayer. A miracle, really. Asking her to marry him and her saying yes. Such a beautiful moment full of God's goodness. He almost smiled at the memory of Paisley's response to his proposal. How she dropped on her knees in front of him and initiated a sweet kiss. Thoughts of his wife would keep him sane in this box. As was relying on the Father who he knew loved him.

I need Your peace, God. He closed his eyes. This time when he prayed the Lord's Prayer, he meant it.

A while later, he heard voices. He sat up. A woman yelled. Paisley? She said something about knowing a secret. That she'd tell everyone if he didn't— The deputy interrupted her gruffly. Was he denying her the right to talk to Judah?

"Let me in. I demand to see my husband!"

Yes! Paisley was insisting that she wanted to see him. He couldn't interpret Brian's low-toned reply. Did he tell her no? Did he inform her that Judah was in solitary confinement? He stood and banged his open palms against the bars like he did before. "Paisley!"

"Juuudaaaah!"

Sounded like a scuffle. Deputy Brian restraining her? He'd better not touch her! A fresh fire burned in Judah's gut. He hit the bars again. "Paisley!"

"Let me go!" she yelled.

"Corbin, leave her alone!" He crossed his arms against the bars, pressing his forehead against his wrist. He felt so helpless. Useless.

A phone rang.

Then a strange silence.

He hated the not knowing. Had Paisley been kicked out of the building? Did she give up and go home? He groaned. How did his life come to this? One problem after another. Now jail? He never would have imagined himself here. And yet, he wouldn't allow himself to get swallowed up in doubt and despair, or in vengeful thoughts, either. But wasn't that how he'd been thinking? Wanting to fight Craig. Enraged at his father.

Ugh.

God, I overreacted with Craig. I felt justified in standing up for my wife, but I let pride take over. I need You. I don't like being locked up. I hate it. Please get me out. And be with Paisley. Give her peace and assurance. I said I'd be there for her. I feel so—

An overwhelming sense of being stuck in the claustrophobic room, behind bars, pressed in on him, like the walls seemed to do a few minutes ago, until he wanted to weep. But then, he shook himself, barely averting panic. Wasn't God in control of his life? Even of this situation? Wasn't he still trusting the Lord? God had a good plan for him and Paisley getting back together and becoming a family again. For that he was thankful. *Focus on that, Grant.*

He dropped back onto the cot and closed his eyes. A long afternoon and night lay ahead. He quoted a few verses and prayed silently.

Some time passed. The door rattled. Who—?

He sat up, expecting lunch. Instead, Deputy Brian shuffled toward the bars, keys outstretched, his cold expression unreadable. The lock clunked as the keys engaged. "You're free to go."

"What?" Judah leapt to his feet. "Really?"

Brian shrugged, gazing at the floor, whether embarrassed or disappointed Judah couldn't tell.

"Well, okay, thanks!" He strode past the deputy and scrambled into the empty office.

"Must be nice having friends in high places."

"Must be. Is Paisley here?"

"Was." Brian dropped onto the chair behind the wooden desk covered in paperwork and plopped his shoes on top. "She made such a fuss, I told her to leave, or I'd make you stay twice as long. Would have, too, if not for—" He shrugged, glanced away.

Her standing up for him made Judah proud.

The deputy withdrew a plastic bag from the desk drawer. "Your belongings."

Judah grabbed his cell phone and stuffed his wallet in his back pocket. "Will this be on my record?"

"Charges are dropped if you keep your nose clean."

If? Why were the charges dropped? Did his father intervene? Or was it something Paisley said? "Glad to hear it." He just wanted to get out of here.

As soon as he hit the sidewalk, he ran. Had to find Paisley. A half block ahead, she stepped out from behind a bush. She dashed toward him and they met in the middle, hugging and clinging to each other.

"Oh, Judah." She sounded near tears.

"I'm okay. Everything's going to be all right now." He was out of jail. Holding the woman he loved. Thank God!

"Brian wouldn't let me see you. He's such a jerk. Always has been."

Judah couldn't argue with that. He stepped back and clasped her hand. "Let's hurry back to your dad's. I want to get the upstairs fixed."

"Wait a sec." She chuckled. "You get thrown in jail and the first thing you want to do when you're released is work on my father's house?"

"Yep. The sooner I finish up there, the sooner I can get the cottage done. Maybe, then, you'll want to come home with me, hmm?"

He heard her soft gasp. Her eyes moistened.

He smoothed the back of his knuckles along her cheek. He pictured himself sitting in the jail cell, missing her. "Actually, the only thing I want to do is this." He leaned in and kissed her, breathing her in, tugging her closer. "Or maybe this." Loving that he had the freedom to touch her, to hold her, he deepened the kiss like she was food, or air, and he couldn't get enough of her. Then, remembering they were in a public place, he pulled back, clearing his throat. "I needed this. You and me being together." Forget working on the houses. Maybe they could talk to Pastor Sagle today.

"Me too." She sighed and smiled up at him with such happiness or contentment that his heart melted. Then her expression changed. "Why did Brian let you out? He said he'd detain you for as long as the law allowed. He threatened to make you stay longer, even when I told him I'd tell everyone what he did on graduation night."

"So that's what the yelling was about." Nice of her to stick up for him like that. He led her up Front Street, moving farther away from City Hall and the jail.

"Yeah. Although, he acted like he didn't care."

"He mentioned something about me having friends in high places."

"The mayor?"

"Probably, but I won't question it. I'm just glad to be out." He glanced over his shoulder, making sure no one followed them. "Good thing I didn't get into a fight with Craig again. I sort of went crazy."

"Sort of?" She snickered and stopped walking. "Yesterday, when you saw him talking to me on the porch, he was telling me something about the mayor. That there were things about him I should know."

"Like what?" Not that he trusted anything Craig said.

"Something about the night—" She shook her head. "I don't know. Did you catch how he and Craig directed the meeting away from their involvement with the riot?"

"I did. Instead, they threw blame on us staying in Basalt Bay."

"Seems fishy."

"Yep."

They continued strolling down the sidewalk, holding hands.

"I'm sorry for getting you into trouble by staying here through the storm." She slowed down the pace. "If I didn't stay in Basalt—if I didn't come back—"

"Hold on. Please, don't say that. Come here." He wrapped his arms around her and kissed the side of her head. Her hair smelled good. Like freshly picked berries in the summer.

She laid her cheek against his sweatshirt. He sighed. This was how he wanted them to face all of life's difficulties—together, his arms around her, her leaning into him.

Too soon, she pulled away and strode forward again, tugging on his hand. "What do we do now?"

"Fix up your dad's. Then our place. Help our neighbors." Get married again. Have babies. Live happily ever after. But he didn't say those things out loud.

Almost to Paul's, she chuckled. "Hey, I just thought of something. You lost."

"Lost?"

"The dare. You left the meeting first!"

He forgot about the dare. Didn't give it a second thought. "That's not fair. The deputy removed me from the building."

"Still, I won." She winked and seemed way too pleased with herself.

Playing along might not be such a bad idea. "Okay. Let's say, hypothetically, you won. What one thing would you want me to do for you?" He had a few ideas of his own.

"When you least expect it, I'll tell you what I want." She chortled, and the musical sound filled the air around them.

Thirteen

With a lighter feeling than she experienced in days, Paisley skipped across Dad's still-mucky yard. She didn't care about her muddy boots. Or how the town meeting turned sour. Gladness oozed through her, warmed her. Judah was released from jail! Thank God. Yes, thank God. *He* answered a prayer she didn't even think to pray.

As she and Judah reached the front stairs, they both came to a halt. Aunt Callie and Maggie Thomas sat in the rocking chairs on her father's battered porch, staring at them with matching scowls.

Paisley gulped. "H-hello."

"Paisley." Aunt Callie's eyebrows twitched. "Judah." Her voice deepened.

"Callie, it's nice to see you." He sounded polite. "Maggie."

The innkeeper didn't respond, but by the look of her grumpy expression she was upset about something.

Paisley and Judah shuffled up the three steps like criminals about to face judgment.

"What's going on?" Her dad must be hiding somewhere the way he did whenever his sister or Maggie came around.

"That debacle at the meeting was unbecoming of a Cedars, or a Grant." Aunt Callie puffed up like a helium balloon. "This town needs to pull together, not be jerked apart. And Mayor Grant ridiculing you two?" She huffed. "If my brother knew folks were talking publicly about him, he'd stew in humiliation for a month! Best not to tell him." Her glare turned on Judah. "What were you thinking, young man?"

"That wasn't Judah's fault!" Paisley defended him. "The mess in City Hall was Craig's doing. The mayor's fault. Not his."

He clasped her wrist. "However, I'm sorry if my remarks offended you."

"Hmph." Aunt Callie exchanged a disgruntled glance with Maggie.

The innkeeper's nose rose higher.

These two gossipmongers took their haughty attitudes too far.

"Aunt Callie, Judah stood up for me and Dad. I wouldn't call that a debacle. I call it heroic." She would take on both harpies if they said another word against him.

His fingers clutched hers. She returned an answering squeeze.

Maggie's gaze zeroed in on their clasped hands and her scowl deepened. What? She didn't approve of a couple giving each other a second chance? Maybe Paisley wouldn't invite her, or any of her family, Aunt Callie included, to the vow ceremony. Eloping worked fine the first time. Might be fine again.

Her aunt rocked furiously in the old chair. "Who does Mayor Grant think he is?"

With each back and forth motion, the rocker clunked

against the wooden floor. Should Paisley warn her that the porch furniture was archaic and weakened by flood waters?

"Bringing his own son to task during a community meeting?" Aunt Callie harrumphed. "And my niece too! I'm appalled a leader of our city would behave in such a despicable manner."

"He's a disgrace to Basalt Bay." Maggie kept her chair's rhythm going too.

How was Judah taking this? He rolled his eyes, giving her his silent answer.

Aunt Callie shuffled her backside deeper into her chair as if settling in for a long stay. "It's about time the mayor came down a notch. I have an inkling of just how to achieve that."

"Me too." A sinister expression crossed Maggie's face.

"Maggie, Patty, and I say he should be replaced. Impeached!" Aunt Callie nodded her double chin. "I don't care if he is your father-in-law, Paisley Rose, I'm going to stand up for my town, my family, and do something."

By the way she plopped her palms on the chair's handrails, it looked like she might stand up and do something right then. Instead, she stared hard at Judah. He cleared his throat and shuffled his shoes as if he felt awkward. No wonder. How could Paisley get these two gadabouts onto a different tangent? While she supported the idea of ousting the mayor, she cared about Judah's feelings, too.

"We'll start a citywide recall petition." Maggie's gray hair fluttered in the wind. She brought the rocker to a stop. "Would you sign such a document?" She cast a squinty-eyed glare at Paisley.

"Oh, well, I—"

"Brilliant idea, Maggie." Aunt Callie clapped. "We'll get

everyone in Basalt Bay to sign. Cheer on the agreeable. Pressure the reluctant. Who doesn't have a beef against Mayor Grant?"

Who, indeed?

Judah cleared his throat and stared at the ground.

Maggie stomped her foot. "Even Deputy Brian disagrees with the mayor's storm protocol. The way he stayed in town when everyone else left was wrong. Does the mayor picture himself the king? And what about the business with the riot? I witnessed him and Masters leaving for the barricade. I'll testify against both."

"But you don't know for sure what happened, right?" Judah spoke softly. "You weren't at the entrance of town that night."

"W-well, I-I"—Maggie stammered—"I h-had a right to speak up at today's session. To state my opinion. That's why I went to the meeting, but Mayor Grant shut me down."

"The man had an agenda, that's for sure." Aunt Callie pounded the air with her index finger. "I smelled a rat as soon as Masters opened his mouth. His sitting next to my niece made me itch." She scratched both armpits as if to prove her point.

"The rumors are flying too." Maggie huffed.

Aunt Callie whirled around and faced Paisley and Judah so fast it was a wonder she didn't get whiplash. "What do you two know about it?"

Judah shuffled closer to Paisley.

She grasped for a distraction. "Did you ask Dad for some sweet tea, Auntie?"

Her aunt's eyes widened. "Haven't seen Pauly. I bet he's hiding. But when I first climbed those rickety stairs"—she glared at Judah—"I heard something inside. You got tea?"

"There's no ice." Paisley grinned at her success in redirecting the topic. "However, since the electricity is on, I can whip up some hot tea."

"That would be nice."

"I'll be right back." Paisley nodded at Judah to follow her inside.

"Ladies." His footsteps clomped across the floorboards behind her.

She put the teakettle on the front burner and Judah leaned against the sink with his arms crossed. She grabbed teacups and enough tea bags for the ladies and herself. "What do you think about what they said?"

"Kind of a sensitive subject. Not for you. You can ask me anything." He gave her a reassuring smile, although the lines around his eyes still looked tight.

"Okay. So, how do you feel about it?" Maybe she shouldn't push, but they were trying to be more honest with each other.

"I hate the thought of an uprising in Basalt Bay. We're just getting over a gigantic storm and its destruction. The town ought to be pulling together." He sighed. "Kind of like us, you know?"

She did.

"Then there's my dad. What would he be, if not the mayor?" His shoulders rose then fell. "I'm not defending him. Just saying."

"I understand. He's your father."

She took a couple of steps to where he stood. Wrapping her arms around his waist, her cheek came to rest against the soft fabric covering his chest, her favorite way to be close to him. No matter what trouble the women on the porch might be instigating, she was thankful that Judah was here with her and not in jail. His head leaned against hers as they stood silently, hearts connecting, until she heard the teapot's whistle.

"Would you check on my dad?" She made a couple of furtive

nods toward the stairs, giving him an alternative to going back outside.

"Thank you." His voice rose in volume. "I should check on Paul. We need to get the bathroom door unstuck." He winked at her before taking the stairs two at a time.

She grinned and added plenty of honey to the cups. She scooped up the tray with the three teacups rattling against each other, then hurried to the porch.

"Finally," Maggie grumbled.

"Sorry for the wait."

Both ladies sipped their tea in silence. A blessed silence. Leaning against the porch column, Paisley drank her hot beverage, wishing she made herself coffee instead.

"Now, for answers!" Aunt Callie sent her one of those spider-killing scowls.

What else could she use as a distraction? "Everything okay at the inn, Mrs. Thomas?"

"No. Someone stole a boat from my property." She squinted at Paisley like it might have been her.

She took a long swallow of tea. Once, a long time ago, she borrowed Maggie's boat.

"I made a full report with the deputy." The innkeeper managed to rock the chair on its uneven rails and sip her tea without spilling. "Someone broke into one of my rental units, too."

Aunt Callie stomped her foot. "Paisley Rose, tell me about your sister and that man!"

"That hunk, you mean?" Maggie spoke without cracking a smile.

Paisley nearly choked on her tea.

"You think he's handsome?" Aunt Callie coughed. "He's

a menace, that's what. Now, tell me what you've heard about this romance. Is your sister involved with the brute?"

"I haven't spoken with Paige yet."

"What?" Her aunt's jaw dropped.

"Craig told me they're not married. Otherwise, I don't know what's going on." Other than the cozy way they acted when she first saw them together.

"Of course, they're not married." Aunt Callie scoffed. "I would have heard about that. What they're doing together at all is what I'm determined to find out. And I will find out."

Me too. Paisley waited until the last slurps signaled the two women finished their tea. She held out the tray for them to set their teacups down.

Maggie shoved off the chair. "See you tomorrow, Callie."

"I'll call folks. Stir the pot." Aunt Callie remained in her chair.

Maggie descended the stairs, glancing back as if to say something. Then she must have tripped. Her hands flailed in the air and she thudded onto her backside. She groaned and whimpered, sitting on the last step and her legs on the wet grass.

Paisley dropped the tray on the railing then rushed to her. "Are you okay?" She squatted beside Maggie, laying her hand on her shoulder.

"No, I'm not okay," the woman snapped. "Terrible steps."

"I told you those stairs were unacceptable." Aunt Callie harrumphed.

They felt sturdy to Paisley. This was just an unfortunate accident.

"You okay, Maggie?" Aunt Callie sounded worried.

"I will be." Maggie ran her right hand down her hip, squinting at Paisley. "Nothing's broken, good thing. Bruised though."

"I'm so sorry." What else could she say? Hopefully, Maggie wouldn't sue Dad for her misstep.

Judah ran out of the house. "What happened? I heard—" He drew in a sharp breath. "Mrs. Thomas, what happened?" He rushed to her.

"She fell on the steps." Paisley met his gaze and cringed.

"Can you stand?"

"Probably." Maggie whimpered.

Together, Judah and Paisley helped her to a standing position, their arms supporting her back.

"How do you feel?"

"How do you think I feel? I hurt! I want to go home. You should have warned me about those uneven steps." Maggie nailed Paisley with a biting glare. "Your negligence wreaks havoc again."

"I'm sorry you got hurt. Really, I am."

"How about if I drive you home?" Judah seemed to know how to deal with the irritable woman better than she did.

"I wouldn't say no." The innkeeper drew in a sharp breath. "Ooh. That hurts." She limped a couple of steps.

"Do you need to see a doctor?" Judah helped her get into his truck. Over his shoulder, he shrugged at Paisley as she followed behind them.

"Just a sprain, probably." Maggie moaned.

Judah ran around and hopped into the cab.

"Sorry," Paisley said again and shut the door.

Hopefully, Maggie wouldn't cause them legal trouble. Blaming Paisley for her woes? That seemed inevitable.

Fourteen

For the next two days, Judah worked on Paul's house, hefting the greater workload since his father-in-law wasn't quite strong enough. Paisley worked alongside him too, but her well-being concerned him, also. Their trio of carpenters made an unlikely group. Paul with his insulin deficiency. Paisley with her hypothermia scare. And him recuperating from his leg injury.

But they accomplished plenty, even scraping out some time to help their neighbors. And with assistance from James and Brad Keifer, who showed up after the town meeting to check on Judah, they repaired the damaged roof. Eventually, it would require a massive re-shingling. For now, it was mended.

After Judah watched a few YouTube videos, they tackled the damaged bathroom ceiling and doorframe. They stabilized the walls and beams in a way that Chip Gaines might even be proud of.

While Brad held up a board, he razzed Judah. "So what's with the public family feud, Grant?"

"Beats me."

"Never saw anyone so red faced as you when the deputy hauled you off to the slammer." He guffawed.

"Yeah, yeah. I'd rather forget about it."

"No wonder. Can't imagine sitting down to Sunday dinners with the mayor." He hooted. "Pass the peas, but first you have to vote on whether they should have been sautéed or steamed."

Judah put up with the teasing, since he appreciated Brad's help. But he was glad when the conversation moved on to other topics.

Now, he and Paisley were teamed up, tackling the removal of damaged sheetrock from the lower portion of the walls. A fine white dust filled the air. They'd scrounged up dust masks, one from Paul's toolbox, and one borrowed from James. As Judah pried boards off the walls, his thoughts wandered.

Earlier today, he tried convincing Paul to leave the house while they attacked the boards and the ensuing dust that could potentially harbor mold. The older man balked, arguing that he could handle any task they could. But when James stopped by and invited him to a salmon bake—he'd gone fishing at the lighthouse and caught a couple of silver salmon—it was too much for Paul to resist.

Judah knew that today would be his last day of working here, and he was hoping for a few minutes to talk with Paisley. Oh, he'd pop back over if they needed him to do something. But it was time for him to tackle the repairs at the cottage. Although, he hated leaving his wife here.

Soon they'd share the same house and bedroom, he kept reminding himself. Some days that seemed like an impossible dream. Other times, when he caught her gazing at him, or she slipped her palm against his and linked their fingers, or even stole a quick kiss, then the impossible seemed possible. Those blessed moments gave him renewed hope. And hope was a beautiful thing that made the sunset more brilliant, the sunshine brighter, and lightened a man's spirit. Truly.

They were on a journey, the two of them. Having her come home to him, to want him with her whole heart, for her not to run anymore, was worth every second he waited for her. And he would continue to wait, however long it took. So help him God.

Paisley stepped next to him, blinking, the dirty mask covering her nose and mouth. She nodded toward the door. Her dark eyes gazed at him through the plastic safety glasses, a question in her expression. An invitation, it seemed.

He could use some clean air to breathe and some time alone with her. He followed her outside. About ten feet from the house, he dusted off his clothes before he pulled off his mask and safety glasses. He inhaled deeply.

She did the same, dusting herself off. "What a mess, huh?" A white layer covered her hair, making her look like a fairy princess.

"Yep." He whisked white dust from her upper lip. He let his fingers dawdle near the right corner of her mouth. Gulp.

Their gazes held. Her warm expression thrilled him, made him want to forget about working and kiss her. His heart rate hit hyperdrive fast. *Take this slowly, Romeo.* He didn't want to scare her off. Didn't want her assuming romance was the only thing on his mind. Not the *only* thing. He chuckled to himself.

They were staring into each other's eyes more since his jail release. Smiling. Flirting. He considered those moments treasures. Each one made him want more. He hoped they kept acting romantic long after they renewed their vows. He'd make sure they did, this time.

"I'm beat. How about you?" She wiped her forehead.

"Take a break. You should catch up on some rest."

She laughed. "As long as you're working, buddy, so am I. Can't get rid of me."

"Never." A little dust caught in his throat. Or emotion. He coughed. "I've been meaning to talk with you about something."

"Oh?" Her eyes darkened.

"Nothing bad. Just stuff about the cottage. So much work to be done out there also."

"Oh, right. You're probably in a hurry to get started. With all this"—she swayed her hand toward Paul's house—"I've kind of forgotten about the cottage. Not to mention working off past bad behavior with a certain neighbor."

He toyed with a strand of her hair. "You've done a good job with trying to make amends. Building bridges. About the beach house? Would you mind if we went out and took inventory?"

Her white-dusted eyebrows furrowed. "I want to help. Really, I do."

He lowered his hand and brushed off his jeans.

"Dad still needs me here." Her cheeks hued the rosiest pink. "Also, we haven't discussed our vow ceremony. When it will be. What expectations there might be."

Expectations? Did she think—? "I didn't mean for us to stay out there together, yet."

"You didn't? Oh, well … things are so hectic." She looked flustered. "The ruined sheetrock. Mudding. I still haven't talked with Paige."

He recognized her nervousness by the way she chattered.

"I understand." Although disappointment clogged his arteries. He stared down the block at people hauling garbage to both sides of the street, tidying up, making their properties look better. Like he should be doing at the cottage.

Paisley's hedging about coming with him stung. Just a setback, though. They were separated for three years. Adjustments needed to be made. He was the one in an all-fired hurry. But didn't he ask for a quick engagement? Didn't she agree?

Inwardly, he groaned. Maybe it was busyness and chores that kept them from moving forward. Nothing more. Nothing else he should read into it. And, she was right, they hadn't talked much about the future. Did he avoid discussing certain things with her, afraid those topics might set them back further? Was she, perhaps, avoiding things too?

She gazed down at her shoes. Gnawed on her lip. Was she feeling shy around him, now? Had they already gone backwards in their relationship?

"Hey." He caressed her shoulder. "If you want to hang out here with your dad for a while longer, you should. No worries on my account."

"Really?" She blew out a breath. "Thanks for understanding."

"Of course." He nodded, making sure he smiled, even if it didn't quite reach his heart. He'd continue being patient, but he couldn't deny feeling a tad disappointed by the delays.

"When this is over"—he rocked his thumb toward her father's house—"will you go on a date with me? A real, get dressed-up sort of date?"

A smile crossed her lips—lips he refrained from meeting with his own. "Yes, of course, I would love to go on a date with you."

"And after we go on a date together ..."

"Mmhmm."

"And after we do some talking ..."

"Yes?"

"Then will you marry me again?" His heart lay exposed on his sleeve. What if she thought she made too hasty of a decision about them getting back together? What if she changed her mind again?

She stared into his eyes, making knots twist and tangle in his chest. He didn't sever the invisible cord. Wouldn't. Could barely breathe as he kept his gaze glued on hers.

"After we have a date, or two or three"—she spoke almost musically—"and after we do some serious heart-to-heart talking, I will marry you, Judah Grant. I promise."

The air whooshed out of his lungs. "Sounds great." Perfect. Magical. He wanted to scoop her up in his arms and kiss her breathless. But they were covered in dust. And she said a date or two or three. More delays. "Guess we should get back to work."

"Guess we should."

He linked his fingers with hers. Dust or no dust, he needed to feel that bond between them. Then it hit him. Three dates? Shoot. Three dates could happen in twenty-four hours. Breakfast. Lunch. Dinner. No problem.

However, Bert's—the local diner with the best burgers on the West Coast—was closed. As were most businesses in town and even in some of the nearby coastal cities. He'd have to drum up some creative ideas about where and when to date her.

First, sheetrock removal at Paul's. Fixing things up at the cottage. Then focusing on the most important thing—winning back the love of his life.

Fifteen

Having electricity and hot running water made a huge difference in the ease of life after their disaster existence of the last twelve days. Following two cups of coffee, showering with lots of hot water, and eating real food, Paisley felt more human, even if she slept in her childhood bedroom that conjured up too many thoughts of the past. Three days had passed since the fateful town meeting when Judah went to jail. One day since he returned to the cottage.

She already missed him. She was used to his being around, winking at her, sneaking kisses, touching hands. The little flirtations—she missed those.

She could have gone to the cottage with him, so she had no one to blame but herself. But she chose to stay with Dad. He needed her, she kept telling herself. Yesterday, James came over and the three of them cut and hammered sheetrock into place. Today, mudding and taping loomed. She'd never done either.

She stared out the kitchen window into the backyard. No more debris or tree limbs were scattered about. The swampy water remaining on the grass for days finally evaporated or was absorbed into the ground. The sun shone. A great start to this fall day.

Yesterday, the grocery store opened. As did Miss Patty's hardware store. The shop owner still hadn't thanked Paisley for her help. Might never acknowledge it.

Dad entered the kitchen dressed in his usual flannel shirt and stained jeans. A dust mask hung around his neck. "Ready to get started?"

"Sure. The sooner we get done the better." She stayed to help him but, today, her heart was elsewhere.

For a few moments, she got lost in thoughts of Judah working alone at the cottage. Probably fixing the roof—that's what he told her. What if he slipped and fell? Or injured himself with a power tool? As quickly as the dire thoughts came, she felt silly for thinking them.

Judah was smart. A strong worker. He had a cell phone. If he encountered a problem, he'd call someone, even if it wasn't her. As soon as she got her first paycheck—whenever she found a job—she'd buy a cell phone. Priority number one.

Speaking of work, what kind of job did she want to pursue? Serving at the diner? An image of the sailboat thrust through the front window of Bert's Fish Shack dampened the notion. The local restaurant would probably be closed for a while. Although, it wouldn't hurt for her to walk by and inquire.

"Paisley?" Dad called from the living room.

"Coming." She tromped into the front part of the house. Hours of smoothing mud over sheetrock tape lay ahead of her. Would her efforts pass her father's inspection?

Much later, her knees ached as if she walked a mile on them. Her shoulders were stiff. Mud was caked around her fingernails. She mentally griped at the inventors of tape and joint compound, and Hurricane Blaine. Dad hinted that she redo several of her first mudding attempts. Sigh. After two hours of intense labor, she got the hang of smoothing out the mayonnaise-like mixture. However, she wouldn't choose to do this type of work again.

Someone clomped up the front steps. Judah? Paisley stood and scowled at the dried mud on her jeans. Did she have joint compound on her hair and face, too? She licked her lips. Tasted mud. Blech.

"Are we expecting someone?" Dad smoothed the trowel across the mesh he installed over a hole.

"Not me." Unless it was Judah.

The door swung open. Paige stepped into the room, then stopped and stared at Paisley. Her gaze swung toward Dad. "I need h-help." Her voice broke.

"What's wrong?" Dad dropped his tool. Mud flecks splattered the wall where he worked. He wiped his hands on a cloth and shuffled over to his youngest daughter.

Paisley didn't move.

"Where's Piper?" He patted Paige's shoulder, getting mud on her too. "Is she okay?"

"She's playing at the neighbor's house." Paige squinted toward Paisley.

Did she want to talk to their father alone?

"I can go upstairs. I could use a break anyway. Wash up." She moved toward the first step.

"No. Wait." Paige moaned. "I need you to hear this too."

If she was in trouble, family came before Paisley's grudge

about the kind of company her sister kept. "What is it? What's wrong?"

"Mayor Grant—" Paige's face puckered up.

"Is he sick? Having a heart attack?" She could imagine that with his high stress level.

"No. He … he …" Paige covered her face and sobbed.

Dad wrapped his arms around her. "There. There. It can't be that bad."

"But it *is*." Paige wailed. "He bought my *building* from the bank." She pressed her hand to her mouth. "I d-don't know w-what to d-do."

Paisley tried to catch up with her sister's problem. "Bought it as in … you must get out, today, or what?"

"He says I can either rent from him or get out." She hiccupped. "He's doubling the cost. I'm still waiting for the flood insurance money. And there's all the artists to reimburse." She sniffled. "I don't know how I'll survive. I have to provide for Piper."

"Of course, you do," Dad said.

"Why would the mayor even want your old dilapidated building?"

Paige glanced at her sharply.

"Oh, um." She didn't mean to sound disparaging. "Why would he invest in the gallery when it's so damaged?"

"He's scarfing up buildings all over town." Paige swayed out her hands. "He even tried to get Bert to sell to him."

"No way. Burt would *never* sell his place to Mayor Grant." She would bet big money on that, but just the idea of the mayor taking over the town, being even more in control, riled her.

"That's what I thought." Paige wiped her nose with a tissue she took from her coat pocket. "I didn't have a choice in the matter since I'm leasing. But I planned to buy it someday."

"What can we do to help?" Dad shuffled his glasses up his nose.

"I thought Judah might be here. Might know what to do." Paige rubbed her hands over her coat sleeves.

"Like what?"

"Maybe stop his dad from taking over the town." Paige stared back at her.

"Not likely." Paisley almost laughed, but her sister's glare stopped her.

"He's good with this kind of stuff. Standing up for a cause. I thought he might jump in and help me."

Sure, Judah might offer her advice. But go against his dad? Paisley doubted that. Especially after his stint in jail and the mayor possibly influencing his release.

"Mayor Grant's taking advantage of folks who are already in a bad way." Dad pulled a multi-colored hanky out of his pants pocket and blew his nose. "Such a shame."

Taking advantage of others sounded just like Edward. But why would he bother with the ruined gallery? Was he stockpiling real estate? Was the building even worth his investment?

"Where is Judah?" Paige glanced around the room.

"At the cottage working." Paisley toed a bump on the floor where the linoleum bulged. "The same as everybody and their brother's doing in Basalt today."

"Oh, right. I should have known. Sorry to have bothered you guys." Paige whirled around and stomped toward the door.

Dad glared at Paisley.

"What?"

"You could have been nicer."

This wasn't her fault. Just because Edward happened to be

her father-in-law didn't mean she had access to his evil brain. Besides, what could Judah do?

Still, she needed to work things out with her sister. "Hold up." She followed Paige to the porch. "I didn't mean to sound insincere. I'm sorry about your building getting into the mayor's greedy paws. I can't imagine that tyrant as a landlord."

Paige nodded. "Thanks."

Dad's footfall landed just behind hers. "If you want to talk to Judah, call him."

"That's right. His cell phone should be charged now." Although Paisley still doubted that he could do anything to change the situation with the art gallery.

Paige's lower lip trembled. She sighed a long, weary-sounding sigh.

"What do you need us to do, Sis?" Dad clasped Paige's hand, surprising Paisley with his show of affection. Even his voice sounded gentler when he spoke to his youngest.

A dig of jealousy from long ago twisted in her heart. Silly childish feelings.

"Um, would you"—Paige nodded toward Paisley—"be willing to come with me to talk to the mayor?"

What? "Where?" Not to his house. Please, not to his house. "To his office. Or maybe his house. I don't know." Her voice rose. "You're still his daughter-in-law, aren't you? I mean, you can talk to him, right?"

Paisley snorted. "Technically, yes. However, we don't get along." Understatement.

Dark brown eyes mirroring hers shimmered back. Some said she and Paige could be mistaken for twins. She never bought into the assessment. They were too unalike.

"Aren't you and Judah back together?"

The question riled her a little. She had her own questions to ask Paige. *Are you dating Craig? Is he Piper's daddy?* Instead, she took a breath and answered truthfully. "We're working on it."

"Judah asked her to marry him again." Dad pumped the air once with his fist.

She expected Paige to frown or roll her eyes. Instead, she wrapped her arms around her. "I'm happy for you." She backed up, folding her hands in front of her waist. "By now you've probably heard I have a little girl. Piper."

Paisley nodded. "She's perfect."

Paige's face creased into a beautiful smile. "She's the best thing I ever did. The most holy version of life I will ever experience."

An image came to mind of Paisley holding her premature stillborn daughter in the hospital. Touching her tiny fingers. Her sweet little face. Had anyone tended the miniature grave where she put flowers before she left Basalt three years ago? Did the storm surge do any damage to the gravesite? Terrible thought. She'd check as soon as possible. Fortunately, the cemetery was at a higher elevation than most of the town.

"I look forward to meeting Piper." She forced the words past the lump in her throat.

"She'll love you." Paige gazed at her. "About the mayor? Will you come with me? Maybe if I can explain how important the gallery is to me and other artists in the area, he'll listen."

Tension seeped through Paisley's pores like a fever, spreading fast. She inhaled, then exhaled, controlling her breathing. "I guess I could."

Dad walked back to the door. "How did you get the news about the buyout?"

"Certified letter." Paige stuffed her hands in her coat pockets.

"They warned me. The bank gave me ten days to drum up the cash. But when the second hurricane hit, how could I?"

"Edward knows that. He's a reasonable businessman." Dad shrugged. "Go talk to him."

Reasonable? Paisley coughed hard.

Dad frowned. "Even if we don't see eye to eye, he didn't get voted into office for being a sleaze. The people of this town trust him."

She had a much different view but bit her tongue.

"Before Blaine, Mayor Grant came to the gallery and helped me. I thought he was a decent guy, being neighborly." Paige scowled. "I was naïve. Should have known he was interested in my troubles for his own gain."

"A shark in kitten's fur," Paisley muttered then strode to the rocking chair. She pushed it back and forth, listening to it clunk against the aged wood beneath.

"The art gallery is my livelihood. I have to do what I can to save it." Paige lifted her shoulders as if to make herself taller or braver. "I can do this. Mayor Grant isn't the monster some make him out to be."

Right.

Even though Paisley's legs quaked, and her heart beat double time at the thought of facing her father-in-law, if her sister needed moral support, she'd go with her. Maybe the mayor wouldn't be at his office or his house. Was that too much to hope for?

Sixteen

Paisley lifted her fist in front of the mahogany door of the mayor's house, then froze. Three years had passed since her last visit here. Anxiety ratcheted up her ribs. Shivers crawled across her neck, chilling her. If she didn't faint, this would be her lucky day. What would the mayor say when he saw her? Accuse her of being unfit to marry his son, again?

Paige stood next to her, their arms touching. If only her sister knew of Paisley's great fear. How her knees knocked. How much she wanted to run away from this property.

"Did you bring a cell phone?"

Paige nodded.

"If anything happens to me—"

Judah's mom opened the door. Not the mayor—what a relief. She must have heard the car drive up because Paisley's knuckles didn't connect with the door. Her mother-in-law's eyes and mouth widened. "Oh, my. Paisley! You're here. I've wanted to talk to you." Bess's arms surrounded her in a warm embrace.

"I'm so glad you came home, honey. So glad for Judah. For all of us."

The woman's kindness soothed some of her nerves, acting as a balm to an inner wound she couldn't quite identify.

Bess glanced at Paige. "Oh, hello, dear. Welcome. I'm Bess Grant."

"Thanks. I'm Paige, Paisley's sister."

"I remember you."

The two shook hands.

Heavy footsteps thudded toward them. Bess cringed and mouthed, *"Sorry."*

"What's going on here?" the mayor thundered as soon as he came into view. He yanked Bess roughly away from Paisley. When he released his grip, Bess stumbled backwards. She clutched her arm and massaged the area where the ogre manhandled her. Paisley wanted to go to her and see if she was okay. But crossing the threshold? Edging past him? No, thanks. However, she would if he dared to touch Bess again.

Paige linked arms with Paisley. Fear and dread bound them together.

Could a woman marry a man and not claim his father as a relative? She would do that in a heartbeat. She tightened the crook of her arm snugly around her sister's.

"What do you two want?" Edward growled, crossing his arms over his dark gray sports coat. A red stain marred his light gray tie. Jam? Wine? It would serve him right to wear a dirty tie all day and no one mention the stain. Then, later, for him to see it in the mirror. "I'm just about to leave. Say what you came to say, then go."

Paige cleared her throat but didn't speak. She gnawed on her lip and stared at the ground.

Paisley squinted up at Edward, despite his domineering stance that was surely meant to intimidate them. Where did Bess go? Hiding in the shadows? Poor woman married to such a man.

"My sister needs to talk to you about the certified letter she received in the mail today." She nudged Paige's arm.

"Go on." Edward's voice deepened.

Paige lifted her chin. "Mr. Grant"—her voice came out quietly—"I want to keep my business. It's important to the artists in our community. I've put a lot of money and work into it. Please, let me keep my lease."

"What business?" He scoffed. "Your little enterprise is washed up. You and half the town. You should thank me for rescuing you from your financial mistakes and ruin."

"Rescuing me?" Her voice rose. "Are you crazy?"

Edward's nostrils flared. The pores on his nose expanded. His hands clenched at his sides. One of the soles of his leather boots tapped the cement landing. He reminded Paisley of a bull preparing to attack the matador. She let go of her sister's arm and shuffled slightly in front of her.

"You may view me as someone who needs 'rescuing.'" Paige pulsed her index finger. "But if you think I'll let you take control of what I've worked hard for, dreamed about for so long, you are mistaken! I'll fight you with every breath in my body."

Go, Paige! Paisley was bursting with pride that her docile sister would stand up to the mayor like that.

"Do you imagine a wisp of a woman like you can rail against the mayor of Basalt Bay and get away with it unscathed?" He guffawed. "Just try it. You'll fail."

Was that a threat? Paisley squeezed her fists. Bopping the man on the nose passed through her thoughts. As did bragging about it to Aunt Callie and Maggie, ladies who'd consider it a badge of honor to spread such a story all over Basalt.

Paige glared at Edward. "How you purchased my building, and other buildings in town, and whatever little insider tricks you're playing while businessowners are down on their luck, is indefensible. Inhumane."

"You have no idea what you're saying. You should leave. Go!" Edward thrust his hand toward Paige's car.

A fifteen-second standoff of grimaces ensued.

"I plan to report your unethical acts to … to Deputy Brian."

What? Paisley swiveled toward her sister. Why did she bring up Brian Corbin? Wasn't he one of the mayor's pawns?

Edward guffawed. Then he lunged forward, his finger jabbing the air. Paisley and Paige jumped backward. "Don't you dare accuse me of unethical behavior. You Cedars girls—" He spat. "Your precious deputy is nothing. A wart on a toad. If I want him fired, he'll be fired within the hour."

Precious deputy? What was he talking about? And how he rushed at them, yelling, threatening, made Paisley's blood boil. Wait until Judah heard about this.

"You're disillusioned to think people respect and admire you." Paige glowered at him, not giving up her fight. "They let you have your way because you're the mayor and you're rich. Not me. You can't take what's mine." She stomped her foot.

"Just watch me." He snorted. "You left the gallery ransacked. Abandoned. You broke your contract."

"I did not abandon it!" she yelled, surprising Paisley. "Everyone left their homes and businesses during the hurricane. It was the law. Didn't you prove that by having your own son thrown in jail?"

A tic twitched in Edward's jaw. "Get off my property! And don't come back."

"Edward!" Bess rushed forward from wherever she'd gone. "He doesn't mean it. You're both welcome here."

"No, they're not. Stay out of this." Edward lifted his hand as if to subdue her, then he squinted at Paisley and stuffed his hands in his pockets.

The cad. Anger burned through her. She clenched her fists until her nails dug into her palms.

He stepped toward her with a menacing gleam, but she didn't back away.

"Come on. He's crazy," Paige whispered then ran for her car.

Paisley didn't move.

"You're always welcome here," Bess said in a soft tone.

"No, she isn't." Edward thrust his finger toward his wife. "Stay out of my business!"

Bess and Paisley exchanged a meaningful glance. Something was wrong here.

"Paisley, let's go," Paige called from the driver's seat.

Just then, a loud engine roared up the hill. Judah's white pickup swerved around the corner, coming to a screeching stop next to Paige's car. He thrust open the door and leapt out. He strode across the gravel and came straight to Paisley. "You okay?"

She nodded. How did he know she was here? Did her dad tell him?

"What's going on?" Judah crossed his arms and stood opposite his father.

"Hello, Son." Bess rushed forward and hugged him. "Thank you for coming."

Oh. Did she call him?

"Mom."

"Why are you here?" Edward's voice didn't sound as mean, now.

"Because my wife is here." He reached back and clasped her hand.

She squeezed his fingers. She owed him big time for this.

Paige scurried back over, apparently bolstered by Judah's arrival.

"Is something going on that we should discuss as a family?" His voice had a hard edge to it. "Paige is my sister-in-law."

"Just business. A misunderstanding." Edward huffed. "Nothing to concern yourself with."

"Paisley and her sister are my concerns."

The mayor shrugged. "Want to come in for coffee? Your mother made scones."

Seriously? After threatening Paige and ordering them off his property, he wanted them to come in for snacks?

"That's right." Bess wrung her hands. "We can sit down and have a pleasant conversation."

How could they ever have a pleasant conversation?

An awkward silence followed.

Judah glanced at Paisley. She shook her head discreetly. Even if half the house belonged to Bess, she refused to tiptoe through Edward's half.

"Not this time. But thanks." He gave his parents a tight smile. "When I finish fixing the beach house, we'll have you over for a barbecue."

Paisley would make sure to have a job by then so as not to be home. Maybe even request the late shift.

"Dad." Nodding at his father, Judah drew Paisley toward the vehicles.

Paige slipped behind the steering wheel of her car and started the engine.

"Paisley, wait!" Bess hurried over to them, patted Judah's arm, then faced Paisley. "I wanted to say, again, how happy I am that you came home. I hope we can be friends."

"I'd like that too." She clutched her mother-in-law's hand.

Judah must have gotten his sweeter side from her. Not from his dad.

Bess hugged Judah. "Don't stay away too long."

"Love you, Mom."

"Bess, let them go," Edward yelled.

Bess glanced toward Judah, then Paisley, with an agonized glint in her eyes.

"Is she going to be okay?" Paisley whispered as he opened the passenger door of the car for her.

"What do you mean?"

"Your mom. I'm worried about her."

"She's up here on the mountain by herself way too much."

Bess being up here *alone* wasn't what had her worried.

Seventeen

Two days later, Paisley and her dad were almost finished painting the living room walls with a cream-colored paint that resembled sage more than tan when it dried. The taping and mudding had turned out okay. Not professional, by any means. But she wouldn't have to hide her section of work behind a couch or deny her part in the project, either. Dad touched up some of her earlier efforts, but she didn't mind. With practice she got better at smoothing out the joint compound.

The next task was tackling the kitchen. Fortunately, it had fewer walls.

She wished Judah could help them still, but he had his own property to fix. Their property. She sighed. A few days had passed since they last spoke about their vow ceremony. Was she just imagining an emotional gap widening between them? Yesterday, he followed her back to her dad's house after they left his parent's place. But then he waved and drove off. Presumably to the cottage, but she'd wanted to talk to him about his mom.

She rolled more paint. This slow, tedious work gave her too much time to think. Did Judah even remember about the date nights they were supposed to be having? Spending time together alone, talking and planning, should be a priority, right?

Suddenly, Dad groaned and slumped to the floor next to his paint can.

"Dad, are you okay?" She dropped her roller and rushed over to him. "Can you hear me?"

"I … hear … you." His eyes opened. "Just tired. Weak." He leaned his forehead against the back of his paint-splotched hands resting against his knees. He exhaled a loud, throaty sigh.

"You're working too hard, Dad. You need to rest." She rubbed his shoulder. "Why don't you take a breather? Go upstairs and lie down for a while."

"Still too much to do."

"There's no rush." She gulped. She'd been pushing herself to get tasks finished, too. She didn't want her dad overdoing it. Better for her to step up and accomplish more. "Your health is important. Take it easy, okay?" She should take him to the doctor since he hadn't been checked since his low blood sugar collapse.

"You're one to talk." His tired gaze washed over her. A paint smudge decorated each cheek and the tip of his nose.

"I feel better now." She grabbed the paint cloth dangling from his back pocket and wiped some of the paint off his face. The rest dried already. He was right that she didn't rest as much as she should have after her near-death experience. But what about his diabetes? Was he testing himself? "Dad—"

"Don't start harping again."

"I'm worried about all the work you're doing." She took

the risk of inciting his anger. "See how tired you got. Are you testing yourself daily like Craig told you to do?"

By his answering growl, the question frustrated him.

"Are you?"

"No! I didn't test today. Or yesterday." He scooted away from her on the floor. "Happy?"

"Are you kidding me? Of course, I'm not happy." Irritated? Yes. "So"—she tried speaking calmly—"you've been testing all the other days, right?"

"Mostly." He wiped the back of his hand over his chin which caused another smudge.

They weren't getting anywhere. "Let's take a break, huh?" She stood and held out her hand to him. "Then you can test yourself and we can both rest. Deal?"

Dad wobbled to a standing position.

He didn't want to be mothered. She got that. But she cared about him and wanted him to be around for a long time. Why was he so stubborn about his health? After the storm, she took up the mantle of pushing him toward taking better care of himself. But sometimes it seemed as if she wasn't making any progress.

After she washed the paint off her hands, she fixed them both a salad. Fortunately, the grocery store had fresh vegetables in stock. She took Dad's portion up to his room where she found him sitting on his bed with his back against a pile of pillows, reading.

She trudged back through the house, picked up her salad topped with balsamic vinaigrette and headed for the front door. Outside, she dropped onto the rocker and plopped her work shoes on the railing. Sighed. She stuffed a couple of forkfuls of spinach into her mouth. Then closed her eyes and chewed, savoring the food and relaxation.

"Paisley!"

She peeked an eye open. Maggie Thomas barreled across the street toward her. The woman's injury from her fall must be a lot better. What did she want?

Paisley chewed quickly. Heaven help her if she smiled with broccoli stuck between her teeth.

"Didn't you hear me?" Maggie's cranky-sounding voice climbed an octave. "I've been yelling your name."

"Hello, Mrs. Thomas." Paisley swallowed, then swished her tongue over her front teeth. "Did you need something?"

"I do." Maggie stood at the bottom of the stairs, huffing, glaring at her. "Pardon me if I don't climb those awful stairs again."

"Right. Um. How can I help you?" She dropped her shoes to the porch floor and stood, holding her plate.

"I heard from Patty Lawton that you're making the rounds. Sign me up!" Maggie's squinty eyes glowed. Her gaze darted from the stairs to Paisley and back to the stairs. Was she trying to make Paisley feel guilty about her fall?

The woman's words registered. "What rounds?"

"You know"—the innkeeper twirled her purse like a policeman's nightstick—"making amends. Community service to pay for your past misdeeds. Where do I sign up for the free labor?"

Paisley bit off a groan. "I offered to help Miss Patty, that's all." Working for Maggie Thomas? No deal.

"You wronged me too. If you're volunteering to make amends, I accept."

Paisley coughed. Goodness. Work for the crabbiest woman in Basalt? The same woman who accused her of stealing some gawdy heirloom jewelry?

"Well?"

"What, um"—she could hardly form the words—"what did you have in mind?" Alternative responses blared in her thoughts. *I will never work for you! I didn't steal your crummy jewels.*

"Can you start immediately?"

"No!" She had a lot of work to finish here. A lot. "I'm helping my dad. He needs me."

"I'm sure he does. But 24-7? Pshaw." Maggie tapped her foot. "Meet me at the inn tomorrow at nine. I have repairs lined up for you."

"But I'm not ... I can't—"

"Patty says you're a tolerable laborer. Nothing to brag about. I'm tickled to be on your indebtedness list." The woman nearly frolicked down the sidewalk. "Too-da-loo. Until tomorrow."

Paisley groaned. Of all the sinister twists. Of all the people she didn't get along with, Maggie Thomas was at the top of the list. Right next to Craig and Mayor Grant. Her appetite gone, she dropped onto the rocking chair. She should have defended herself. Or told Maggie she'd rather clean barnacles off the rocks with her teeth than to work for her.

But she had promised herself she'd do whatever was necessary to make amends. But working for the innkeeper?

She took a bite of salad as a past wrong flitted through her mind. Regret flipped over like a pancake in her gut. As a teenager, she had pelted Maggie's inn with mud balls and took her skiff without asking. Did Maggie find out about that?

She stuffed a cherry tomato into her mouth. Perhaps she could volunteer for one hour. Two, at the most. Then any past misdeeds would be paid in full. Sigh. Even if she worked twenty hours, Maggie probably wouldn't let her live down whatever it was she held against her.

She carried her plate into the kitchen. The house was quiet. Did Dad fall asleep? If so, she'd let him keep sleeping.

She picked up the paint roller and resumed her position by the living room wall. More painting meant more time to ponder stuff. More time to wish she hadn't started this making amends business. Then there was the way Edward treated Bess. Paisley couldn't let another day go by without telling Judah about that.

And she still hadn't collected on her dare. Maybe it was time to ask him for that one thing.

Eighteen

Judah took a long guzzle of ice-cold sweet tea. Ahhh. It hit the spot. For the last half hour, sweat trickled down his neck and dripped between his shoulder blades as he hauled rolls of tar paper up the ladder for the cottage's roofing job. An hour ago, he yanked off his shirt and hurled the soaking wet fabric over the side. A couple of boats passed by in the bay, and one enthusiastic female boater even wolf whistled at him. He'd snickered.

He took another long swig of tea before resuming his work.

Ever since Mom called two days ago, telling him to come and save his wife from Dad's wrath, he'd been mulling over what she said about his father buying up businesses, including Paige's. On the day Blaine hit, Judah had gone by the gallery to help his sister-in-law. Even then, he felt suspicious of his dad's interest in the art establishment. Perhaps the mayor wasn't as altruistic as he tried to make people believe he was.

Judah unrolled another row of roofing paper, hoping this one didn't blow off the side like the last one did thanks to strong gusts coming off the ocean. He still needed to go down and retrieve it and haul it back up here. Using the battery-powered stapler, he zapped the thick black paper a bunch of times as he moved down the line paralleling the roof's ridge.

He heard a car engine. A door closing.

"Judah?" Mia Till's voice.

Oh man. Why was she here?

If he remained quiet, would she think he wasn't home and leave? Not a nice way to treat someone. But Mia put him on edge. She flirted too much with him, along with every guy she met, it seemed. And here he was not wearing a shirt. Just great.

"Judah, you up here somewhere?"

The ladder swayed. Was she coming up in her high heels? If so, she could seriously injure herself.

"I'm on the roof. Stay where you are. Be right down." He leaned over the edge, waved. "Hey, Mia."

"Well, *helllooo*." She put her hand over her eyes, shielding them from the sunlight. She smiled brightly. Her gaze pulsed to his chest. "My, my, don't you look yummy!"

His cheeks burned. Why did he throw his shirt to the ground? He'd never felt more uncomfortable being bare chested than he did right now.

Mia fanned her face with her hand. "Judah Grant, you do impress a girl."

"Just get off the ladder, okay? And be careful." He wasn't in any mood to tolerate her flippant, flirty behavior.

"Hurry and join me. I have news!" Her voice almost got lost in the wind gust. "Oops."

"Everything okay?" He peered over the side. She held down her skirt. And, yep, she wore spiked heels.

"I'm okay." She waved and giggled. She backed down the rungs and stepped off the ladder.

Relieved, he sighed and made quick work of descending. As soon as he reached the sand, she hugged him. Hugged him! Sweaty torso and all.

"Excuse me." He disengaged himself. Then he jogged around the cottage to grab his t-shirt. He yanked it over his head, smoothing the damp fabric over his chest. Dirt smudges clung to the material, but he ignored the sweat and grit. "How are you?" he asked when he saw she followed him.

"Fan-tas-tic," she said in three exaggerated syllables. She pointed toward the roof. "How's the maintenance going?"

"Should be less leaks this winter." He tried keeping things light, still waiting to hear why she drove to the south side of town.

She ogled his t-shirt for so long he squirmed. She smoothed her hands down a pink short skirt with a hot-pink belt over a tucked-in white shirt. A dangly necklace swayed in front of her. Those heels sure were tall.

"What brings you out this way on a workday?" He needed to resume his roof repair. Lots to do before nightfall.

"I'm here to see you, of course. I miss you at work." She stepped toward him, placing both palms lightly on his arm.

He stepped back, freeing himself from her touch. Awkward.

"Mr. Linfield sent me here on official business." She giggled like she was here for anything but professionalism.

"What's up?"

"Other than this amazingly beautiful blue sky?" She gazed up at the heavens and squealed. "Wouldn't you just love to be out on the water on such a gorgeous October day?"

"Sure."

"C-MER's in business again, you know, and we need our right-hand people at the helm." She winked. "Good looking ones, if you know what I mean."

"Mia." He growled. How many times did he have to remind her that he was married? That he didn't want her flirting with him.

"Okay, okay. Can't a girl have a little fun?" She huffed. "I'm here waving a white flag, if you didn't notice."

"White flag? How so?" While working on the roof, he contemplated his job loss. He figured it turned out okay since he had the time that he needed to fix things up at Paul's and here at the cottage.

"Mr. Linfield sent me. Surprise! He wants you back." She clapped her hands.

"But Craig—"

"Has been demoted."

"What?"

She bobbed her head. "Mike sent me to extend an offer to you, Judah Grant, to take Craig's supervisory position. You'll have an office and everything."

"No way." He wiped his hands down his jeans. "What's this really about?"

"I'm serious. He's offering you the position."

"Craig's position?" He couldn't wrap his brain around it. "What about him?"

"Don't worry about him." She chuckled in a tinkly tone. "Good thing I'm not taking an employee photo. You are one big mess. One hot mess, Jude."

"Judah. And don't talk to me like that, please." He walked toward her sports car, hoping she followed. He needed some time to think about the job offer.

"Don't get your feathers all in a knot. What do you say? I'm supposed to bring back an answer." She fell into step beside him. "Interested?" She quirked her eyebrows.

"You're serious that Mike sent you?" He wouldn't put it past her to fib. He opened the driver's door and waited for her.

"I'm serious about the job, your good looks, everything." She winked.

"Stop with the flattery."

"Some guys wouldn't mind."

"I do. I'm married." He held up his hand with his ring to validate his point.

"Right." She gazed toward the ocean, still not getting into the car. "Lovely view you have here."

"Mmhmm. Why did Craig get demoted?"

"For firing you." She grinned. "And he was a naughty boy. Rumor has it, he did something that got him in heaps of trouble with the bigwigs." She clasped her hands in front of her hot-pink belt. "So, are you in or not?"

"I should, um, talk with Paisley first."

"Good grief. The woman left you. Why ask her anything?"

He scuffed his shoe in the sand. "She's my wife. Of course, I'll talk to her. Then I'll come by and talk to Mike myself." He wouldn't take anything Mia said at face value.

"Fine." She put one foot into her low-slung vehicle. Her short skirt flipped about in the wind. She grinned like she knew her power over men.

Judah averted his gaze. Wouldn't fall for her tricks. Would be on guard if he went back to C-MER.

"Did your dad mention I'm the chairperson for the town's reconstruction committee? I can't wait to work with him. He's such a great guy." She dropped into her car. "See you later,

Jude." She backed up fast, her sports car spitting sand, and zoomed off.

"Judah." But he knew she didn't hear him.

Did Mike Linfield really want him back? It seemed the winds of change might be blowing.

Nineteen

Paisley stood near the door and perused their accomplishments. The living room walls were dry and looked nice. The flooring was a different story. She and Dad still needed to talk some more about that. He wanted linoleum, and she hoped to convince him to go with laminate or vinyl planking. Something easy to install.

He strolled into the room carrying a pile of Mom's old canvases. Uh-oh. He must have been scrounging through the pantry.

She cringed at the thought of the paintings she abhorred as a kid displayed on the walls again. Weren't those canvases ruined with the other flood-damaged items? "Are you going to put those up?" She heard the cranky tone of her voice. Couldn't help it. Those paintings brought out the worst in her. "I mean … they're really … ugly." Her voice dropped off.

His black glasses slipped down the bridge of his nose. He huffed. "It's my house. I can decorate how I want."

"That's true."

However, if he hung the one of the giant eyeball, or the one with black lips and a bleeding nose, she'd avoid this space like the plague. She never understood Mom's obsession with abstract-impressionistic art.

"Your mom loved her paintings." His voice sounded wistful.

"Doesn't mean she was good at it."

He glared at her.

"Sorry." If only she could explain and get some things off her chest. Yet something held her back. Maybe the grief in his eyes. The sadness as he gazed down at a painting of a child—or a dog?—hanging upside down from a tree. Were they comforting for him to look at? A hard leap for her to imagine.

She trudged into the kitchen. They replaced the sheetrock. Now it was time for more taping and mudding. Thankfully, the room was small. However, if people kept stopping by asking for help, she might never get Dad's house finished.

"Someone's here," Dad called from the other room.

See, people kept stopping by.

The front door creaked open.

"Hey, Paul."

"Judah!"

Judah? She peered around the dividing wall between the kitchen and living room. The two men shook hands.

"Good to see you."

He waved at her. "Hi, Pais."

"Hey." She smiled back. He looked good. Probably smelled good. With his damp hair, he must have just gotten out of the shower. He shaved his beard too. His smooth reddish face appeared sore after his two weeks of not shaving. He wore crisp jeans and a button-up shirt. He wasn't picking her up for a date, was he? She glanced at his black, steel-toed work boots. Nope. No date.

"Looks like you two have gotten a lot done. Good job."

"We sure have." Dad led him to a corner of the room and showed him something, maybe one of the flawed sections she worked on that he fixed.

Judah patted Dad's shoulder, then walked toward her. "Hey, beautiful."

"Hi." She smoothed her hands self-consciously down her paint-stained, mud-flecked t-shirt and jeans.

He kissed her cheek. Yep, he smelled spicy and good. He stroked his finger down her cheek. Held her gaze for several breathtaking moments.

"What's going on? You're dressed up. I thought maybe you came by to pay up on your date debt." She pointed at his shoes. "Until I saw those."

"Date debt? Oh." His cheeks flushed. "I'm here to talk with you."

"You dressed up to talk with me? Sounds ominous."

He glanced at her dad. "Can we talk privately?" He nodded toward the pantry.

Like she'd step foot in that room for a casual talk. "How about the front porch?"

"Or upstairs?"

Yeah, her dad would hear them on the porch.

"Sure." She led the way up the stairway. In front of her old bedroom, she paused and faced him.

"Mia visited me today."

That little troublemaker. "Why would she come out to your house?" Mia probably knew he was home alone and took advantage of the opportunity. "How long did she stay?"

"Not long." He blinked a couple of times and stared at her as if assessing her emotional state. "She was flirty like usual. Or more than usual. I just wanted to tell you. Keep things honest."

"Okay." She trusted him. Mia? Not a chance. "So, why did she go out there?"

"Mike Linfield sent her to offer me a job."

He said it so matter-of-factly she had to mentally replay his words. "She offered you a job with C-MER?"

"Yep. Craig got in some trouble, and they're offering me his position."

"You're kidding. A supervisor's job. That's great! Congratulations." She hugged him. When she stepped back, his expression sobered. "It is great, right?"

"Sure. I'm puzzled too."

"About why he sent Mia? Why didn't Mike just call?"

"Right." He spread out his hands. "So, what do you think? Should I take the job?"

"Why ask me?"

He groaned. "Pais, I want us to share in everything." His voice became almost stern. "I don't want us to keep living separate lives. Haven't we done that long enough?"

His pointed words hit hard. She gulped.

He raked his fingers through his damp hair. "Man, I'm sorry. I didn't mean to sound so abrasive." He looked contrite. "I'm nervous. Feeling trepidation about taking Craig's position."

"I understand." Although, his uneasiness set her on edge. He loved his job, so working at C-MER would probably make him happy. Him being around Mia again? That would cause her sleepless nights. And Craig? How would he and Judah get over past differences?

He took her hand. "What's your honest opinion about my

taking another stab at a job with C-MER? Your opinion matters to me." His shoulders lifted. "Being on call all the time. Taking risks on the sea. All those played into our struggles before. Maybe that's why I feel apprehensive." His voice went soft. "Sorry about getting all tense before. I want more for us now, talking about stuff, you know?"

"I know. Thanks for including me in your decision." Even if it seemed by the way he was dressed that he made up his mind back at the cottage. Still, it was nice of him to stop and ask her.

"So—?" His blue gaze danced.

"This is your career. Your hopes and dreams. What do you want?"

He leaned in and brushed his smooth, beard-free face against her cheek. For a second, she wished he hadn't shaved it off. "What do I want? You by my side. Us, together. Forever."

A shiver rustled down her spine.

"I don't want to work somewhere if it's going to keep me from you, or our family if we choose to have one, any longer than necessary."

She inhaled slowly. They hadn't talked about kids in a long time. She disengaged her fingers from his. "You should do what's in your heart. I trust you to make good choices. If something doesn't sit right"—like with Mia, she wanted to say—"you'll figure out what to do."

"Thank you." He sighed. "Pais, what do you want? I mean, what do you really want?"

Why did things get so serious? But maybe this was her chance to take a leap toward honesty. "When I'm with you, I want this." She leaned her cheek against his dress shirt. Smelled his spicy deodorant. Heard the thudding of his heart. "Other times, I'm not as sure."

He nodded. His hands smoothed over her shoulders, her back. "I've missed you."

"Me too."

If he worked at C-MER again, she'd have to accept the receptionist as part of his world. Could she do that without stressing? He smelled way too good and was far too handsome to be in Mia's territory every day.

"Any chance you could fire Mia?"

He snickered. "You have nothing to worry about in that corner. I want to be with only you."

"You say the sweetest things."

"I'm just getting started." He tilted up her chin. His glassy gaze looked like he was going to kiss her. Maybe one of those deep kisses that bonded them together so beautifully. He drew closer, his minty breath on her mouth.

Footsteps clunked up the stairs. She jumped back as if she'd been caught kissing a boy back in high school.

"Excuse me," Dad said gruffly as he trudged past them and entered the bathroom.

As soon as the door closed, they both snickered and scurried down to the first floor.

"So, we're agreed I should take the job?"

She shrugged. "You need a job. So do I. Taking an old friend's position? How do you feel about that?"

"Not good. I plan to talk about it with Mike."

"Is that why you're all duded up?"

"Yes. And to see you." He kissed her chastely on the lips. Not what she anticipated upstairs. But his palms slowly moving down her arms made her want to spring back into his embrace.

She followed him out to his truck. Remembering about Maggie, she told him of the innkeeper's demands.

145

"Want me to have a chat with her?"

"Nah."

He opened the driver's door of his pickup. "She can't make you work for free. Amends are what you choose to do. Not what someone else dictates. Don't let her bully you."

Too late.

As he drove off, she wondered if Mia had anything to do with his rehire. Was the receptionist out to get something for herself? Namely Judah?

Paisley sighed and tromped back inside her dad's house. En route to the kitchen, her gaze collided with the evil eyeball of Mom's painting. A shudder coursed through her. She promised to finish the tasks here, but after that she was moving back to the cottage.

Or else she had to convince Dad to get new artwork.

Twenty

Later that day, Judah stopped by and handed Paisley an unmarked bag. "For you." He grinned. "Actually, it's a gift for both of us."

She opened the package. Inside she found a new cell phone. "Oh, thank you." She hugged him. "It's a wonderful gift."

"Even though we're both busy, I want us to stay connected." He tapped the box with his finger. "Unlimited minutes. We can talk every night the way we did when we were dating."

Hmm. Sounded promising.

He rocked his eyebrows. "I'll whisper sweet nothings in your ear. Say *goodnight* before we go to sleep."

Bridging the gap between them, planting a kiss on his lips, was tempting. But she remembered his job offer. "How did things go with your meeting at C-MER?"

"Better than expected."

"Really?" She should be glad for him. Not focused on Mia and her possible trap to ensnare him.

He made a slight bow. "You're looking at the new supervisor of coastal responders."

"Wow. Congrats." She stroked his arm, letting her palm rest against his elbow. "You deserve it, Judah."

"I'm glad to have a job. A pay raise too." He sighed. "I didn't run into Craig. Mia said he hasn't been back since the conflict."

Would Paisley's stomach clench every time he mentioned the woman's name?

"What is it?"

"Nothing. Silly worries."

"We're still working on 'us.'" He stared at her intensely. Maybe saw her doubts. "Nothing's changing that."

Surely, even he realized the reprieve following the storm was a holiday compared to his hectic lifestyle with C-MER. Since Basalt sat next to the Pacific Ocean, the agency he worked for was on an alert of one kind or another almost all of the time.

She felt him watching her. She stared at the swollen plywood flooring. Avoided his gaze. "What do you think about this wood? Should we pull it up?"

He crossed the empty room, scuffing his shoes over several of the swollen spots on the floor. "Best to replace it." He stopped in front of a picture of a potato-shaped face with a giant eyeball in the center. He squinted at it. "Interesting concept."

She glanced over her shoulder, hoping Dad didn't come down the stairs. "My dad and I disagree about the artwork."

"I can imagine. It could make a kid cry."

"Oh, it did. Believe me."

"I still need to get some work done on the cottage tonight, so I should go." He strode toward the door. Then he rocked on the soles of his black shoes. "Would you be interested in coming out to the house tomorrow? I want to show you what I've accomplished."

"I have that gig with Maggie."

"Oh, right." He stared at the floor. Not leaving but not saying anything.

Why did their relationship feel tentative? A couple of days ago, she felt so close to him. Living separately wasn't helping. Both of them being preoccupied with house repairs at two locations wasn't helping, either. Maybe the cell phone would make a difference.

She sighed. "I could come out for dinner after I finish at Maggie's."

He glanced up, a boyish smile on his lips. "That would be perfect." He took her in his arms, crushing her against him. "Oh, Pais, I miss being together. I want you to come home with me so much."

So he felt the distance too. Here in his arms she felt safe. Her refuge, if only for a few minutes. But he wanted her to take the giant leap. To meet him halfway, perhaps.

"There's so much to be done here. It's hard to just leave." That was true. Not an excuse. "But I am moving forward, trying to wrap things up."

"That's good." He released her. His baby blues hued almost navy. She detected a sadness in them. Loneliness?

Right now, they couldn't resolve the issues that would bring them completely back together. But she had determined to mention something the next time she saw him. "I'm worried about your mom."

He tipped his head. "Why?"

"Was your dad ever abusive?"

"No." His face paled. "Do you mean with my mom?"

She nodded. "You should ask her about it—soon."

He drew in a long breath. "Did something happen that I should know about?"

She adjusted her weight from shoe to shoe, uncertain how to explain. Would he think her view of his dad's rough treatment was due to her bias against him? Even so, she couldn't let it stop her from sharing what she observed. "Your dad grabbed your mom's arm like this." She clutched Judah's wrist. His eyes widened. "Then he yanked her backwards." She tried to demonstrate but couldn't move him.

"You're sure?"

"Absolutely. When you ask her, just be sensitive, okay?"

He stared at her so long she wondered if he even believed her.

Twenty-one

"When you're done sweeping up the broken glass, come straight to my office," Maggie barked. "I need you to haul boxes, lots of boxes, to the storage room. Then—"

Paisley blocked out the woman's third to-do list of the day. At some point, she'd just say she was done and leave. Maybe sprint away during a break, if she got a break. Four hours should be more than enough community service time to pacify the innkeeper. But would anything absolve the woman's grudge?

After Maggie left the room ranting about Paisley not accomplishing expected tasks, not listening to instructions, Paisley grumbled and swept up the broken glass. Earlier, Maggie told her to cover the broken window with plastic sheeting until a glass installer could get here. Since Paisley knew the waiting list for professional assistance in the hurricane and flood-stricken town was lengthy, she tried to do a thorough job.

After she finished stapling the plastic on the outside window,

Maggie stomped over to her. "You're not doing it right!" Her voice screeched.

Paisley gritted her teeth. Free labor shouldn't be ridiculed. "How else do you want it done?"

"Stapled from the top, of course. You left too much plastic hanging over the sides. That part is puckered. Rain will get in!" Her snarky tone made Paisley's stomach churn. "You should have noticed your mistake and corrected it."

Or not done it at all. Or walked away three hours ago.

"I'll try to do it your way, Mrs. Thomas." Why did she agree to this exasperating work? All for the hope of reconciliation? Sigh. Yes, for such a hope. Although, the idea of working off her past mistakes seemed to be epically failing.

She stood on a short step ladder, and Maggie remained right next to her, watching her intensely, as she plucked staples from the wood—not an easy task.

The older woman made annoying tsk-tsk sounds. "Why, I never imagined you doing it like that."

"I've never covered a window in plastic before."

"Get out of the way." Maggie grabbed her arm and pulled her off the step ladder, then climbed up herself. "If you want something done properly, do it yourself."

If Maggie required perfection, then she ought to do it herself.

"What else do you want me to do before I leave?"

"Before you leave?" Maggie whirled around, nearly toppling off the ladder.

"This is such a waste of—" She bit back the words she wanted to say. *My time. My life!* "I have things to do. Helping my dad." And she was having dinner with Judah at the cottage— the highlight of her day.

"You haven't done half the chores on the list." If Maggie's glare could kill, Paisley would be limp on the ground. "I didn't know you were such a slow worker."

Her words stung. "A free worker, Mrs. Thomas."

"Not free." The woman stepped down from the ladder. "Your wrongs have piled up over the years like a canker sore eating away at my soul!"

Whoa. Paisley didn't have to put up with this. "I should go."

"No, you should not." Maggie's chest heaved. "I said I needed your help moving boxes. You have not fulfilled your obligation to me!" Her voice hit a screeching tone again.

"I've done enough." Anger pulsed through her. "More than enough."

"Cleaning up a little broken glass? Washing the bathrooms. Pshaw. You think that constitutes making amends for thievery?"

Paisley wanted to walk away, run away. To not put up with Maggie's antagonistic attitude for one more second. But she forced herself to speak humbly. "I admit I did some foolish things as a kid. But I never stole jewelry from you. *Never.*" It was time she stood up for herself.

"I don't believe you. Will never—"

"Too bad." Paisley cut her off. "I'll help with the boxes, but then I'm done."

When she finally got back to her dad's, although worn out, she jumped in with prying out the old floorboards alongside him. If nothing else, the physical labor helped get rid of some of her angst toward Maggie. *Some.*

Later in the afternoon, she and Dad walked over to the hardware store and arranged for the next day's plywood delivery. Miss Patty agreed to let them add the costs to Dad's account until his flood-insurance money came through for repairs. During the transaction, the two hardly spoke. He stood tight-lipped and grumpy acting. Miss Patty kept her gaze on the computer screen. Their "cold shoulder" attitude toward each other was puzzling.

Finally, a little before five p.m., Paisley put on her boots and hiked out to the cottage. She could have driven dad's VW, but a beach walk sounded perfect. It gave her time to unwind and breathe in the salty air she loved. Time to put aside the unpleasant parts of this day. At the front door, she left her boots beside the entrance. She knocked once to let Judah know she arrived. "Hey. I'm here."

A spicy smell of barbecued meat reached her as she stepped into the living room. "Mmm. Smells great in here."

Judah entered from the kitchen, a giant spatula in his hand. "Hey, Pais. You made it."

"Finally." She heaved a sigh.

"Rough day?"

"Yep."

He strolled straight for her and kissed her cheek. Nice to come home to that every day for the rest of her life. Her thoughts skipped ahead to a simple wedding dress. Some new lingerie. Romantic thoughts danced in her head like sugar plums. Too bad it wasn't Christmas. Sigh. Other things needed to be done first. Things for them to discuss. Their hearts mended. Maybe tired as she was, she felt ready to skip some steps she previously deemed important.

"What made your day difficult?"

"Oh, you know, Maggie."

"Ahhh."

"The work at Dad's was strenuous too."

He nodded like he understood. Then he pointed toward the patio. "Join me on the veranda?"

"Okay." She noticed some of the improvements. "Hey, you already pulled the carpet and removed the damaged sheetrock."

"Yep. Roof's fixed too."

"Amazing." She stepped onto the pavers they installed a few years back. Memories hit her. Judah grilling and them eating meals in front of the sea. Dancing in the moonlight. Holding hands and walking on their beach. She thought of the last time they shared a meal together, here. So much transpired since their breakfast before Blaine hit.

"Excuse the sorry table arrangement." He pointed at a large cardboard box with a square of plywood lying across the top. "I lost our patio set during the storm surge."

"Oh, too bad. This is nice, though. Simple."

Chuckling, he pulled out her chair. "Have a seat. I'll grab the meat."

"If I sit down, I may never want to leave." She dropped into the chair and sighed. Her words hit her. *I may never want to leave.* She glanced up.

Their gazes met. "Sounds perfect to me, Pais."

She gulped.

He set a plate of barbecued chicken between them on the board and her attention homed in on the delicacy. She was hungry after her day's work and then walking out here. Two bowls of food already graced the table. Baked beans and potato salad. Deli specials from Lewis's Super. She recognized those from meals and picnics they shared in the past.

"Looks great."

He sat opposite her. Held her hands and prayed, his gaze facing the sky. When he finished, he asked, "So, really, how are you?"

"I'm okay."

She loved this, his attentiveness, his awareness of her, the way he gazed into her eyes. If only it could last. She recalled how cold things were between them before she left three years ago. Even though she agreed to a second chance with him, and wanted one too, she didn't forget what she hoped to avoid. Would this loving feeling survive another time around?

"I'm not perfect."

What? "What do you mean?" She disengaged her fingers from his. "I don't expect you to be perfect."

His eyebrows raised.

"I don't." Goodness, she knew better than that. She let out a little huff. But his gaze probed hers. She swallowed. Okay, maybe, in some small way even she didn't want to admit, he might be right. Perhaps she expected a smidge of perfection from him. Or for him to be her knight in shining armor like in the princess stories, or something. No flaws. No human weaknesses. But that wasn't fair. She wasn't perfect. Far from it.

"Good. Because at some point I'm bound to fail you." A somber expression shadowed his handsome face. His blue eyes glistened. But his honesty, and his truth, tugged on her heart.

That's what she wanted, right? For him to talk openly with her. For them to be able to discuss the hard parts of life and marriage. It made her want to be honest also. "I'm sure I will fail you too."

"Okay, good." He wiped his hand across his forehead as if wiping away sweat. "We got that out of the way."

She chuckled, feeling disarmed. Is that why he started the meal with the line about failing her?

He passed her the food plates. They ate and chatted about the house projects, his job, and her helping Maggie. Just normal husband and wife stuff. Something felt so right about being here with him with the sea breeze blowing over them. Not comfy like an old pair of slippers. Comfy like she fit. Belonged. The ocean waves pounding the shore, a lovely man in front of her, a bit of honesty exchanged between two wounded hearts. The realization and the hope that their lives were better together made her feel at home, at rest, with him.

It was tempting to stay tonight. To talk under the stars. To dance with him in the moonlight. To let whatever might happen between them happen. They were still married, after all.

"I'm enjoying this." Judah wiped his mouth with his napkin. "Talking like we've been together forever."

"I was thinking almost the same thing."

Did he hear the wispy sound of longing in her words? By the way he gazed into her eyes for a long time, maybe he did.

He shuffled his chair to the side of the table facing the ocean. He motioned for her to do the same. She inched the kitchen chair closer to his but kept some space between them. Maybe she didn't trust herself. Her emotions.

His raised eyebrows hinted that he knew how she felt. Yet his soft smile assured her he'd wait however long it took. Didn't he tell her that once before?

He linked the fingers of his left hand with her right. They sat for a few minutes, staring at the bay. A fishing boat chugged past. An orange-colored buoy bobbed on the distant waves.

"This is nice. The view. Being with you." She nodded toward the table. "Great meal. Thank you."

"You're welcome. And you can come over, or stay over, any time you want." He cleared his throat. "Not trying to push you. Just saying."

If he only knew.

"We can go on a real date, too, as soon as Bert's opens. Or we could drive to a nicer restaurant up the coast."

"That would be great. When do you start working at C-MER?"

"Monday." He made a wry face. "I want to get as much done here as I can, so it will be ready for you to come home." He lifted her hand to his warm lips and kissed her knuckles.

"You're so sweet." She placed her other hand over the top of his. "About the workload, I know you're super busy, but—" She hated to add more to his plate.

"Yes?"

"Would it be possible—and feel free to say no—for you to come over tomorrow and help lay the floorboards? James will be there. Dad and me. A motley crew. If you can't, I understand."

"For you? I'll do anything."

Their gazes tangled. Oh, boy. She couldn't look away. Didn't want to. He stroked his fingers down the side of her cheek, down the side of her neck. The stirrings of love, or desire, warmed her. Kissing him seemed the most obvious thing to do. But, considering her own thoughts about staying, how would she stop the fire once it started?

"Did you, um, talk to your mom?" Maybe they needed a shift in topics. A subject to cool their ardor.

He sat up straighter. His gaze darkened. "Uh, not yet." He cleared his throat. "Have you thought any more about when you might be ready for our vow renewal?"

"When do you want to get remarried?"

"Tomorrow?" He kissed her mouth. One brief kiss with a truckload of promise.

Heart pounding, she took a long breath. "Tomorrow. Is that even possible? There's so much to do." Even though it would only be a small gathering for a ceremony, even that took some planning.

He chuckled. "Wishful thinking, I guess." His face grew serious. "The reconstruction of the town, your dad's house, our cottage, will all take time. Rebuilding is a slow process. Takes time to mend."

Their gazes met and held. Goosebumps raced over her skin.

He broke the rope-like connection. "Is there anything you want us to do before we exchange vows?" He released her fingers and folded his hands in his lap.

"I'll have to think—" She held her breath an extra second. "Oh, I know."

"What?"

"Misty Gale." She pushed the word past the lump in her throat. "Her gravesite. How would you feel about us taking flowers over there together?"

"Of course. I should have thought of it myself."

"You don't mind?"

"No." He leaned back. "Wait. Did you think I might not want to go to my daughter's grave?"

"Oh, I didn't know." She swallowed. "Since we didn't, um, share much in the grieving process before, I'm not sure how that part of our lives will work now. Being at her grave after three years will be tough for me." A tender emotion overcame her, but she subdued it. Wouldn't give in to tears tonight.

He tugged his arm around her, drawing her closer. "For me too, Pais."

Sighing, she leaned her face into his neck. His understanding and sharing in the heartache were good signs. Steps in their healing process. *God, please, let it be so.*

Twenty-two

Judah finished yanking up the last of the ruined carpet from the bedrooms. He already threw out a giant pile of carpet chunks and foam underlayment, mounding it at the end of the short driveway. The city garbage trucks would hit this side of town by Monday or Tuesday, scooping up trash and ruined building materials left over after Hurricane Blaine.

He stomped around the empty living space, inspecting the flooring. Mushy. Not what he hoped to find. He'd have to rip out all the plywood like they were doing over at Paul's. Oh, right. He checked his watch. Paisley asked him to stop by at one o'clock. Almost time.

He heard a car door slam. He strolled to the door, swinging it wide.

His mom stood on the porch with her fist raised as if to knock.

"Mom?"

"Oh, Judah." Her face crumpled and she burst into tears.

Covering her face with her hands, her words came out stilted. "I didn't know ... I didn't know where to go. What to ... to do."

"What's happened? Come in. You're always welcome here." He laid his arm over her shoulder and led her into the bare living room. He'd never seen her so broken up. "What's wrong? Did something happen to Dad? Is he sick?"

"No, no." She wept and muttered something about not knowing how to explain.

He didn't have any furniture to offer her a seat. Other than— "Let me grab a chair from outside." He scrambled out to the patio where he and Paisley dined last night. Grabbing two chairs, he hauled them back to the empty living room. He set them in the middle of the space, facing each other.

Mom dropped into one, her gaze downcast. She wrung a tissue between her hands.

He should be heading over to help Paisley, but this crisis was more urgent. "What's going on? Please tell me." He sat in the other seat and leaned forward, elbows on his knees, facing her, giving her his full attention.

When she lifted her chin, her eyes were red rimmed with tears puddling in them and dripping down her face. That's when he saw an ugly, fist-sized greenish-purple bruise covered most of her left cheek.

"Mmmooooom?" His voice came out strangled. "What happened?"

"I left your father."

"Did he ... did he do this?" Anger ignited his core. His chest felt on fire. His fists clenched and unclenched. What kind of a coward would do this to a woman? To his mother?

"I don't want to talk about it." She wiped a tissue beneath

her eyes. "He's your father." She sniffed a few times. "Even if I never wish to be in the same room with the man again, he's your dad. Always will be."

Judah didn't want to think of his paternal bond with Edward Grant right now. His gaze intent on the bruise, he forced himself to ask, "Did he do this to you on purpose?"

"When h-hasn't he h-hurt me on p-purpose?"

"Oh, Mom." He jumped to his feet. Couldn't sit still. He had to talk to his dad. Get to the bottom of such a horrible act. His father, the mayor of Basalt Bay, struck Mom? Unbelievable.

He rubbed his temples as he paced between his mother to where the kitchen began and back again. He reached out to rest his palms on her shoulders, but she jumped as if his touch hurt her. He pulled his hands back and dropped onto his chair again, trying to appear calm. But he couldn't pull it off.

"Has Dad done this to you before … hurt you?" His heart pounded hard. How could this be happening in his family? His father was a dignified, somewhat respected, leader in the community.

Mom glanced furtively around the room. "Can I stay here? I see you don't have furniture, but I can sleep on the floor. I won't take much room."

"Of course, you can stay. I have some furniture that didn't get ruined." He took her hand, trying to be gentle. "You want some coffee? Tea?"

"In a while, tea would be nice." She waved her other hand toward the back of the house. "Is Paisley here?"

"No, we aren't living together yet." He released her hand and scooted back in his chair. "We're waiting until we exchange vows again."

"That's wise. I'm proud of you, Judah. And Paisley." She

patted his knee. "I'm thrilled you're getting back together. There are things—" She broke down crying again.

How could he comfort or reassure her? If his dad were standing here, he'd have plenty to say to him. *Rat fink coward. Hypocritical cad. Horrible husband and father.* But those thoughts stirred up his anger and weren't anywhere close to the love he should feel toward his parent. He'd ponder that later. Right now, he needed to be comforting and helpful to his mom.

Eventually, she let out a long sigh. "My leaving him will take some getting used to for all of us. I'm sorry to disappoint you. I held it together for as long as I could."

"Don't worry about me." He stared at her bruise again and still couldn't believe this happened. Mom had been the cream in the Oreo between Judah and Dad's relationship for a long time. He avoided his family home for years due to his father's antagonistic attitude toward Paisley. Even when she mentioned her unease about Mom, Judah didn't drive up and inquire. Now, he felt like a heel for not acting on her concerns. "Can you tell me what led to this?" He swayed his hand toward Mom's face, not even knowing how to address the issue.

"Does it matter?" She stared hard at him. Was she offended?

He gulped. "What did I say? Mom, I'm proud of you for staying with Dad. For trying to make it work. You've been a jewel. If he isn't aware of that, if he doesn't know you're the one whose held our family together, he's a fool."

"Thank you." She sighed again. "He'd never admit that. I've prayed for him for years. Hard to give up, even now. But I've endured too much, hoping he'd change." She shuddered and wrapped her arms around herself. "I won't take any more 'accidents' at his hands."

"Accidents?"

"His so-called accidents. Mistakes made during angry outbursts." She coughed, then cleared her throat. "I shouldn't say anymore. You need to have a relationship with your dad that isn't tarnished by my problems with him."

"Too late."

"Oh, Judah."

"No, Mom. I mean, I've had issues with him for years. You know that."

She stared at the wall for a long while. "So, where can I start?" She scooted to the edge of her seat.

"Start what?"

"Helping you. Painting, whatever. How can I assist you in getting things fixed up?"

"Mom, you should rest."

"That's the last thing I need. I prefer busy work. I've been stuck up in the house—" She shook her head. "What's the next thing? Floorboards coming up?" She stood and rolled up her sweater sleeves.

Judah groaned. He could hardly tell her no.

His cell phone vibrated. Paisley, no doubt.

"Um, Mom, I promised to help Paisley with the flooring over at her dad's." He slid his phone out of his pocket and held it up. "I'll tell her there's been a delay."

"No, you won't." She moved her chair to the far side of the room. "Tell me what to do. I'll get started while you help her. Keep your word to your wife." She stared intensely at him.

"Okay. But I'm not leaving you alone." Wouldn't this be the first place his dad came looking for her?

"I doubt he'll show his face here."

"He might." Judah wouldn't put it past him to try dragging her home like a caveman—even in a three-piece suit.

165

"Fine. I'll come with you and help Paul and Paisley."

He saw sincerity and determination in her gaze. And a brokenness he recognized from the way his own eyes looked in the mirror during the years Paisley was gone.

"As long as you don't overdo."

"Yes, Judah." She rolled her eyes.

Her sarcastic tone and eye rolling surprised him. She always seemed content with her life. Passive, even. Did she hide her personality, subdue her true self, because of Dad's dominance? Inwardly, Judah groaned. How well did he even know her?

He tapped out a text to Paisley. *Running late. Be there soon. Mom too.*

"Do you mind if I bring my suitcase in?" She headed toward the door.

"Not at all. Let me help." He ran ahead of her and opened the back of her rig. Only one suitcase rested on the carpeting. Thirty-four years of marriage and she left the house with one piece of luggage?

She set her hand on the hood of the SUV as if she needed the support. "It's been packed and hidden for a long time. I left quickly."

He clutched the suitcase handle with one hand and laid his other arm over her shoulder. "It's going to be okay. You're going to be okay." He'd make sure of that.

But what would happen to their family if she divorced Dad?

Twenty-three

Paisley heard a truck engine pull up. Judah's? She tiptoed across the exposed two-by-eight floor joists to reach the porch. A short while ago, she got a text from him saying he was running late. And that his mother was coming over too. What was going on?

She trudged down the uneven stairs, then scurried across the lawn.

Judah and his mom were just exiting his pickup. Bess reached her first and hugged her. Leaning back, Paisley stared into her mother-in-law's sad-looking eyes. Then she bit back a gasp when she saw a nasty bruise on her cheek. Edward's doing? Her gaze flew to Judah's. He shook his head.

"It's so good to see you." Bess's smile didn't reach her eyes. "Just tell me what to do. I want to help."

"You sure?" She laid her palm on her mother-in-law's shoulder. "Are you okay?"

"I will be." Bess linked Paisley's arm with hers and sighed.

"How's Paul? Judah told me about his health scare on the drive over. How terrifying for that to happen while the town was deserted. I can't imagine what you went through."

"He's better. Stubborn, but better."

"I've met a few men like that." Bess winked at Judah.

Other than some awkwardness as each person glanced at Bess, they had a productive work session. Besides Judah and his mom, James, Kathleen, and even Paige, came by to help. Paige and Paisley worked amicably, hauling boards and hammering nails, even though they hadn't discussed their personal issues yet. No one brought up any controversial topics. Even Dad didn't mention Bess's shiner.

At one point, she noticed Kathleen and Bess talking by themselves. The two women were huddled near the stairway, speaking quietly. Paisley knew Kathleen to be a kind and sympathetic soul. Hopefully, she had some encouraging words for Bess.

She was just about to take a coffee break when someone pounded on the door. His shoulders tense, Judah crossed the newly laid plywood floor and pulled open the door.

Edward stood there glowering. "Judah."

"Dad."

All work came to a halt. Paisley shuffled in front of Bess. Kathleen, with her small frame and slightly bent shoulders, did the same, the two of them forming a barricade. Paige trudged into the kitchen, obviously putting space between her and the mayor.

"Is your mother here?" Edward stepped across the threshold.

"I think it's better if you leave."

"Too bad."

Judah's stiff position, with his arms crossed and legs braced, kept his father from coming any farther.

"Hello, Mayor." Paisley's dad waved as if he didn't sense the tension in the room.

Edward lifted his chin, his pinched gaze traversing the group. He reminded Paisley of the bad guy in a Western about to face off with the sheriff and his posse.

"Where is she?" He stared hard at Judah. "You can't keep me from seeing my wife."

"I can keep you from hurting my mother!"

Edward wiped his knuckles beneath his nostrils. "So, she cried on your shoulder and fed you her lies, did she?"

Judah's muscles flexed beneath his work t-shirt. He opened and closed his right fist. "What lies would she tell me?"

"Some whiny drivel. How she doesn't want me to be the mayor. Doesn't want me cavorting with female constituents. How she tripped and—"

"Liar!" Bess pushed forward between Paisley and Kathleen. "Leave now or I'm calling the police!"

Paisley grabbed her arm, stopping her advance.

"Don't tell me what to do." Edward huffed. "Bess, you've carried on this foolishness long enough." He pointed toward the open doorway. "Come on. I'm bringing you home where you belong. I saw your car at Judah's."

"She's not going anywhere with you," Judah said sternly.

"Stay out of this, *boy*."

Bess lunged ahead like she was ready to do battle herself, but Paisley's linked arm stopped her from reaching Edward. Paige rushed over and clasped the woman's other arm.

"I haven't been a 'boy' in a lot of years." Judah stood almost nose to nose with his father. "You should go. When Mom's ready to talk, she'll call. Leave her alone until then."

"You think you can tell me what to do?"

"I guess I do, *sir.*"

Edward thumped his index finger against Judah's chest. "I call the shots in this family."

"Not this time. You need to leave." Judah's tone sounded gritty as he stepped forward.

Paisley couldn't tell if he shoved his dad onto the porch, or if Edward backed up on his own.

"Every marriage has a few problems." The mayor spoke contemptuously. "You know that more than anyone. You and that whor—"

Judah gripped the mayor's coat and propelled him down the steps. Edward flailed his arms and yelled several profanities.

Paisley's heart pounded in her ears. Her mouth went dry.

Kathleen marched over and slammed the door.

Bess gasped and shuddered, almost falling backward. Paisley supported her arm and back in case she collapsed, even though her own heart rate hadn't returned to normal.

Kathleen brushed her hands together. "That's that. Back to work, ladies and gentlemen. We have things to do." She smoothed her hand over wayward strands of white hair.

"You okay?" Paisley slid her arm over her mother-in-law's shoulders.

Bess shivered like she had a high fever. "I will be. Thank you for your kindness. I didn't mean to drag my son into this. Or you. What must he think?" Her blue eyes, so like Judah's, peered back at Paisley.

"That he loves you. Will protect you, no matter what."

"That's not a son's job." Bess's lips trembled. "Should I go out there and talk to Edward?"

"No!" Paisley, Paige, and Kathleen said at once.

"I'm going to make coffee. Want some?" Paige patted Bess's arm.

"Tea?"

"Absolutely." In passing, Paige squeezed Paisley's free hand. They had things of their own to work out. Big things. But they were sisters. Family. They stood together against Edward twice now—that counted for something.

Male voices rose outside. More yelling.

"Oh, dear," Bess muttered.

"It'll be okay. Would you care to sit down?"

Bess shook her head but kept staring toward the front window. "Edward wouldn't dare hit Judah. He never hit him, even as a boy. I made sure of it."

That made Paisley want to weep. Bess had put up with Edward's manhandling since Judah's childhood? Despicable man.

Paisley's dad and James started hammering again, covering over the voices outside.

After Paige handed teacups to Bess and Kathleen, the two older women trudged upstairs. Maybe Kathleen would show Bess where the bathroom was. Or listen to her plight.

Paisley carefully stepped across the partially nailed flooring to get to the front window. Out by Edward's truck, Judah stood by the driver's door rocking his thumb toward the south end of town as if ordering his dad off Cedars' land. Edward said something that caused his mouth to snarl up. Cussing, probably. Then, the engine revving, the truck zoomed up the street in the opposite direction from where Judah had pointed.

When he strode toward the house, Paisley let out a sigh. "You okay?" she asked as soon as he entered the living room.

"Uh-huh. Where's my mom?"

"Upstairs with Kathleen."

"I'll have to watch her. Be on alert. Who knows what he'll do next?" A tight expression on his face, he trotted up the stairs.

Tension whirled back up into Paisley's throat.

"Crying shame," James spoke.

"What?" Dad fingered his glasses.

"My pop used to treat my mom the same way." He pounded the floor with the hammer aggressively. "Rough. Mean. Especially when he was drinking."

"The mayor's been drinking?" Dad's jaw dropped. "I doubt he's the sort to get drunk during the day."

"It's best if we don't talk about it right now." Meeting his gaze, Paisley nodded toward the stairway.

"Oh, sure. These things usually work themselves out."

They did? When did things ever work out without effort? Three weeks ago, when she returned from her stint in Chicago, Dad hardly spoke to her. If she didn't push and pry to keep the lines of communication open, they still might not be talking.

She glanced at Paige. When would they get their chance to talk? That her sister reached out to her about the banking issue, assisted with the flooring, and her kindness toward Bess gave Paisley hope that they could put the past behind them. Maybe embrace a sisterly closeness in the future.

Especially if Craig wasn't a part of her life.

Twenty-four

Judah leaned his backside against the porch railing and sighed. Tired from the day's work and disheartened by his family problems, he watched as Paisley rocked in the chair and spooned soup into her mouth. A simple act, yet he became mesmerized with the drops of moisture on her lips. Luscious lips he'd enjoy taking possession of, finding comfort in. Blame it on fatigue. Not thinking rationally. He didn't even want dinner. Maybe that was the problem. Too tired. Numb. Needy. "I should go." Before he did something Paisley might interpret as him being too pushy.

"Are you okay with your mom staying with us?" She gazed up at him.

Her tender look tugged on his spirit. Drowned him in another wave of yearning. "Probably." Not really. He wanted Mom to stay at the cottage where he could keep an eye on her. Protect her from his dad, if he dared come around. "Too bad my beds are all torn apart." He didn't think that through when he cleared the floors of all his worldly goods.

"She can stay in Peter's old room. My dad doesn't mind." Paisley scooped another bite of food into her mouth. "You can stay here too, if you want." She whispered the last part.

"With you?"

Her eyes widened. "Oh, w-well, I uh ..."

The altercation with his father still strummed in his gut, blurred his thoughts, made him act unlike his usual level-headed self. The idea of the man laying a finger on his mother— "Sorry. That comment ... I'm just tired."

"It's okay."

He sighed, again. "I appreciate your taking care of my mom. The cottage is a disaster. I need more hours in the day." He ran his hands through his hair, wishing he were home and curled up on a mattress. Or punching a boxing bag. More time in the day? He wanted this day to be over.

Mom shuffled onto the porch. "Shall I head back with you, Judah?"

"It's up to you."

"It felt good to lie down for a few minutes." She pointed at the night sky. "What a beautiful display of stars."

He glanced up. Sighed. How many times did he sigh in the last fifteen minutes? "What do you want to do, Mom?"

"I enjoyed visiting with Kathleen. A new friend. Do you realize how long it's been since I had a friend?"

A more peaceful expression graced her face than he'd seen in a long time. Why hadn't he noticed her strained expression before? Of course, he stayed clear of his parents' house for years to avoid Dad's callous remarks. And he was never good at calling his mom to check in. He clenched his jaw to stop himself from sighing again.

"Kathleen's great." Paisley stood and yawned. "She

comforted me during the town meeting before the storm. Maybe we could have her over for dinner or something."

"Sounds wonderful."

The two women hugged, and such loving expressions rested on their faces that Judah felt the first inkling of peace since his mom showed up at the cottage. During Paisley's three years away, Mom used to call and tell him she was praying for her return. Her faithful reminders were an encouragement during his time of struggle. Maybe he could do that for her also.

"You don't mind if I go out to the house with Judah, do you?" Mom asked.

"Not at all." Paisley shrugged. "Just take care of yourself."

Mom brushed her fingers beneath her eyes. "I will. Things are going to be different now. I'll grab my jacket, then I'll be ready." She strolled inside, leaving him and Paisley alone.

"You knew something was wrong."

She nodded. "I hoped not. But I thought so."

"I'm sorry I didn't do something." He groaned. "If I went up there, if I called and asked her, it might have stopped this latest thing from happening."

"Might have." She clasped his wrist and stroked her thumb across the back of his hand. "Don't blame yourself. Your mom may have denied it. Made excuses for Edward. Or called it an accident."

"Maybe." He shifted his hand to link their pinkies. Being this close to her, sensing her empathy and understanding, was comforting. He sighed again, couldn't help himself. "Thank you for being so supportive."

"Of course. We're family."

Family. He touched his lips to her cheek. It wouldn't

take much to deepen it into a more satisfying kiss, a more needy one, but he refrained. Things were too emotional. Too unsettled.

Mom returned to the porch, zipping up her jacket.

Paisley took a couple of steps toward the door. "Goodnight, you two."

"Night." He faced Mom. "Ready to go?"

"Mmhmm. I'll sleep good tonight."

"Me too." Unless his brain kicked in with more frustrating thoughts and questions.

During the truck ride home, he broached the subject he avoided all afternoon. "Do you mind telling me how you got the bruise? What did Dad do?" He didn't have to know, but he hoped to better understand the situation.

Her lengthy pause either meant she didn't want to talk about it, or she was pondering her answer. She let out a breathy sigh. "He yelled and threw a couple of hardback books at me. One contacted my face."

"Books? On purpose?"

Her glare, even in the darkness of the cab, reached him.

"I'm sorry. I didn't mean to sound like I disbelieve you. It's just ... a book?"

"He's been acting more aggressive. Enraged about everything." Almost to the beach cottage, she spoke again. "He forces me to stay at the house."

"What do you mean?"

"He doesn't want me to talk to anyone. No phone calls. No coffee visits. Not even with you."

"Why would he treat you like that?"

"I might say something that'll embarrass him. Tell someone he's a selfish hypocrite."

"I'm so sorry for what he's put you through." He groaned. "And I'm sorry for not seeing it."

She shivered like she was freezing even though he turned the heat up as high as it would go.

"When he came to Paul's house demanding that I go home with him, he meant it. He'll come after me again. You can count on it."

"You're a grown woman. He can't make you do his bidding. You can do what you want."

Her sarcastic laugh didn't even sound like her. "I haven't done what I wanted in years. Until today." She sank back into the seat. "For now, I'm free."

For now? "You can stay with me as long as you want."

She patted his hand where it rested on the steering wheel. "You've been so hospitable, welcoming me into your home. Thank you for that. But you and Paisley have your own lives. I'm looking forward to your vow renewal. Wouldn't miss it for anything. And I won't get in the way by hanging around your cottage too long."

"We've got a lot to do before then." He swallowed the dryness in his throat. "I confess to being impatient. I want to get on with being married."

"Of course, you do."

"I've waited a long time to get my wife and my life back."

"Yes, you have. I'm so proud of you for waiting. For accepting her back."

"I love her. She is a part of me."

"She's a lucky woman." After a pause, Mom continued. "Your dad and I used to love each other too. There are things—" She shook her head.

177

"What were you going to say?" He pulled into his driveway and shut off the engine.

"Some things are better left unsaid." She opened the door.

Judah opened his. "Even though Dad's being a jerk, I'm sure he loves you."

"Loves me? You must not have heard a word I said. Edward Grant loves Edward Grant. He's no longer the man I married."

"Why didn't you leave him before?"

"Because of you, our wedding vows, and my lack of courage." She sighed. "I held onto hope that things would improve. That he'd change. Like you've wished about Paisley for the last three years."

He and Mom had more in common than he realized. "And now?"

"I'm all done living in fear." She trudged around the other side of the truck, meeting him near the engine. "I am sorry for disappointing you." She clasped his hand, her fingers icy.

"I'm the one who's sorry for not recognizing what Paisley did. For not believing what she told me."

"She's a lovely girl."

"I know." His words came out hoarsely.

At the front door, she spoke, "Paisley recognized what you couldn't because of her own past with abuse."

A cold nausea rushed through his middle. "I never abused her. Would never—"

"Not you. Of course not." She patted his coat sleeve. "You're a good man. A loving husband."

Nice to hear. But how did she know about Paisley? And what had she heard about his wife's past?

Twenty-five

Someone pounded on the front door. Judah groaned and grabbed his cell phone. Six a.m. Still dark out. He pushed himself off the mattress he placed on the floor last night and pulled on his jeans. The banging continued. "Okay. Okay."

"Judah?" His mom's voice sounded faint, weak. Scared? "Do you think it's—?"

"Uh-huh."

"I can get up and speak with him."

"No. I'm dressed. I'll take care of this." He shoved his feet into his slip-on shoes. "Stay put." He rushed by the guest room where he set up the twin bed for her.

Striding past the kitchen, he flipped on the light switch. He'd go out on the porch. No way was his father coming inside. But as soon as he cracked open the door, Dad shoved past him and barreled into the empty room.

"Dad. Wait." Was that alcohol on his breath at this time of morning? "Hold on. You can't just—"

"Where is she?"

"This is a safe place for her. Lower your voice. Stay calm." What if Judah couldn't contain him? He'd call Deputy Brian if he had to.

"Bess! Bess, get out here!"

"Stop yelling." Judah grabbed his arm.

"No one tells me what to do!" Dad yanked free of his grip then stomped around the room. His hands chopped back and forth, his eyes bugging, tension rippling along his shoulders. "Bess! Get out here before I come get you."

"Dad, stop. Quiet down or leave."

"Don't tell me—"

"This is my house. You're an intruder. I *will* tell you what to do." He braced out his hands toward the older man, prepared to do what he had to do to stop him.

"Get your mother before I—"

"She's not going anywhere with you."

His dad nearly butted noses against his. That's when Judah got a strong whiff of the man's horrendous breath. Smelled like a distillery.

"This is a squabble between her and me. Butt out of my affairs."

Affairs? Judah winced.

"Bess, come out here right now." Dad clambered toward the bedrooms.

Judah stomped after him, grabbing his arms.

His father yanked away, punching the air in front of him. "Don't do that again."

"Don't do what you did to Mom ever again." His temper ignited. "Don't manhandle her. Don't hurt her. Treat women with respect, isn't that what you taught me?"

"Get your mother, *now*, or you'll be sorry."

"I won't." He stiffened himself to resist a punch or whatever Edward—he didn't even want to think of him as "Dad"—intended. In the past, he experienced a plethora of angst-filled moments with this man. None compared to how he felt now.

The guest room door creaked open. "Judah?"

"Mom, stay back." He glanced over his shoulder as she stepped into the short hallway.

Edward's gaze homed in on her. He didn't smile, but he sighed, perhaps relaxing a little.

Mom wore a sweatshirt and a pair of pajama bottoms. Her arms were crossed over her middle. "I'll talk to him for a minute."

"Not here in the hall. Not like this."

"Fine." Edward stomped into the living room. "Get in here, Bess." His commanding tone left no doubt he expected obedience.

"You don't have to do this," Judah spoke to her. "He's been drinking. Might be volatile."

"He'll just keep coming back if I don't talk to him." Her shoulders sagged. "Don't worry. I'm not going with him."

Judah set his arm over her shoulder and felt her tremble. If she had a teaspoon of the adrenaline rushing through his veins, she'd possess the courage to face Edward with her chin held high and boots ready to kick him in the rump.

"Grab your stuff!" Edward yelled. "We're leaving."

Take a hike—Judah wanted to say. But as much as he wanted to interfere, he wouldn't except to defend his mother.

"I'm not going with you," Mom said quietly.

"Judah, give us some privacy." Edward rocked his thumb toward the front door. "This is none of your concern."

"I'm not moving." He crossed his arms. "And use a nicer tone when you address Mom."

"So, what's your plan, Bess?" Edward's voice came out snarly.

"I said use a nicer tone!" Judah took a step toward the man he wanted to kick out of his house.

Mom squinted at him as if she was surprised by *his* tone. "I'm staying here until Judah and Paisley's ceremony."

"That could take months." Edward thrust out his hands.

Not quite.

"Then what?"

"I'll find another place to stay. Rent a room." She shrugged. "Maybe buy a condo."

"A condo?" Edward roared. "With what?"

"Savings." She squinted at him. "How about with alimony?"

Edward inhaled like he had a fish bone stuck in his throat and couldn't cough it up. "Not this side of the Pacific, you won't." His voice rose a couple of decibels. "Taking a break from our marriage is one thing. Present company did that." He sent Judah a piercing glare. "Getting divorced is out of the question."

Judah gritted his teeth, fighting the urge to respond.

"See this bruise?" Mom's voice rose. "You did this."

Edward jerked, then huffed.

"You will never hurt me again. Just so you know"—she tapped her cheek—"I took photos of it."

Edward shuffled his shoe against the raw board. "Ah, Bessie"—he whined, sounding much different than moments ago—"I didn't mean to hurt you. I love you. You know that, right?"

She made a strangled cry. "You didn't mean to sprain my wrist a month ago, either. You didn't mean to leave bruises on my shin before that." With each indictment, her voice got louder. "You didn't mean to throw the pottery plate at my head and cause the scar I've kept hidden beneath my hair. Need I say more?"

Judah's stomach roiled. "Dad?" His voice sounded just as strangled as Mom's.

His father didn't answer. Didn't refute her statements, either. His shoulders slouched. He appeared a decade older than yesterday. He swiped the back of his hand beneath his nose. "Come home with me, please. I'll make it up to you. I promise to never do those things again."

"You said the same thing last time." Mom exhaled a loud breath. "And the time before. Just go … leave me alone."

"I agree. You should go." Judah pointed toward the door, his hand shaking. "Before I do something I'll regret."

Edward didn't budge.

Judah stepped closer. "Don't make me force you to leave, because I will. Do what's right."

Edward glared at him like he was going to refuse, but then he trudged toward the door. With his hand on the doorknob, he paused. "What am I supposed to tell people? What do I say?"

Leave it to him to worry what others thought instead of being concerned about losing his family. His marriage. His wife.

"Figure it out yourself," Mom said. "I'm done caring what other people think."

Edward opened the door and trudged outside. As the cool air hit Judah, something sharp twisted in his gut. He had been guilty of indifference in his marriage. He contributed to Paisley's feelings of being lonely, sad, and unloved. But how did Mom put up with her husband's violent actions? How did she survive? Had she ever confided in anyone?

"I'll be back tomorrow." Edward stomped across the porch.

"No!" Mom yelled after him. "Don't come back. If you talk with a counselor, or a pastor, I might speak to you. Otherwise, I never want to see you again."

Edward pivoted on the steps, his eyebrows raising to his hairline. "What do you mean? Expose my failings to a stranger?"

"Pastor Sagle is hardly a stranger."

"To me he is!" Edward shouted then marched through the sand to his rig.

Judah had one more question to ask him. "Mom, I'll be right back."

"Don't try to intervene. This is our business. Your dad's right on that point."

Even so, he closed the door then jogged out to the truck.

The window rolled down. Glaring eyes peered back at him. "What? Haven't you caused enough grief?"

"Are you ... are you having an affair with Mia Till?"

Edward slapped the steering wheel. Swore. "What kind of a question is that for a son to ask his father?" Smoke seemed to spew from his ears. "I'm not telling a traitor like you anything."

Judah ignored his lashing out. "Are you?"

Edward grabbed the gearstick. The engine revved. "I'm the mayor of Basalt Bay. That blond, while gorgeous and flirtatious as all get-out, is young enough to be my daughter."

Judah couldn't forget her implications. "An emotional affair, perhaps?"

Edward hawked and spat, just missing Judah's face, then gave the truck too much gas, spinning the tires, pelting sand in the driveway. Once the vehicle reached the road, its tires squealed. The rig flew down the road.

He shouldn't even be driving. And he didn't answer Judah's question.

What kind of trouble might he cause next?

Twenty-six

Paisley strode across the empty living room to answer the door. She'd had her morning coffee. Had a mental list of things she needed to accomplish. Text Judah. Check on Bess. Finish the mudding and taping in the kitchen. Gut the pantry—could she just burn down the dreadful room? She opened the front door.

Paige stood on the porch holding Piper. "Good morning."

"Hi." Paisley's gut reaction was to shut the door. A ridiculous response. She wasn't a child to run from trouble. These two were family. Her sister and her niece. Still, their appearance made her feel unsettled. "Come in." She backed up. "Dad hasn't come downstairs yet."

Paige stepped inside. "Piper wants to see him." She smiled at her daughter. "Don't you, Piper? You want to visit with Grandpa?"

The girl nodded, then hid her face against her mother's sweater.

"She's shy."

Paisley shut the door and followed Paige into the kitchen, wading through awkwardness a foot deep.

"Is he awake yet?"

"I haven't heard any noises from upstairs."

Paige set the toddler down and squatted beside her. "Piper, this is your Auntie Paisley."

Auntie. Gulp.

Paige and Piper gazed up at her. Seeing the sparkly-eyed child filled her with yearnings for motherhood. Or aunthood. Was this her sister's olive branch?

She squatted beside them. "Hi there, Piper. I'm glad to meet you." She held out her hand.

The girl hid her face against her mother's clothes, keeping her hands tucked between them.

"She's not good at shaking hands with people." Paige stood.

Paisley stood also. "I hope we can be friends." She patted Piper's shoulder.

"Auntie Paisley is married to Uncle Judah."

"Unca Dzuda! Unca Dzuda!" Piper danced around and ran for the front window.

"She loves Judah." Chuckling, Paige strolled to the bottom of the stairs. "Dad! I brought Piper over. Can you come down and say hi?"

"Be down in a minute," his rough morning voice called.

Paige lifted her shoulders. "It's our routine."

"You come over every morning?" Dad didn't say anything about it. Were they staying away because of her?

"Most days. Not every day."

"So, did you know about his illness?" Maybe she had it wrong. Perhaps Paige worked with him, trying to get him to take his insulin, taking part in his care.

A shadow crossed her sister's face. "I'm sorry to say I didn't. He's been slowing down. Aging. Normal stuff, I thought." She sighed. "I wish I recognized his decline sooner. I guess I've been preoccupied with being a single mom while you were gone."

While she was gone. The sting.

Paisley lifted her chin, pride filling her empty chest cavity. But then her angst melted. She didn't want to cling to grudges anymore. "When I came back, I saw a difference in him. Aloof and disinterested, but not sick, you know?"

Paige nodded. Perhaps relieved for them not to fight about their father's health. Paisley did, after all, leave town without warning. Stayed away for three years. Things for her to remember when she talked with her sister about reconciliation. Although, there was still the matter of Craig.

Dad shuffled down the stairs, his hair sticking up, and his unbuttoned flannel shirt revealing a stained t-shirt beneath. "There are my girls."

His girls. Was he including Paisley? Or just referring to Paige and her daughter? Who wouldn't love a dolly like Piper? Misty Gale may have even looked similar with darker hair. Where did the two-year-old get the blond hair? Most of the family had dark hair. Even Craig's was dark brown.

"Hi, Dad." Paige hugged him when he reached the main floor.

Piper squealed and charged at her grandfather. He scooped her up and bounced her. She asked him to take her to the window so she could show him something.

"Care for some coffee?" Paisley strode to the coffee machine, needing a task.

"No, thanks. I drank plenty already." Paige pointed toward the lower walls of the kitchen. "Looks like you have lots of work to do."

"Never-ending tasks." Paisley watched the coffee maker drip brown liquid into her cup, searching for small talk. Maybe something about the ocean. Or her time in Chicago. Or Paige's art. What did sisters talk about after three years of no communication?

"When are you and Judah going to have your c-ceremony?" Why the catch in her voice? Paige gazed out the kitchen window as if her thoughts traveled a million miles away.

"We haven't set a date. Still catching up on house repairs after the storm."

"Oh, right." A pause. "I hope I'm invited." Her tentative expression reminded Paisley of the young sister who used to sit at their mom's side doing art, painting, sketching, trying to appease the difficult woman by doing everything right. Such a burden.

She, on the other hand, had never been able to please or appease Mom. But why regurgitate that subject when she was trying to let it go? "Of course, you're invited."

"Good. Thanks."

When they were growing up, she and Paige were never close the way she and Peter were. Nor was there a horrible clash. Not until she didn't attend Mom's funeral. Then the two hurled insults spanning twenty-some years of sisterhood. Did Paige remember that awful day?

"You're selfish and unkind"—Paige's words. *"You only think of yourself. She wanted to talk to you, make things right before she died. But you couldn't set aside your blame. Your hate!"*

Paisley stared out the window, putting emotional distance between them. From then, and now.

"I should go." Paige shuffled a few steps away. Maybe she felt the gap too.

Paisley poured creamer into her coffee, stirring, contemplating what the future might be like if everything were different. If she went to the funeral. Never met Craig. Never left Judah. Didn't go to Chicago. Mind boggling what-ifs. Irreversible decisions that affected more than her. Maybe she should just jump in and ask Paige about Craig. Get the conversation over with. Wasn't he the elephant in the room?

Instead of walking away, Paige retraced her steps. "I wanted to tell you that I plan to speak with someone at the bank today. And maybe a lawyer." She nodded toward the living room. "I can't let Mayor Grant control my business affairs, threaten me and others in town, without putting up a fight."

"Sounds good." Paisley grabbed her mug. "It's about time someone put the mayor in his place."

"You don't care?" Paige looked uncertain. "Even though he's your father-in-law? Judah's dad?"

"With the obnoxious way he acts? Hardly."

"Good to know. I'll talk to you later." Paige lifted her hand.

Childish squeals came from the other room. Laughter. Goodbyes. Sweet sounds.

Paisley sipped her coffee and stared out the plastic-covered window, imagining what Misty Gale would have been like as a four-year-old.

Her phone vibrated. She focused on the screen.

Had a visit from Edward. Judah's text.

How did it go? She tapped in, noticing he didn't say "my dad."

Not good. Demanding as ever. Typical Mayor Grant.

How's your mom? She cared about Bess. Edward could take a long walk off a short dock.

Mom wants to stay here. She told him to get counseling.

Good for her! She inserted a happy-face emoji.

I'm going to work here today. Start the job on Monday.

Two days. Not much time for them to talk about sensitive issues they still needed to face, or to go on one of those dates.

Sorry I can't be in two places at once.

No worries. Look after your mom. Make sure she's okay. Same as me with my dad.

What a pair we make, huh?

She thought of his warm kisses. Of the way his arms surrounded her and made her feel at home with him. Of the spicy scent of his deodorant and aftershave lingering on her after she hugged him. Yes, they made quite the pair. Even though the tone of his texts was serious, she decided to send him a flirty one. He could use something lighthearted. So could she.

Tell me one thing you like about me. She sent an emoji of a girl shrugging.

He sent four emojis. A heart. A rose. A kissing face. Two hearts.

Tell me one thing, she persisted.

I love the way you gaze into my eyes like you really see me.

Her breath caught in her throat.

I love your smile.

The way your heart beats in time to mine.

That was three things. His responses stirred up deep emotions in her.

She tapped the screen. *You're a sweet man. I love that you love me.* She held her breath, waiting.

I do.

She exhaled. Soon they'd exchange those two words in a ceremony. When would that happen? Her thoughts skittered in a different direction.

I'm still waiting to cash in on our dare. She couldn't let him forget about that.

Bring it on!

She laughed and ended the texting session.

She and her dad worked for a couple of hours in the kitchen. Yesterday, when Judah and James came by, they cleared out the fridge and stove, leaving easy access to the walls.

"I hope we never experience a hurricane again." Dad moaned. "My father would be outraged to see his house flooded. Walls torn apart. The tree he used to climb chopped up and gone."

"It's been rough. But, other than the tree, things are nearly as good as new, right?" She spread some mud with the trowel.

"Never the same."

"No. But what if it's better the second time around?" For her, speaking up took a step of faith, a chance to look for something positive in the middle of the hardships. "If we never had the storm, we wouldn't have had all this time to work together. Time to talk."

Unexpected tears flooded her eyes. What if he had died after the hurricane? What if she never got the chance to make things right with him? A grief she didn't realize she still carried twisted in her chest, followed by a sorrowful moan. She set down the trowel and pressed her fist against her mouth to subdue it. She bent her head so her dad wouldn't see her tears. Silly tears.

"What's wrong?" He tipped his head down, staring at her.

He wouldn't understand. Goodness, she barely understood.

His arms came around her. "What happened, Paisley-bug?"

Paisley-bug? His pet name for her was her undoing. She leaned into his flannel shirt and cried.

"Did I say something wrong?" He sounded baffled.

"I'm just so sorry for leaving the way I did."

His arms stiffened. He pulled back. He probably didn't want

to dig up old memories. Neither did she. Yet, the moment seemed to be glaring her in the face.

"I know I hurt you." She gripped his wrist, preventing him from moving farther away. "I regret that."

"We talked about this the day of the storm. What's done is done."

She leaned back with her legs folded beneath her and faced him. "But you didn't accept my apology. We still ... need to talk ... until we can make things right."

"Don't see why." He slapped some mud on the wall. A few splatters hit the floor.

"I disappointed you when I didn't attend the ... Mom's ... funeral."

A tic throbbed in his jaw. His bluish gray eyes squinted at her. "Why discuss what can't be changed? Are you sorry you didn't attend your mother's funeral?"

"Yes."

He jerked like the word startled him.

If she could go back and fix that part of her life, of course, she would. "I'm sorry for the bad decisions I made. For hurting you. Mom. Paige."

He gazed at her with a softer look, nodding like he understood. Finally.

Another issue came to mind. Should she say something? Would there ever be a better time? She took a deep breath, knowing he probably wouldn't appreciate her question. "Why didn't you ever rescue me from the pantry?" The words tore from her lips, from her heart. A weight pressed down on her chest.

Dad released a slow breath. "She"—he cleared his throat—"called it a quiet place. Somewhere for you to mull over your actions. I didn't see any harm in it at first."

His words nearly sent her heart into palpitations. She grabbed a wet cloth and wiped mud off her trembling fingers. "Did you question that a dark locked room wasn't a healthy place for a child?" She kept her voice as calm as possible. "Did you?"

"I—" He bit his lip. "I can't speak ill of your mother."

Powerful emotions surged through her. "Please. I've waited a long time to hear your explanation."

He stared into the mud bucket. Lost in thought, perhaps. "I questioned her. Told her to let you out."

"You did?" The tension squeezing the air out of her throat eased. One by one, chains unlinked. Air flowed more freely into her lungs. Easier to breathe. "And—?"

"I said you were small. You shouldn't be left alone." He stared at the wall as if watching a scene in the past. "You weren't a bad child. Adventurous. Sometimes mischievous. Not bad."

He stuck up for her? Defended her! Oh, goodness. This changed everything. Everything! She linked her arm with his and leaned her cheek against his shoulder. "Then what?" She felt like a little girl and her father, the man she trusted, was telling her a story with great meaning. A story about her and him.

"We fought. Terrible arguments. She said I was gone from the house too much to pass judgment on her parenting." He picked up the mudding tool and spread some goo on the wall as if Paisley's arm wasn't still linked with his.

She lowered her hands to her lap, shuffled back a little. "Didn't you argue for your right to have a say in your daughter's upbringing?"

"Yep. Slept on the couch for a week." He gulped. Staring at her, he sniffed. Was he fighting his emotions? "I told myself you'd be okay. You had a fiery personality. You were okay, right?"

Such a travesty. Such a loss. "No, Dad, I wasn't. I'm still not okay."

His lips trembled. So did his hands. His eyes filled with moisture. "I'm s-sorry t-too." His face crumpled into a grimace that tugged on her heart. "I n-never would have p-put you in there. Never. I hated it more than I hated anything in the world." His shoulders shook.

She leaned forward and wrapped her arms around him, pressing her face against his shirt. In her heart of hearts she knew her loving father could never have approved of that treatment. Yet she blamed him, too. Her heart ached for the parent who saw injustice and didn't do anything to stop it.

So many times she begged God to send Dad or Superman or Jesus to free her from the pantry. The remembered walls closed in on her now, reminding her of their power. How could she cross the bridge to peace? Toward healing? Judah would probably say it started with love and ended with grace. Was it that easy?

If so, why did it feel so difficult?

Twenty-seven

Judah received an email that a community meeting was scheduled for five o'clock tonight. He deleted the notification. After what happened last time, he wasn't attending anything at City Hall. He'd rather keep his distance from the mayor. And Mom wouldn't want to attend, so he'd stay home with her.

Any chance you're coming to the town meeting? Paisley texted him later in the day.

Not planning on it.

I could use a shoulder to cry on.

What? His stomach lurched. *What's going on?*

Stuff with my dad. Paige.

There must have been a conflict for her to say she needed a shoulder to cry on. Did she mean it literally? Did she need him to go to her?

You want me to come over now?

Nah. I'll be alright. She sent a sad-faced emoji. *Just wanted some sympathy. A great big shoulder like yours.*

You got it. Going to the meeting? Even though he didn't want to attend, he could stop by for a few minutes to see her.

Dad wants to. Thought I would. But I hate to run into certain people.

I know what you mean. I'll meet you there.

Really? Have I told you lately that you're a nice man?

Not enough, he thought, then sighed. Did he dare leave Mom alone?

An hour later, after she assured him of her well-being and shooed him out the door, he slid into the seat next to Paisley in the community room at City Hall. She clasped his right hand with both of hers and squeezed.

"You okay?"

She nodded, shrugged. Not much to go on. When she shuffled closer to him and leaned her head against his shoulder, his heart hammered. He slid his arm around her, and she nestled her cheek against his chest. Did she hear his heart's reaction? How many more days until she came home? Until they could start their lives together?

He glanced toward the front of the room. Wait a second. Why was Mia Till behind the podium? Where was the mayor? He perused the crowded room but didn't see Edward anywhere.

Oh, no. Did he make a terrible mistake by leaving Mom alone? He couldn't stay with her all the time, but he had felt conflicted about whether he should remain at the cottage with her or come here to be with his wife. What if Edward showed up at the beach house? Hurt Mom or coerced her into going back to their place. He groaned.

"What is it?" Paisley whispered.

He shook his head. He should go now, but he hated to leave when he just got here.

"Hey, everyone!" Mia tapped the microphone and laughed.

"I'm the chairperson for the town's reconstruction committee."
She pulsed her arms in the air like she was doing a dance
move.

A few people clapped. Mia bowed, hamming it up.

Judah lowered his arm from Paisley's shoulder, about to
explain why he had to go.

"Why do we need a chairperson?" Maggie Thomas called
out. "Who's paying for the luxury? Better not be me."

"Me, neither." A female voice in the back sounded like
Paisley's aunt.

Judah edged forward in his seat, but Paisley tugged on his
hand. What made her feel so vulnerable tonight? She didn't
care for these meetings or City Hall. Maybe that's what troubled
her.

At the podium, Mia rocked on her heels. "I get paid ten
times what the last volunteer received. Get it?" She laughed
and waved at some people—probably men—in an unprofessional
manner. Judah recognized her way of smoothing over uncomfortable topics with a flirty grin.

"Where's the mayor?" Brian Corbin leaned against the
back wall, not in his deputy uniform. A few coworkers and
neighbors stood at the back also.

"Hey, Deputy." Mia waved. "Mayor Grant will be here
shortly. He's been detained."

The man was never late for official functions. Judah's dread
deepened.

"Why summon us to a meeting he doesn't value enough to
attend himself?" Maggie Thomas stood quickly. "What a waste.
I'm leaving."

A rustling followed. Others stood as if leaving too.

"Hold on! Wait, please." Mia waved her hands. "Come on,

you guys, I have important news. Even if the mayor doesn't make it back tonight, you've got to hear this."

Why wouldn't Edward make it back? Where was he? Judah clenched his jaw.

"Sorry I dragged you to this fake meeting," Paisley whispered.

"It's okay. Just worried about my mom." He nodded toward the back of the room. He'd explain later.

"Go." She nudged his arm. "I shouldn't have sent such a desperate text."

"I want you to reach out to me." He whispered goodbye and waited for his chance to exit without much notice.

"We're starting a brigade of neighbors helping neighbors," Mia spoke. "The group you'll be assigned to depends on where you live." She clicked a remote and a PowerPoint slide of a map of the city flashed on the wall behind her.

Some of the people who stood up before sat down, mumbling. A ruckus of some sort happened at the back of the room.

"Let me by. Get out of the way." The mayor stomped up the aisle, strumming his fingers through his messy hair, then straightening his jacket and dusting himself off.

Where had he been? And what detained him? Since he was here, Judah might as well stay a while longer. Wait. Did the mayor have on mismatched cowboy boots? One, tan. One, brown. Good grief. He was going to be embarrassed about that.

"Let's give it up for Mayor Edward Grant—father, husband, friend, and town hero!" Mia clapped her hands high over her head like she was welcoming a celebrity.

Judah's gut clenched as he pictured Mom's bruise. Some hero.

A few loyalists joined Mia's enthusiastic welcome. The mayor bowed his head as if he were a humble leader.

Paisley clutched Judah's hand again. Then it hit him like a two-by-four across the head. Had Mia been warming up the crowd? Filling in time until the mayor arrived?

Edward cleared his throat. "I apologize for my tardiness."

"Something wrong with your eyes, Mayor?" Maggie Thomas cackled. "Got stars twinkling in those orbs so bright you can't tell the difference between brown and tan?"

"Whatever do you mean, Maggie?"

She pointed ostentatiously at his boots, garnering laughs.

The mayor glanced downward. His face paled. "Oops. Happens to the best of them." He shrugged like he didn't mind, but Judah knew better. "Tonight, I want you to hear a message from my heart."

This ought to be good.

Regret burned in Judah's gut for how badly he felt toward Edward. But it dueled with his anger over the unconscionable way the man had treated Mom. Deep in his heart, he knew that whatever deplorable ways the mayor acted, he was still his father. And the love of God constrained him to love everyone, including Edward Grant. *Mercy and grace.* However, he didn't feel either of those kindnesses right now.

Hopefully, Edward didn't go by the cottage. Didn't harass Mom. Judah sat on the edge of his seat. Should he head back to the house and check on her, or stay with Paisley?

"Some of you have questioned my loyalty, my involvement in what happened at the barricade the last night of the evacuation." Edward swayed his hand toward the back of the room. "The deputy and I have come to an agreement about that."

"Hold on, Mayor." Deputy Brian cleared his throat. "No discussing an ongoing investigation."

"Right. I only meant to say, all the citizens of Basalt Bay have an obligation to help our neighbors, to come alongside each other and do what needs doing for the good of our town." His voice rose and sounded more refined than usual. Was someone coaching him? Mia, perhaps?

"Here. Here." Another male voice. Craig's? Was he still schmoozing the mayor?

"What Miss Till shared with you about the way we've split up the town into brigade's—her brainchild, by the way—will benefit all of us." The mayor clapped in Mia's direction, saying something indistinguishable to her. Judah imagined him grinning like a fool.

Mia laughed and winked.

Gag.

Paisley leaned forward, her elbows on her knees, closing her eyes as if she couldn't stand to watch the proceedings any longer. That's how Judah felt too.

"I have served as mayor of this fine town with a dedication few could fault." Edward clutched his lapels and rocked on his boots like he was giving a stump speech.

Few could fault? Right.

Whispers and snickers reached Judah. He glanced back. Callie and Miss Patty chattered a couple of rows behind him. Callie tugged on Miss Patty's arm. The store owner shook her head. Then more whispers. Were the gossipers getting ready for some mudslinging?

He tuned into his father's words. "I beseech you to listen to Miss Till's presentation with an open mind and a loving heart toward your neighbors. Then we'll split up into groups and make plans for our town's ongoing reconstruction."

Good ideas. Excellent ideas, even. Didn't Judah and Paisley

talk about doing something similar in the aftermath of the hurricane? However, he didn't understand the change in Edward's demeanor. *A loving heart toward your neighbor?* Not his MO. Was he overcompensating because his marriage was on the rocks? Trying to act more compassionate so, when people found out about him and Mom, they wouldn't be quick to blame him?

Or was the sprucing-up-the-mayor campaign Mia's doing? If so, even she wouldn't condone his faux pas in the shoe department. What would she say, what would the townspeople think, if they discovered the extent of the mayor's cruelty and lack of honor toward his wife?

Wasn't a public servant supposed to be held to a higher standard?

Twenty-eight

Before church started the next day, whispers passed from one pew to another about a mayoral-recall signature drive. Murmurs reached Paisley, sitting between Judah and her dad. By Judah's tense posture and the way he leaned forward with his eyes closed, he probably heard too.

Bess, seated on his left side, appeared relaxed. She waved at a couple of people and smiled. Would she condemn her husband, if given the chance? She might be glad if he lost his leadership position in Basalt. Might even vote against him.

As delighted as Paisley would be if Edward Grant got kicked off his high horse, she cared more about the two Grants sitting next to her. It was unlikely that the three troublemakers—Miss Patty, Aunt Callie, and Maggie Thomas—would drum up enough signatures to impeach him, anyway.

The plan Mia introduced last night for the town's renovation came to mind. Paisley still wanted to talk with Judah about that, since he left to check on Bess before attendees split into neighborhood groups. She didn't know why Mia insisted that Paisley and Judah participate separately. Something was strange about her rise to leadership with the whole reconstruction thing, too.

After they sang a few worship songs, Pastor Sagle stepped behind the pulpit and read a familiar verse about love not failing. She and Judah used to have a plaque with that quote on their living room wall. The idea that love might not fail was intriguing. But with the shortcomings of mankind, how could it not break apart the way everything else did? It would take a powerful love to be so resilient that it never caved.

Pondering how Judah kept saying he loved her, watched out for her, and risked his life to save hers, a tender feeling rushed through her. She linked her fingers with his. She didn't want to interrupt him from hearing the pastor's words, but she needed to feel connected with him.

He leaned back against the seat, met her gaze, gave her a small smile. His eyes looked so tired. She wished she could encourage him the way he did with her so many times.

The silver-haired pastor who gave her a ride to Dad's the night of the horrible storm perused the congregation with a thoughtful expression. He glanced in Judah and Bess's direction, then sighed. "Friends. Neighbors. Flawed humans. Broken, all."

What a strange way to address them. Paisley sank against the wooden seat and scooted down a little. Quite a few years had passed since she darkened a church door on a Sunday morning. Today, since her dad asked her to attend, and she didn't want to tell him no, she came along. Also, Judah texted her that he was bringing his mom. Did she want to join them? Of course, she said yes.

But coming to the old church where she attended growing. up? Entering the place where she remembered how some of the meanest people could act spiritual, then later say horrible things to her, made her shudder. Running out the door was tempting.

Pastor Sagle remained silent for a good thirty seconds. He perused the congregation so intently that she wanted to slink down lower and hide, lest his gaze cross hers.

A restlessness prevailed in the room. The sound of shuffling and rustling of fabric on wooden seats grew louder. A few coughs. Whispers.

"Love is a beautiful thing."

All rustling stopped.

For ten minutes, Pastor Sagle spoke in a quiet voice about a tender love that transcended all human loves. A perfect love that went beyond failings or duty or pride. Far above wealth or a name or a person's bank balance. Beyond hurts. Beyond the cares of this world. Beyond disappointments and loss.

Some of his points felt like the pastor had been reading her mind. She knew he spoke of God's love. Of sacrificial, selfless love like Judah sometimes talked about. But several times it seemed like he was referring to intimate love between a husband and a wife, too. Then Judah held her hand a little tighter. Sending her a message? Reminding her that he was eager to restart their marriage? Sigh.

Pastor Sagle ended his talk with, "The purest love any person can know, the most satisfying and eternal, is the precious love of God." He closed in prayer.

After the benediction, the congregation dispersed. Paisley and Judah strode down the center aisle. He seemed in a hurry to get outside. Bess and Kathleen walked slowly behind them.

At the foot of the outdoor steps, Paisley's dad stopped and chatted with James.

When she and Judah reached the parking lot, she slowed down their pace. "Pastor Sagle's brevity surprised me."

"He doesn't preach long but says a lot." His gaze met hers. "What did you think of what he said?"

"I, well, I think there are lots of forms of love." Her grin felt a little impish. "I love coffee. I love walking out on the peninsula."

"I love your eyes." He leaned toward her as if he might kiss her.

She batted his arm. "We're in the church parking lot, silly."

"So?"

"So let's not give people something else to talk about."

He groaned and slapped his hand to his chest.

"Not that I wouldn't enjoy ..."

"Yes?" He tilted his head.

"You know. Us. Kissing."

"Uh-huh." He grinned.

Heat rose in her cheeks. "But people ogling us? Gossiping about us. No, thanks."

"All right. I get that."

They strode the rest of the way to the truck. She leaned against the driver's door. "What about the whole Father's love business? He meant God, right? It's hard to grasp unconditional love."

"We've both had challenges with our parents."

"Exactly." The things he was dealing with about Edward and Bess came to mind. "I'm sorry. Maybe I shouldn't have said anything."

"Nothing to apologize for. You can talk to me about anything. I mean it. Anything, anytime."

"Okay. Thanks."

Both stood quietly for a few minutes.

He started up the conversation again. "I believe God's love is greater than anything you or I have experienced in our families. For me, my mom's love comes closest. But she's human. Fails like we all do." He slid his arm over her shoulder. "Just like we talked about before, I'm bound to mess up and fail too." He leaned his chin against her head. "But God's love, Pais, it's amazing. He's always there for us. He's a good Father who loves us. The songs say that, but I've found it to be true in my life."

She met his gaze. "You're different now. More peaceful. Kind. I mean, you were always a nice guy. Not perfect by any means."

He chuckled.

"But since I've been back, you've shown me such grace and love, it's remarkable."

He linked their pinkies. "I want you to know that I love you. But I also want you to know God's love. For all the times I can't be with you, can't make things better—even though I want to—He will be there. Loving you. Forgiving you. Holding you up."

See, he was being so sweet.

She was talking to God more. But this thing about accepting His love … believing that He cared for *her* … might take a leap of faith she wasn't ready for.

"I finally talked with my dad." She changed the subject.

"The text about needing my shoulder?" He moved and leaned against the door beside her. "How did it go? The talk, I mean?"

"Hard. Good. We cried." She groaned. "I asked him about my lockups. Why he didn't do something. He said he was sorry."

"I'm glad it went okay." He gave her a sympathetic hug.

Just then, while his arms were around her, three older women approached the car parked next to his truck. They stared at them until Paisley pulled away and trudged to the back of the pickup.

"Ladies." Judah followed her and they both leaned against the tailgate. "Did you reach some closure with your dad?"

"Kind of. I wish—"

"What?"

"I wish forgiveness and getting over things was easier."

"Yeah, me too. That petition stuff was embarrassing. I almost walked out. Too much to handle after the last few days I've had with my parents."

"I'm sorry. Must be hard."

"Yeah, but I'm glad I stayed. People will talk regardless." He leaned in and briefly touched their lips together, maybe making a point. People would talk about them no matter what, also.

The car with the three ladies in it backed up with the driver squinting at them like they were doing something wrong.

"You and I still have some things to talk about." He swept a strand of her hair back as if he didn't notice they had an audience.

Paisley sighed in relief when the car moved away. "Yeah. I'm nervous about that discussion." She didn't want to talk about it now, either.

"Maybe, after we chat, you'll feel more comfortable about setting a date." His statement sounded like a question.

"Maybe. Oh, look, it's my dad." Was she too obvious that she wanted to change the subject? "Ready to go?"

"I'm ready for lunch." Dad jiggled his car keys, heading

toward the burnt sienna Volkswagen in the next row. "Leftover potpie calls."

"Too bad Bert's isn't open." She glanced at Judah. "Maybe I should try to get a job there."

"If that's what you want to do." He frowned like he was puzzled by the switch in topics.

"I need to do something. Work somewhere. I can't just"— she blew out a breath—"mooch off my dad. Or you. Or do a big fat nothing."

"Paisley, you've worked ever since the hurricane." He stuffed his hands into his pockets. "There's still a lot to do at the cottage. And in town."

"But that doesn't help us or my dad financially."

"No. But—" He shuffled his shoes against the broken pavement making a scratching noise. He moved a little farther away from her. It seemed a coolness settled between them. "I should go." He rocked his thumb toward the church. "I'm picking up my mom in front. We'll talk later, okay?"

"Yeah. Sure."

He hopped in the truck and started the engine. What bothered him more? Her talking about getting a job, or that they still had things they needed to discuss? For her, it was the latter. Why, she didn't have figured out.

Twenty-nine

On Monday morning, nineteen days after Hurricane Blaine hit, Judah strolled into C-MER as a supervisor, not just an employee. That awareness, and the sense of greater responsibility, settled over his shoulders. Was this God's plan for his life? Being a leader in this company? If so, why wasn't he more enthusiastic? What happened to his peace? Maybe he had a bad case of nerves, that's all.

He needed a job for provision for him and Paisley, maybe even for Mom. But something about the way he got this position, or the way Mia sprang the news on him, smacked of underhandedness. He despised that.

Four of his previous cubicle buddies waved. Then each one dropped out of sight behind their divider walls. Avoiding interactions with him? Were the guys feeling loyal to their previous supervisor? Perhaps, they judged it unfair that Judah got promoted. He sighed and glanced around without finding Craig. The receptionist's desk had been empty when he walked in, too.

He trudged into Craig's, er, his, small office. As soon as he crossed the threshold, a bad smell hit him. Something rotten. Just great. Papers were scattered across the desk. A dirty coffee cup and empty pastry packages littered the space between the laptop and the papers. The garbage can spilled over with scrunched up papers, empty soda cans, candy wrappers, and store-bought sandwich packaging. Was that the cause of the stench?

Judah removed his jacket, draped it over the back of the black office furniture, then gathered up the garbage from the floor. He could barely tie a knot in the heaping, bulging trash bag before setting it in the doorway. He stacked loose-leaf papers, files, and mail into a single pile on the desk. He'd sort through it later.

Two coworkers scurried past the open door, muttering. Were they also disgruntled about the change in command? Craig did great work for C-MER, even Judah admitted that. Too bad the guy acted so erratic lately and got himself into trouble. Something soured in Judah's stomach. Perhaps he took the supervisory job without enough forethought.

He dropped into the swivel chair and pinched the bridge of his nose. *Lord, did I make the right choice in coming back here?*

He pictured his mom at the cottage. When he left this morning, he told her to bolt the locks and stay inside. She rolled her eyes like she didn't take his warning seriously.

But if Edward heard through the grapevine that Judah returned to work, he might make another unannounced visit. Mom said he had shown up at the beach house the night of the community meeting. That he apologized and asked her to go to City Hall with him, for appearance's sake. She declined—good thing.

Judah talked with her about the possibility of getting an

emergency restraining order against Edward. Beneath her makeup, she still had the bruise to prove the domestic abuse. But she said she didn't want to create more hardship for him. Go figure. Didn't he give up that right?

Judah gripped a paper cup and squeezed until it was flat before throwing it away. Then sighed.

Lord, I've been caught up in a lot of frustration about my family, and now with this job. Could you watch over Mom? Give her peace. And me too.

"You're already here!" Mia rushed through the doorway, sidestepping the garbage bag. She dashed around the small space, scooping up the stack of papers, grabbing Craig's coat and a few other items. "Too many things going down. Sorry for the mess."

"No problem."

She scurried out the door, grabbing the trash bag on her way, nearly running on her high heels. About thirty seconds later, she reentered the room. Scuttling from one side of the small office to the other, she filled her arms with loose items. She tossed Judah a smile. "I would have cleaned this up for you. Sorry it's such a disaster."

"It's okay." Craig should have done it himself, but he probably left the building upset. Or was escorted out. "You said stuff's going down. What stuff? Can I help?"

Her movements came to a halt, and he caught a whiff of her overpowering floral perfume. She touched his arm. "You're so thoughtful. We're going to get along just fine."

He moved out of her reach. She stepped closer. He backed up against the file cabinet in his attempt to keep his distance.

"If there's ever anything—*anything*—I can do for you, just push 'one' on the phone." She lifted her index finger. "I like being Number One, if you know what I mean." She winked then whirled around, her dress flouncing as she sauntered away.

Good grief. He'd hit "one" on the phone only as a last resort.

"There you are." Mike Linfield stopped in the doorway, still wearing his jacket.

"Mike. Good to see you."

The older man with silvery slicked-back hair swayed his thumb toward the east side of the building. "Meet me in my office in five?"

"Sure thing."

The manager took furtive glances over his shoulder, acting jumpy, then dodged away. What was up with that?

Ten seconds later, Mia popped back into the office. "Just wanted to warn you. Craig's here. I'd avoid him if I were you."

Did she expect thanks for the warning? If anything, her popping in and out telling him things annoyed him. He yanked open a couple of drawers to inspect the contents. Oh, nasty. Something had rotted. *Peeuuw.* An apple? Yep. And more empty candy wrappers. Even a moldy sandwich.

Mia rushed forward. "Let me do that. You have a meeting to prepare for." She extended the drawer with the disgusting items as far as it would open. "Craig, what were you doing?" She grabbed the trash can and dumped in the offending wrappers and packages.

"That wasn't necessary. But thanks."

"You're welcome." Her blond multi-hued waves bobbed as she exited. At the last second, she whirled around. "We're still friends, right?"

"Uh, I guess." Some things she did in the aftermath of the storm flitted through his thoughts. Still bugged him. Her touching his cot at the storm shelter. The way she stroked his hand, implying more than simple friendship was going on between them. How she kept minimizing his relationship with Paisley.

"I'm so glad you're back"—her lips spread in a wide red grin—"I could just hug you."

"Please, don't."

She held up her hands as if in surrender. "Don't worry. I've learned my lesson."

"Good."

She palmed the doorjamb, glancing back at him and grinning, then scurried around the corner. She said she learned her lesson, but he'd be on guard. Why hadn't anyone taken her to task about her flirtatious behavior on the job? Had she and Craig been involved? Her and Edward? Better not go there.

He dropped into the swivel chair and pressed the power button on the computer. An oceanic scene appeared on the screen. What was the password? Each of the company's devices had individualized passwords that were changed monthly. He opened the desk drawers searching for a scrap of paper with a series of numbers or a code. Nothing. Maybe he'd have to call "one" after all.

He felt someone's gaze on him. He glanced toward the door.

Craig leaned against the doorjamb, a deep scowl creasing his face. His dark eyebrows almost touched his nose.

"Morning." Judah took the initiative, even though their last interactions didn't go so well. He pointed at the screen. "The password is—?"

"A mystery, apparently." Craig stomped away.

Just great.

By mid-afternoon, Judah had sat through three meetings, avoided calling Mia, and missed lunch. One long planning session was with Mike. Two others were with different department heads. He'd never been in a supervisory position before, so he spent most of the time listening. Mike told him about a dispute among some employees concerning Craig's demotion. That accounted for his coworkers' aloofness. Craig had filed a complaint with the parent company, and Mike was expecting a call from the leadership before day's end. Judah's job might be in question—not a great thing to hear on his first day back.

When he returned to his office, he plopped down in front of the computer—which he still didn't know the password to—and bemoaned his situation. How could he work here, if they allowed him to continue in this role, and regain the trust of his coworkers? What they weren't aware of was that Craig was drunk when he fired him. That Judah tried stopping him from stealing a skiff, or possibly getting killed or injured in a boating accident. What if the higher ups sided with Craig?

A long sigh rumbled out of him.

Mia popped in with a note from an outside agency inquiring about access to the harbor. Judah took the opportunity to ask her about the password. She promised to hunt it down.

When the end of his workday arrived, he drove away from the C-MER building thankful it was over. Hungry and exhausted, he stopped to pick up groceries at Lewis's Super. Grilled steaks sounded fantastic. As did relaxing in front of his ocean view and forgetting about the office problems he encountered today.

"Judah!"

Mom? What was she doing here? She strode toward him wearing a green Lewis's Super apron and carrying two loaves of bread.

"What's going on? What's with the apron?"

"I got a job. Isn't it great?" She grinned and set the loaves on the shelf next to the other bread.

"You took a job here? Does Dad know?"

She shot him a disparaging glare.

"Oh, uh …" Mentioning his father wasn't the best thing to say. And he reverted to thinking of him as "Dad."

"Why should your father care where I work?"

"I, well, um, because he is, well, he will—"

"What?"

"Never mind. It doesn't matter what he says, right?"

"No, it doesn't." She lifted her chin.

But wait until he hears.

"I had to do something." She shrugged. "I can't sit around your place painting my toenails all day."

No, she couldn't do that, not after she'd been a prisoner in her house on the cliff. His telling her to lock the doors and stay in the house probably didn't help, either. "I'm proud of you, Mom."

"Really?" Her wide grin made her appear younger.

"Of course. This is a brave thing you're doing, working at Lewis's." He didn't mention that if the mayor walked in, every customer, perhaps everyone on the block, would hear him yelling. No doubt, he'd holler at Lewis, too, demanding to know why the store owner dared to hire the *mayor's wife*. He pushed those thoughts aside. "How do you like the job?"

"Love it. I enjoy all the people. Chatting now and then. It's therapeutic." She smiled at a customer walking past and seemed a natural at interacting with people.

How long had it been since he saw her so happy? He nodded toward the groceries he collected in his cart. "Thought I'd fix steaks for us."

215

"Sounds heavenly. I'll be done at six."

"Bess Grant." A male voice announced over the intercom. "Clean up needed in aisle four."

"That's me." She rushed down the aisle, calling over her shoulder, "Duty calls!"

He didn't know what to make of this new development. If her working here surprised him, he hated to think what his father's reaction might be.

Thirty

Judah and his mom sat down on the kitchen chairs he returned to the patio. A well-done steak rested on each of their plates along with a dollop of potato salad and a small pile of green veggies. This was his favorite type of meal: grilled food, a fabulous view, and the wind moving through his hair. Maybe that wind would blow away his work-related angst.

"What a treat. These look fabulous." Mom picked up her fork and steak knife, her eyes gleaming.

Before Judah took a bite of his steak, a loud engine and a blasting horn alerted him to someone's arrival. He groaned. He'd been afraid of this since finding Mom working at the local grocery. His gaze collided with hers.

"He's here." Her steak knife clattered to her plate.

"Yep." A knot tightened in his middle. He stood and shoved his chair from the makeshift table. Before he reached the sliding glass door, his father barreled through the living room and stomped outside onto the pavers.

"Dad."

The mayor didn't pause or address him. He strode to the table, parking himself across from Mom with his hands fisted at his hips, wheezing like he ran to get here. "What's the meaning of this?" He huffed and leaned forward, eyes bulging. "I heard you took a job at Lewis's."

"Hello, to you too, Edward," Mom said crisply.

"Care for some steak?" Judah would split his if it would soothe the tension between his parents. He remained standing in case he had to intervene somehow.

"No, I don't want your food." Dad's chin jutted out. Beneath his reddened eyes, dark baggy skin revealed he wasn't sleeping well, or else was drinking too much.

"What has you worked up this time?" Mom picked up her knife and cut her meat. Apparently, she was used to dining in the middle of stress.

Not Judah. He couldn't sit down and eat as if his father wasn't standing here, glaring and huffing. All the anticipation of a fine meal was thwarted.

"Worked up, you say?" Dad snorted. "How could you humiliate me by taking that kind of a job? My wife working as a grocery bagger. You've got to be kidding me!"

"Humiliate you?" Mom pulsed her knife in the air. "I'll have you know I put in a hard day's work. I'm pleased with my labor. So is Lewis, I think. And I'll work anywhere an honest person who isn't intimidated by you will hire me." She stuffed a chunk of meat into her mouth and chewed. "Mmm. Good steak, Judah."

He almost snickered.

"No wife of mine is going to work!"

Mom groaned.

"Come on, Dad. It's the twenty-first century."

"Doesn't matter." His father pounded the unsecured tabletop with his hand. The cardboard swayed and dishes rattled.

Judah grabbed hold of his plate to protect his steak.

"I'm the leader in this family. What I say goes!"

Mom laughed outright.

"Stop howling, woman." Dad leaned his fists on the table which made everything sway to that side.

"Don't ever speak to me like that, or tell me what to do, again." Mom stood, glaring at him. "Watch out, or I'll tell people the whole story about you. What do you say to that, *Mayor* Grant?"

He sucked in great gulps of air as if hyperventilating. Would Judah have to make his father leave? Take him to the ER?

"*If* you must work, where you work matters." He shot Judah a glare before resuming his intense stare toward Mom. "The type of job this family has matters to my constituents."

"Hogwash!" She grabbed her glass and gulped some water.

What did he mean by "the type of job?" Did he speak to Mike Linfield? Pressure him to—? "What did you do?"

"Nothing." The older man's eyes twitched. "I'm here to tell your mother I don't want her working in Lewis's Super, that's all." His gaze fastened on Mom's. "Do you understand me?"

Still standing, her fingers gripped the glass so tightly her knuckles turned white. "Do I understand that my estranged husband is commanding me not to work in a place he deems unfit?" She harrumphed. "Want to know what I think about that?" She jerked the glass toward Dad, and water splattered his face. Liquid ran down his jacket and dripped onto the table.

He sputtered and yowled, swiping his sleeve across his mouth and cheeks.

Judah couldn't believe what he just saw. What should he do? He wanted to stay close to his mom in case she needed him, but he forced himself to dash into the kitchen and grab a dish towel off the oven door. He scrambled back outside and tossed the fabric to his father.

Mom scooped up plates and food like an agitated busser in a busy restaurant. With her arms full, she stomped into the house.

"I can't believe she did that." Dad wiped his face with the towel and sniffed a couple of times like water went up his nose.

The water drowning Judah's steak and salad, and the emotional outbursts, had ruined his dinner. There was one thing he had to know. "Did you talk with Mike Linfield about my job?"

Dad wiped his face again.

"Did you?"

He dropped the towel on the table. "If I did, be thankful I used my influence to help you out of an unfair situation."

"I'm not thankful! I've been doing fine on my own for a long time."

"Could have fooled me."

Judah gritted his teeth. "Stay out of my business."

"And you stay out of mine." Dad thrust his finger at him. "Harboring my wife. Accusing me of having an affair!"

"Get off your throne." Judah hurled the towel across the patio. "You hurt Mom! How could you? She's the nicest, gentlest woman in Basalt Bay. And you abused her."

The mayor's blustering pride seemed to wither. He shrank before Judah's eyes, sinking onto the chair Mom vacated. "An unfortunate mistake. I never meant for—"

"You need help. Serious help."

"I have it under control. I promise it won't happen again."

"And tonight's display? Another example of you being under control?" He pointed in the direction of the driveway he couldn't see from the patio. "You probably drove like a maniac to get here. Stomped through my house. Barreled outside as if you intended harm. Yelled at Mom. She's a woman. Your partner in life. Maybe ... maybe you should start respecting her."

"How am I going to get her to come home?" His voice sounded small and weak.

"She might not be willing to go with you, ever."

Dad glanced up. "That's odd coming from a man whose wife left him for four or five years."

"Three." Judah gritted his teeth. His father knew how to push his buttons. He sighed and sat down. Maybe he could say something meaningful that might get through to his dad. Worth a shot. "I didn't know if or when Paisley would come home, but every day I prayed for her. I loved her with all of my heart, even when she hadn't returned yet."

Dad stared at him with a dull expression like he couldn't comprehend his words.

"I had to change. Me." He pointed at himself. "A little humility in your heart might go a long way toward reconciling, too."

"I can act humble." The mayor's chest puffed up—with hot air, no doubt. "Didn't you see me stroll into the community meeting? Affable, congenial, a regular guy next door. People love me."

Judah groaned. "I didn't say *act* humble. Humility is the opposite of pride. The opposite of how you behaved tonight."

"So, things still working out between you and—"

"Paisley. Yes." He paused. Should he say anything else? Was his dad even listening? "You know, you could pray too. Ask God to help you to be a better husband."

Dad laughed harshly. Then he marched across the sand and rounded the corner, out of sight. The Grant men's way of dealing with uncomfortable things—walking away, not talking, not being vulnerable. A good reminder for Judah of how he never wanted to act again.

He listened to the sound of the truck engine, the vehicle's revving, and the acceleration as the rig rumbled out of the yard. If his father were willing to sacrifice his pride and self-righteous attitude for his wife's happiness, he might salvage his marriage.

But it seemed he was too stubborn for that.

Thirty-one

Paisley swept the kitchen floor and admired the finished walls, glad that her dad didn't display any of Mom's paintings in here. She inhaled, smelling the scent of paint even though the walls were dry.

This morning Dad and James went to Eugene to hunt for secondhand appliances and furniture. They probably wouldn't find many used items with so many residents along the coast searching for similar pieces. Her dad's Plan B included visiting a furniture store and applying for a payment plan to tide him over until the insurance money arrived. Fortunately, a lot of businesses were offering discounts to hurricane victims.

For the last ten days, Paisley's focus had been on assisting her dad with his remodel, but now she needed to expend some good faith on the cottage. Soon, it would be her home again. Since Judah went back to work, he wouldn't have as much time for completing the renovations. Or talking or dating. A little dig gnawed at her middle.

His mom still lived with him, which Paisley understood and supported. But it meant they didn't have many opportunities to hang out or share their hearts the way they did after the storm. If she spent more time at the cottage, maybe they could go on some beach walks and talk when he got home.

She finished a few more chores, then threw on a sweatshirt before heading outside. She planned to drop by Bert's and have that chat about getting her old job back.

As she strode past Miss Patty's rental, Kathleen rocked in a chair on the front porch. "Why, hello! Are you renting this house?"

"Paisley, good afternoon." The older woman smiled and waved. "Yes, I am renting it. I hope to get into something bigger soon, but it's been great for just me." She gestured toward the one-story beach house. "How about a cup of tea?"

"Oh, no, thank you. Another time, perhaps."

"You sure?"

"I'm on a mission. Soon, though, okay?"

"Very well." Kathleen rocked in the chair. "I'll keep enjoying this beautiful fall day."

"Me too." Paisley waved and continued walking. Next door, she saw Sal in the souvenir shop knee deep in debris. Poor man. His merchandise and building were ruined. The roof had partially fallen off and landed on the ground. She sent the storekeeper a sympathetic smile. He could use two of the volunteer brigades to help him.

She strode past Paige's art gallery. Loud voices reached her through the open plywood door, and she paused. A man and a woman were arguing. Who was in there with her sister? Edward?

Craig barreled out the door, muttering to himself. Paisley stepped back against the wall. He stomped past her as if he didn't see her, grumbling and biting off words. He marched down the block, almost colliding with Miss Patty who carried an armload of bags in front of the hardware store. Heated words were exchanged between the two.

In the shadowy doorway, Paige started to close the door of the gallery. Her gaze met Paisley's. "Oh, hello." Her eyes were red. Her face blotchy like she'd been crying.

"Are you okay?"

Paige's expression crumpled. "Not so great. Did you want to come in?"

"Oh, um, sure." Paisley trudged into the dark room. The empty space appeared the same as it did the last time she was here, except for the swept floors. "I'm on my way to talk to Bert. Ask for my old job." She chattered, filling in the awkward silence.

Paige walked to the center of her destroyed studio. "Here's my dream. My storybook ending. Until Addy and Blaine destroyed everything." She covered her face and groaned.

"I'm sorry for your loss. This has to be a harrowing experience." Paisley remained in her place, not breaching the distance between them, between their hearts.

Paige shuddered, lowering her hands. She shook her head like she was clearing her thoughts. "How are things at Dad's?"

"We're almost finished with the interior. He and James went to search for appliance bargains."

"Good luck with that."

"I know, right?"

Paisley wanted to ask her about Craig. But how could she without sounding like a snoop or being insensitive? She trudged to the open window and stared out over the sea. A gust of wind billowed against her. Turbulent waves pounded the rocky beach below. Seawater exploded into the air like foaming fireworks. If she reached out far enough, it seemed she could touch the sea spray.

Had Paige and Craig fought? Broken up? She took a deep breath and faced her sister. "So, what's with you and Craig?"

"Nothing." Paige's shoulders buckled. "Everything." A pitiful cry wrenched from her.

This time Paisley didn't hesitate to go to her. She wrapped her arms around her sister, and Paige cried into her shoulder for a few minutes.

"It'll be okay." Paisley tried to reassure her, even though she didn't know what was wrong.

"Sorry." Paige sniffled, wiping her shirt sleeve over her face. "So many things are hitting me at once." She took a few steps away.

"Want to talk about it?"

"Not really." Paige shook her head but kept talking. "The mayor's playing dirty. Telling me what I can and can't do with a building I thought I'd own. Threatening if I don't do what he says—exactly what he says—he'll evict me. Craig's his henchman."

"Really?" Hadn't he warned Paisley about the mayor? He didn't seem sympathetic to him then. However, he did stick up for Edward at the community meeting.

"He says if I don't comply with Mayor Grant's wishes, the powerful man will cause me more trouble than it's worth. That I should get out. Yield to Edward's plans like every person on this street will do."

Not Bert. He would never go along with the mayor's intimidation tactics. "Edward has big schemes, huh?" If it came to a takeover, would the town council stand up to him? Did anyone ever go against Edward Grant's wishes? Other than Maggie Thomas.

"He's amassing properties. Taking over Sal's. Bought Casey's. Rumor has it he's pressuring Bert too."

"No way." Paisley paced to the window and back. "Bert and the mayor don't get along. I can't imagine him doing anything just because Edward says to."

"If he goes under financially like the rest of the business owners, he might not have a choice." Paige wiped her fingers beneath her eyes, then stooped over and picked up a shell. She flung it out the broken window. "The strangest things made their way inside during the storm surge." She picked up something else. Tossed it.

"I wonder what the mayor's endgame is."

"To possess the whole town." Paige sighed. "Probably rename it Grant Bay."

"Or Edwardsville."

At least she and Paige were talking. Maybe this was how reconciliation would work between them, by fighting the powers that be together. She nodded toward the damaged door. "Judah and I could help you fix that."

"I'd appreciate the help."

"I should go and talk to Bert." Paisley took a couple of steps toward the door. "I'll find out if the mayor's strong-arming him."

"If I could offer you a job, I would." Paige followed her and clasped her hand. "We're sisters above all else, right?"

"Right." She'd have to remind herself of that the next time Craig came between them. She released her hand, started to turn away.

"I broke up with him before the second storm."

Paisley glanced back. "You did? So, you're not with him?"

"No."

"Not dating or anything?"

"No. Just friends."

What a relief. Yet they had been arguing. Craig left angry. Paige cried. "What about Piper?"

"What about her?"

"Isn't he—" She swallowed back the question. "She seems to like Craig."

"She does."

"Is he ... is he her father?"

Paige's mouth dropped open. "That's none of your concern." She grabbed a box from off the counter and stomped into the coffee shop area. "Ancient history."

"I'm sorry. I just—" She shouldn't have said anything. Must be a sensitive subject.

"Craig told me you two had a fling." Paige eyed her from behind the counter.

"That's a lie." Even so, her heart skipped a beat.

"He said you flirted with him before you left Judah. That you were ... passionate toward him." A dark look crossed her face.

"He'd say anything to make himself look better."

"He told me he loved you."

"That's not true!"

Paige gnawed on her lower lip. "He says you may have loved him, also."

"He's just making up stuff." She gulped. "Okay, he's right about my flirting three years ago. I was seeking relief from grief. In alcohol. In male company." She drew in a breath. "I wish it didn't happen. And I've explained it to Judah."

"Did he believe you?"

"Yes. He forgave me."

"So, when you and Craig stayed together after the storm"—
Paige's words sounded rushed—"did you push for more to
happen between you?"

"What? No! Why would you think that?"

A familiar emotional wall rose between them.

"He said you're to blame that he succumbed."

"Succumbed to what?" This conversation was getting worse
by the second.

"Kissing. Emotional entanglement." Hurt blared from Paige's
gaze. "You and him."

"There's no him and me." Paisley would have laughed
at the idea if her sister didn't look so anguished. "There's no
entanglement. You have to believe me, Paige."

"Oh? I should believe the one who couldn't be bothered
to visit our dying mother?"

An old wound twisted in Paisley's chest.

"The one too absorbed in her own life to attend Mom's
funeral or care that others were hurting, too."

Her words were arrows hurtling into Paisley's heart.

"What I'll never understand"—Paige's voice rose—"is how
you could kiss another man while you were married to an amazing
guy like Judah. A man who's waited for you like a lovesick
puppy. Even when women have thrown themselves at him, he
remained faithful. And you—" She shook her head like she was
disgusted. "If you'll excuse me, I have work to accomplish."

So much for reconnecting, or sisterhood. Paige could fix her
own door. With a heavy heart and leaden feet, Paisley trudged
across the room. She paused in the doorway. "This is what he
wants."

"Who?"

"Craig." She drew in a long breath. "I never kissed him during the storm. He terrified me. Still terrifies me." Another breath. "I love Judah. I never loved Craig."

"Not even three years ago?"

"Not even then. He was a diversion, nothing more." Should she tell her the rest? "Just so you know, he tried forcing me to go against my vows to Judah. Ask Mayor Grant if you want proof."

She strode out of the gallery. She had enough of sisterly bonding.

Thirty-two

Mia Till buzzed into Judah's office and plopped down in the chair on the opposite side of the desk from him. She crossed her legs and swung her high-heeled foot, grinning with an I've-got-something-up-my-sleeve look.

"Can I help you?"

"I'm sure you can." She batted her thick black, fake eyelashes. It didn't take long for her to reestablish her flirtatious ways with him.

If he ignored her, maybe she'd grow weary of rejection and leave. "I'm busy." He pointed at his laptop. For the last hour, he'd labored over a report to headquarters about their evacuation procedures during Hurricane Blaine. What worked. What failed. He made a list of suggestions for future evacuations. Even if he couldn't keep this job, he wanted something to prove that he had the experience and the smarts to fulfill it.

"I have a big favor to ask. Any chance you could escort me to an event?" A confident smile stretched across her mouth.

"Escort you? Are you kidding me?" He stood, hands on

the desk, leaning forward. "You know better than to ask me that kind of question. I'm married."

"Don't overreact." She frowned. "I never realized how much you're like your father."

That stole some of his thunder. His dad's recent behavior came to mind. He sat back down. "So, explain yourself."

"I'm in a jam. I need an escort to a function at City Hall tomorrow. Please, pretty please, would you come with me?" She clasped her hands together and puckered her lips in a begging pose. "Paisley won't mind."

He doubted that.

"You two staying in the same house yet?" She tipped her head one way, then the other. "Last I heard the mayor's missus crashed at your place. How's that affecting your love life?"

"Watch what you say." A second more of this and he'd order her out of his office.

"Fine." She sighed as if weary of the conversation. "Your father suggested that I ask you to escort me, so I thought I'd give it a shot."

His dad? That was even more suspect. "Why would he do that?" Other than to cause trouble between him and Paisley. Or to get back at him for inquiring about an affair.

"You'll have to ask him yourself."

"What's the event?" He kept his tone aloof. He knew better than to sound curious.

"It's an appreciation dinner for the leaders of the brigades." She grinned. "You're the best leader material we have in Basalt, Jude."

"Judah." He chose to ignore her flattery. "Thank you, but I decline." He pointed toward the door. "Let's get back to work, huh?"

"Calling the shots, now, *Mr.* Grant?"

He couldn't tell if she was being flirtatious, kidding, or insubordinate. "Yes, I am. You know the chain of command?"

She stood, gave him a mocking salute, then clicked her heels across the room. At the doorway, she paused, her hand on the doorjamb. "Come to the dinner, Jude. Tomorrow night at six. No escort required." She scurried out the door.

"Don't call me Jude!" He groaned. Why would his father encourage Mia to coax Judah into attending a dinner with her? Dirty manipulator, trying to control everything. He still hadn't broached the topic of how he might have gotten the job with Mike Linfield. Did his father coerce the manager into giving him the position?

If he influenced that, what about other suspicious things? Like Mia being at the same storm shelter with Judah. Her cot next to his. Her offering to drive him to Basalt when no one else would help him. Was that too farfetched to think his father could manipulate those things?

He pulled out his cell phone even though company policy restricted employees from texting during work hours.

Had the strangest visit from Mia. He punched in the letters and sent a text to Paisley. *She invited me to dinner at City Hall.*

???

As her escort.

As in DATE?

Maybe.

His phone vibrated.

"Hey."

"Mia Till asked you out on a date?" Paisley's tight voice. "The little snake!"

"She said 'escort.' I labeled it a date."

Craig strolled by the doorway, glared at Judah, then continued toward Mike's office.

"I have to go."

"Sorry. I had to call."

"That's okay." He got an idea. He swiveled the chair so his back faced the doorway. "What would you say to us crashing the dinner Mia just invited me to?"

Paisley snickered. "Are you kidding?"

"Nope. Will you be my date?"

"You bet!"

"Then I'll pick you up tomorrow evening."

Judah arrived to pick her up just before six the next day. Seeing her in a sexy, sleeveless royal blue dress, he whistled. She blushed and giggled. An excellent beginning to their evening.

On the front porch, he clasped her hand and kissed her cheek, wishing he brought a bouquet of flowers to celebrate their night out. "You look amazing."

"Thank you." She smiled, a little wide-eyed, like no one had complimented her in a long time. "You look pretty nice yourself." She touched a button on his pale blue shirt.

"Oh, yeah?" He nuzzled her ear with his nose, eliciting another chuckle. If he had more time, he'd kiss her with some sizzle she'd remember. Maybe later. He escorted her to his truck.

"How is this going to work? You didn't tell Mia you planned to attend, or about me coming with you, right?"

"No. If I did, we couldn't crash the party." He gave her what he hoped was a reassuring smile. "Don't worry. It'll be fun." He closed her door and dashed around to his side of the truck.

"Why are we doing this, again?" she asked when he was seated.

He started the engine. "Getting to the bottom of some things." He drove down Front Street and recalled what Mia said about him being a leader. It was silly to be pleased about that since she was only flattering him. Still, it stuck in his mind. "What neighborhood brigade are we in?"

"I'm with my dad, James, and others on their block."

"What about me?"

"Mia put you with the southern group." Her voice got quieter. "Same as Craig."

Judah groaned. "You and I are married. We should be in the same volunteer group."

"I know." She made a huffing sound. "I tried, but the mayor's Girl Friday wouldn't listen."

Hearing Mia called his dad's *Girl Friday* had the power to sour his evening. Something he couldn't let happen. Even if he and Paisley were assigned to different committees, he planned to enjoy his date with her. "I'll just sit in on your group."

"You will?"

"Of course. You and I are sticking together." He winked at her.

Their gazes held for a moment. When he pulled into a parking space next to the art gallery, Paisley turned toward her sister's building and let out a long sigh. Was something wrong?

"Ready?"

"Sure."

Inside the community hall, rectangular tables were spread with navy tablecloths. Mia and a couple of ladies bustled about setting out dinnerware.

A woman with long red hair—he couldn't place her name—wearing a white apron rushed up to them. "More Grants? Do you have reservations with the committee?"

Why the tone? Paisley's hand tensed in his, but she didn't say a word to the other woman.

"I have a place reserved." He released her hand and put his palm on her back. "My wife is attending with me. You remember Paisley?"

"How could I forget?" The redhead deadpanned. "Paisley."

"Lucy."

Ah. Lucy Carmichael. The two of them had some high school feud, if he remembered right.

"Can you make room for two?" He smiled at the server, hoping to dispel some of the tension.

"Mia won't like it." Lucy rolled her eyes. "Mia's in charge of *everything*! But since you're the mayor's son ..." She shrugged. "Whatever. Wait here." She rushed toward the far-left side of the room.

He rubbed his palm over Paisley's tight shoulders. What were the weird vibes between her and Lucy?

The redhead switched a couple of name tags and shuffled plates and glasses at one of the tables. She waved them over. He kept his hand at Paisley's back as they walked between the seated guests. He nodded at a couple of people.

"Lucy"—Mia skidded to a stop beside the woman rearranging chairs at the table—"what are you doing?" She spoke through clenched teeth.

"Making room for her." Lucy jerked her head toward Paisley.

Mia squinted at Paisley with a snobbish gleam that spiked Judah's irritation. "We didn't plan on *your* attendance. But, since you're here, protocol be tossed in the sea, right? Paisley, so nice of you to join us." Her tone turned sugary and fake sounding. She readjusted the name tags Lucy had switched. "This will never do." She grabbed one and thrust it into the redhead's hand. "Find another place for him."

Lucy strode down the center aisle and dodged around a few tables.

"Thanks for understanding, Mia."

"I understand. But will your father?" Head held high, she traipsed after Lucy.

He pulled out a chair for Paisley. "Sorry about that."

"It's okay."

Plates of food were soon placed in front of attendees. Roast beef and rice with a creamy gravy on top looked delicious. Smelled great too. One chair remained empty at their table.

Speeches commenced as brigade leaders introduced themselves and told success stories about people working together in the neighborhoods. They shared how tasks were getting accomplished as people pooled resources and assisted each other—all thanks to the mayor's and Mia's initiative, yada yada.

Judah recognized some of the points from the C-MER training manual. Their mission as a company included taking care of neighbors during storms and disasters. Did Mia take ideas from the workplace and bring them to life in the community? For the welfare of others? Or was there a more selfish reason behind her charitable actions?

Craig entered the community hall and strode toward their side of the room. Oh, no. The empty chair. Who planned this? Mia didn't know about Paisley attending. But she asked Judah. Did she place Craig across from him on purpose?

As soon as his coworker dropped into the chair, Paisley's troubled gaze flew to Judah's. *Don't panic*—he tried to convey. With her hand shaking, she lifted her fork of beef to her mouth. He might have to make their excuses and rush her out of the building. Take a beach walk to calm her.

Craig squinted toward them. Judah tried not to replicate his negative facial expressions.

Brad Keifer took the podium. "I'm sure some of you are surprised to find me here. I hate these meetings."

Folks laughed.

Judah nodded, surprised at the fisherman partaking in any civic duty.

"The thing is the beach is a mess all along the coast. We need volunteers to befriend our sea animals and help with cleaning up the plastic and debris-strewn beaches after the hurricanes."

He had Judah's interest.

A minute later, Paisley's brusque tone distracted him from Brad's speech.

"You're despicable," she stage whispered.

"What have I done now that displeases you?" Craig smirked.

At the front of the building, Brad appealed to locals to join forces and combat the trash plague. Judah focused on Paisley. Other than Craig being at their table, why was she so upset?

"You're a troublemaker and a dirty liar!" She wrenched her body and kicked Craig under the table.

What in the world?

Craig jerked and clenched his teeth. "Tame your wife, Judah."

"Paisley." He leaned toward her. "What's wrong?"

She clutched the edge of the table, her livid gaze aimed at Craig. "Why are you telling Paige falsehoods? Trying to hurt her? Or me?"

"What are you talking about?"

"What you told her. What you invented. It's all lies!"

Judah smoothed his hand over her shoulder. "Sweetheart, this isn't the time."

"No?" She shot to her feet, glaring at Craig as if he'd done the vilest thing imaginable. "Stay away from my sister! Stay away from me!" Her voice rose. "And keep your stinking lies to yourself."

Brad stopped speaking. Silence filled the room.

"Is there a problem here?" The mayor's voice bellowed over Judah's shoulder.

He stood slowly. His plan to crash the party was over. "Let's go," he whispered to Paisley, putting his hand at her elbow.

"What's going on?" someone asked.

"It's that crazy Cedars girl." A feminine voice guffawed. Lucy?

"Get her out of here," the mayor ordered.

His father's command tempted him to sit back down. Let Paisley kick the snot out of Craig. But if he did, he'd regret it later. So would she. He led her away from Craig, away from the mayor, away from the whisperings traveling from table to table.

"This is a nightmare." She jerked from his grasp, ran from the room, from the building.

He followed her into the night air. Laughter came from the assembly behind him.

Why did he think it would be a good idea for them to attend this meeting? "I'm so sorry." He unlocked the truck door and helped her climb inside.

She pulled away from him like she didn't want him touching her.

Just great. He ran around the rig, then climbed in behind the wheel. "What did Craig say to you?"

"He's a dirty, filthy, lying scum."

"Yes, but what did he say to you?"

She pounded her fists on top of the dashboard, groaning. "If only I were a man—"

Judah didn't put the key in the ignition. "What happened? Tell me."

She gave him an anguished look. "He told Paige that I ... that I kissed him. Loved him." She stared forward again, her hands buffing her arms. "Things were starting to get better between Paige and me. Now, this. When he sat with us, I couldn't stay silent. Couldn't do nothing."

"Of course, you couldn't. Come here." He scooted across the seat and pulled her into his arms. "Pais, I'm sorry. I wouldn't have wanted any of this to happen."

She leaned into his chest, shivering.

A thunderclap of adrenaline raced through him as he pondered her words. "Did he mean three years ago?"

"No. After the storm." She swallowed. "Paige is so mad at me. But I did not, would never, kiss that scumbag."

"I know." He sighed. Anything he said could be the wrong thing, but he had to try to comfort her. "I understand why you got upset. You and Paige will work this out. It'll be okay."

"How can it ever be okay again?" She drew in a raspy-sounding breath. "I'm getting blamed for things I didn't do. Paige ... she doesn't understand."

He had the urge to retrace his steps, grab Craig by the collar, and haul him outside to answer for his words. That would make him feel better. Wouldn't help Paisley. He needed to focus on her. "Do you want to come out to the cottage?"

"Why?"

"To talk things through." He smiled, trying to lighten the mood. "Drink coffee. Eat chocolate. Sit on the veranda and listen to the ocean."

"I have a better idea." Her eyes suddenly sparkled. "Do you know where Craig lives?"

"Uh, no. Why?"

"I want to cash in on that dare now. Remember, you owe me one thing."

"I do, but—"

With that mischievous gleam in her eyes, he wasn't going to like her idea.

Thirty-three

"What does the dare have to do with Craig's house?" Judah shuffled his hands over the steering wheel.

"We're going to bombard his house with mud!" She made a squealing sound.

"Wait a sec. Paisley, no way."

"Come on. I need your help." She reached out and clutched his right hand. "Please, help me do this. It'll be fun. You and me and mud …"

For a fraction of a second, he got lost in her coaxing tones. Lost in the idea of doing something so radically bizarre … with her. But taking revenge on a coworker's house with mud? That could get them into a lot of trouble. It wouldn't be very Christlike, either. "Sweetheart, throwing mud balls at someone's house isn't going to make the problem with that person go away."

"Of course, it won't. But it will make me feel better. Us, right?" She gripped his hand tighter. "You owe me for the dare." She challenged him with her gaze.

Of all the mischievous things she ever concocted, this one took the cake. How would he talk her down without making her angry with him?

"Couldn't you contact someone?"

"What do you mean? Contact who?" He slipped his hand away from hers. Started the engine. Giving himself time to figure out what to do next. What to say. Stalling. Someone had to be rational here.

"How about Mia? Call her and ask for Craig's address."

He couldn't believe she would suggest that he call Mia. "I will not." That's all he needed was for the receptionist to tell people—his father, or Deputy Brian—that he called and inquired about Craig.

Paisley clicked her fingernails against the dashboard, then pulled something out of her handbag. She held up the cell phone he purchased. "I'll check online for an address."

Groaning, he put the truck in gear and made a U-turn in the middle of the street.

"Where are you going? Judah, you're heading the wrong way." Her voice went higher. "He lives on the south side."

"I know. I'm taking you back to your dad's." He clenched his jaw. He'd rarely gone against something she wanted to do. But this idea of hers could get them both into a lot of trouble. Neither of them was spending the night in jail, if he could help it.

She lowered the phone. "So you're not going to help me?" She scowled, her mouth tugging downward into a pout.

"You told me you weren't doing these kinds of things anymore. That you changed." While true, that might be a sore subject for him to bring up.

"But Judah—"

"No, you came back here to make amends."

"Yes, but not with Craig." She groaned. "He caused me all kinds of trouble. He's lying and getting away with it."

"I know." He clutched the steering wheel. While he was aware of the evil things the guy had done, he couldn't give in. Wouldn't.

"Paige might not even talk to me." She slammed her phone down on the seat. "I can't find anything on him. Seems to be invisible."

"Let's go back to your dad's and talk. Maybe sit on the porch, okay?"

No answer.

"Paisley, I'm sorry. I just can't throw mud at someone's house."

"Because you're the mayor's son," she said in a snarky voice.

"No, not because I'm the mayor's son." He gritted his teeth at his own sharp response. "Because it's not right. And I'm trying to act like a Christian. A caring person in our community."

With jerky movements, she scooted to the far side of the seat, her back facing him.

"You shouldn't be doing those things, either. You're an adult."

"No kidding." She mumbled something about him not understanding her.

Terrific. Their first argument since getting back together was about Craig. "Paisley?" He kept his voice soft.

She didn't respond. He almost snickered at her slumped over, pouting position. He didn't. Of course, he didn't.

He parked next to Paul's house and shut off the engine. "Pais?"

While she didn't answer, she didn't leap out of the truck, either.

"I'm sorry Craig hurt you and Paige again. That makes me mad too." Frustration simmered in his chest, close to reaching the boiling point. Didn't he nearly go back into City Hall and take the jerk to task? But hurling mud at his house? Not happening.

She sniffled and cleared her throat as if suppressing her emotions. That twisted more angst inside him. What could he do to make peace between them? This night had turned out all wrong.

Then an idea came to mind. Something that might help to soothe her hurt feelings. Might make things better between them.

"I'm sorry for the lousy first date." He touched her back with the tips of his fingers. "I have an idea. Want to hear it?"

"No."

"It's a good one."

"I don't want to go out to the cottage with you."

"I know."

"Then what?" Her tone still sounded sharp.

"How about if we change into some grubby clothes, then we can talk about it?" He opened his door. "Meet me on the porch in ten minutes."

She whirled around. "You changed your mind?"

"Maybe." He hoped she wouldn't be too upset with his fudging.

She leapt out of the truck and sprinted up to her dad's porch. Her agility in her fancy dress and heels surprised him.

Inside the house, he talked to Paul and asked if he could borrow a change of clothes that might get messy. Paul agreed and told him where he could find a flashlight, too.

Ten minutes later, dressed in holey jeans and a thick flannel shirt with rips in the elbows, he scrounged in the shed for an old bucket. He also located two gardening spades. With Paul's flashlight in hand, he waited for Paisley on the porch.

She exited the door dressed in leggings and a long baggy sweatshirt. At least, she had her own clothes here. "Did you find out where Craig lives?" Her wide eyes sparkled like a kid on Christmas Day.

"Not quite." He hated to disappoint her. He placed the handle of the bucket over his right arm, still gripping the flashlight. Then he reached out his left hand toward her.

"What?" She frowned, not taking his hand. "We're not going to Craig's?"

"No, we're not." He nodded toward the beach. "Come on. This'll be fun too."

She groaned. "Where are you taking me?"

"I owe you for that dare and for the bad date."

"And?" She trudged warily beside him.

"It's low tide. Great mud on the flats."

"Really?" Her eyes widened. She may have cracked a smile. She walked faster.

He had to hurry to keep stride with her.

"What are we going to throw mud at?"

"We'll figure that out."

He kept the flashlight aimed toward the rocks as they descended to the beach below. The surf roared in the distance, but low tide would be perfect for gathering moist mud.

Once they reached the beach, she took off running toward the ocean. He ran too, glad his leg was improving, and relieved that she seemed distracted from her previous plans for retribution.

Just ahead, she squealed and laughed, sliding in a section of wet sand. "This will be perfect." She dashed back and grabbed one of the spades from him. Her eyes glowed in the light. "Come on." She took his hand this time.

She dropped to her knees next to a large muddy section. He set the flashlight on top of a two-foot rock, aiming it toward them. He shivered in the chilly air as he dropped beside her and set down the bucket.

For the next fifteen minutes, they dug up mud with their spades and formed balls—like snowballs without being frozen—with their hands. They laughed and joked, tossing around ideas about where they might hurl their collection, and he was relieved their previous tension seemed to be gone. He mentioned City Hall. She suggested Maggie's. Then she admitted she never wanted to do community service hours for that woman again.

Eventually, their bucket overflowed with globs of pressed mud. A pile rested on the beach too.

Judah stood with dirt-caked hands outstretched. Paisley stood also and showed him her muddy hands. Then, unexpectedly, she brushed her fingers against his cheeks, laughing.

"Hey!" He swiped his shirt sleeve over his face.

She cackled and ran in a wide circle, still within the light's glow. He chased after her, feeling like a teenager flirting with the cutest girl in school. He laughed and the wind chafed his cheeks, but the exercise kept him warm. He caught up to her and grabbed her hands. In the flashlight's beam, and beneath the brilliance of the moonglow, he kissed her. He didn't care if he still had mud on his face—and if he did, she was getting some of it. He might have even rested his palms against her cheeks.

She snuggled against his borrowed shirt. He wrapped his arms around her, holding her, being careful not to get any more mud on her.

"That was fun." She giggled. "But it's not over."

"No, it's not."

She pulled away. "Come on. Let's find our target!" She scooped up the pile of mud balls from the ground. "Where shall we throw them? Other than where I want to throw them?" She still had a mischievous gleam in her eyes.

He grabbed the flashlight, the small shovels, and the over-flowing bucket. "How about at one of the boulders on the peninsula?"

"Okay, but I'm going to pretend it's Craig's house."

"All right." He chuckled.

Their arms were full as they crossed the flats to the peninsula. The chilly wind pounded against them, but it didn't hamper their enthusiasm. When they got within throwing distance of some big rocks, Judah set down the items he held. He propped the flashlight so that it faced a boulder he hadn't classified with a letter of the alphabet before Blaine hit. "How about that one?"

"Looks good." She dropped her mud balls in the wet sand. "Are you game for a contest?"

"Uh, sure. What does the winner get?"

"Um." She gazed at the dark sky. "To set the date?"

His heart skipped a beat. "Our vow renewal ceremony date?"

"Mmhmm. Just remember, I'm good at this."

Living with this woman would never be boring. "You're on." He scooped up three mud balls the size of tangerines. One immediately disintegrated in his grip. "Oops."

Paisley snickered and compacted a wad of mud, working it between her hands. "My hands are freezing. How about yours?"

"Yep." He pressed one of the balls in his hands, following her lead. "Ready?"

"Ladies first." She hurled a mud ball straight at the boulder. Thud. It slammed hard against the rock and mud chunks flew outward. She cheered.

"One point for you." He threw the next mud ball. Thud. "Yes!"

"One to one." She hurled two in a row. Thud. Thud. "Take that, Craig Masters!"

Judah chuckled at how she was still getting her feeling of revenge but using a safer route. Since she threw two, so did he. Only one hit. Man. One point behind her, he had to focus.

"Three to two." She chortled.

"So it seems."

They used up their pile of mud balls faster than he could have imagined. Too bad they didn't make more of the muddy spheres. It was a blast throwing them. The score was eighteen to sixteen. Paisley missed once. He missed three times. Once because his mud ball fell apart before it reached its destination. He called for a mulligan, but she disagreed. Said they had to take what life gave them. Maybe she was trying to tell him something. But he remained intent on catching up and winning this contest, then he could set the date for their ceremony.

Four mud balls remained in the pile.

Paisley threw one. Missed! She groaned.

He didn't comment, but he was back in the game. He hurled the next one as hard as he could. Splat.

"Eighteen to seventeen!" She pulsed her fist in the air. "One more each."

"We could m-make some m-more." His teeth chattered. She must be cold too.

"Nah. Winner takes all." Easy for her to say. She wound up and flung the mud ball overhand. Smack. She whooped and hollered, leaving no doubt she hit her target.

249

No way to even the score now. He threw his last hardened clump of mud. At least it hit.

Paisley cheered. "I won!"

"You sure you don't want to make some more? Best of two rounds?"

"I'm ready to wash up and get warm."

"Yeah, me too."

She scooped up the pail and dropped the spades in. He grabbed the flashlight.

"So, you get to decide on the date." If it was up to him, he'd pick tomorrow, no doubt about it. But she won. He'd be a good sport about it.

"Yeah." She sighed. "That was fun. Safer than pelting Craig's house."

"Sure was." He took a chance. "Feel better?"

"Uh-huh. Sorry for getting so grouchy."

"Fifteen years ago, I would have gone along with you to Craig's."

She nudged his arm. "I didn't think you were that kind of teenager. Edward Grant's son. The perfect kid."

He balked. "Not perfect. I keep telling you that."

"Right. Right."

They climbed the rocks beneath the beach houses. Once they reached Paul's, they used the outside spigot to wash off the grit.

"Brrrrr. That water's freezing." She splashed liquid on her face, removing dirt smudges.

"I'll grab my clothes, then I should go." He rocked his thumb toward the street. "I have lots to do tomorrow."

"Okay." She tugged on his shirt sleeve, then leaned up and kissed his cheek. "Thank you."

He smiled, wanting to ask what she had in mind about a date for their vow renewal. But he'd be patient for a while longer.

Thirty-four

At first light, Paisley buttoned up her jacket and headed outside. Low tide made the air tangy, almost pungent, but even with the slightly abrasive scent, the roar of the waves in the distance drew her. Called to her.

As she trudged toward the seashore, making her way down the slippery rocks, she mentally rehashed yesterday's events. The trouble between her and Paige. The things Craig said. That kick she gave him was a stupid move. Childish, as Aunt Callie would say. But Judah's solution of making and throwing mud balls on the beach, even going along with a contest, turned out wonderful, and helped ease her frustration and embarrassment.

Now she had to decide how soon she wanted the vow renewal ceremony to be. Surely, Judah would ask her about it when she saw him today.

She kicked an empty white seashell and sent it tumbling into the water. Why did she feel reluctant? She loved him, so what was the problem? Was it her fear of them wandering into the same problems as before? Or of Judah getting so caught up in his career that he forgot about her. Or, maybe, of her dropping into a black hole of despair again.

Inhale. Exhale.

"Trust" skidded through her thoughts and burned a path right to her heart. Could she trust Judah to do what he said? That this time things would be different? Better, even?

She nudged a wad of seaweed with her boot and a crab scuttled down the beach. The waves rolled up the shoreline, crashing against boulders and driftwood, creating a cacophony of sound. A couple of times, she dashed up the beach to avoid getting splashed by the incoming tide. At the peninsula, white water billowed and crashed in such majestic beauty it tempted her to go out there. But she promised Judah she'd head out to the cottage and help him with the remodeling. No time for getting soaking wet today.

Not far ahead, a boulder she climbed on many times as a kid glistened in the morning sunshine. Eagerly, she strode toward it. Almost to the tide line, she climbed up, using her hands and knees for leverage, and centered herself on top of the rock. She shuffled her backside until her back faced town and the full panoramic view—the old cannery to her left, the bay straight ahead, the peninsula to her right—spread out before her in a spectacular display.

She could sit here all day, if she hadn't made plans, watching the waves roll in and pound the shoreline. Bursts of sea-foam exploded into the air near her. Her gaze followed the surf as it rushed out to sea, then rolled back in, the process repeating itself over and over. Like life's rhythms. A storm. The calm. A storm. Then peace.

Was that like her and Judah? What if another storm hit

their marriage? What if she got pregnant and lost their child again? She couldn't bear to think of that. Her eyelids clamped shut as she felt the pain of loss, the agony of grief, pressing in on her. Losing a baby had felt like it almost killed her. She couldn't risk that again. But to never have children because of her fear didn't make sense, either. So where did that leave her?

She opened her eyes, staring at the waves. Judah probably wanted kids. Was that one of the reasons she put off setting a date?

She sat on the boulder long enough for the waves to hit the rock beneath her. Water splattered onto her pants. She pulled her feet higher. If she didn't get off this chunk of basalt, she'd be forced to wade into the sea to reach dry land. And yet, she stayed.

A few minutes later, she heard something. What—? Strong arms wrapped around her. Craig? She twisted, wrenching her upper body, and attempted to free her striking elbow—just in case.

"Whoa. Pais, it's me."

Judah? She exhaled a breath. "What are you doing? Why didn't you say something?" She faced him as he dragged her off the rocky perch.

He grinned, holding her in his arms. "Sorry. I wanted to surprise you."

"Oh, you did."

He waded through knee-deep water. "What are you doing out here? Planning to swim back?"

"Maybe." He smelled good and spicy. Might be nice to snuggle her nose into his neck. Press her cheek against his skin.

He tripped, or else faked tripping, so she had to cling to him tighter. When he reached dry ground, he set her down. "Good thing I came along to rescue a lady in distress, huh?"

She smacked his arm. "Do you see anyone in distress?"

"Not anymore."

"I suppose if I needed rescuing, which I'm not admitting I did, you are the cutest rescuer in Basalt." She kissed his cheek.

"Nice to hear. Want to beach walk with me?"

"Sure." That sounded more inviting than remodeling work.

They strolled across the city beach in comfortable silence. How did he know where to find her? Was he here to ask about the date for their ceremony?

They crossed to the other side of the peninsula, following the rocky shoreline on the west side of town. Noticing the C-MER building up ahead, nestled between some sand dunes, she asked, "How's the job going?"

"Not great." He pointed toward his workplace. "The mayor is taking credit for my rehire."

"What? You're kidding."

"He's meddling and interfering."

"And Craig?"

Judah's eyebrows rose.

"I mean, you have his position. How's he handling that?"

"What you witnessed last night shows how he feels about it." Judah drew her around a large piece of driftwood.

"Is that why—"

"Can we not talk about Craig?"

His abrupt tone surprised her. "Okay." Didn't he say they could discuss anything?

"I'm sorry." Stopping, he rubbed his hand over his forehead.

"When your dad said you went for a hike, I panicked, thinking you might be out on the peninsula."

"So that's why you came to my supposed rescue."

He didn't smile this time. He heaved a sigh.

"What's wrong?"

"I'm just … sorry … for how things came down last night. Sorry that I put you in such an awkward situation at that dinner."

"It's okay. Craig's the jerk."

"We can agree on that. So, we're okay?"

"We're okay." She smiled and linked their fingers. "I enjoyed our target practice."

He nodded toward the roiling sea. "For the last two weeks, everything has been in chaos. But when I'm with you the uncertainty goes away. I just want to be with you."

"You're that for me too." She stepped closer, hoping he could handle her honesty. "But I also have doubts. How things turned out before plays over in my mind."

He nodded, sighed. "Would you mind if we hiked farther? I wanted to show you something down the beach."

"Sure. Are we going out to the lighthouse?"

"Not that far."

"C-MER?"

"Nope. It's a secret." He smiled like some of his tension eased. The problems with his dad and mom must be bothering him. And her saying she still had doubts probably wasn't encouraging for him, either.

The wind picked up and gusted harder against them, but they trudged forward. The waves pounded up the shoreline in a constant roar, rolling closer with the incoming tide. When they headed back, they'd have to climb on the rocks and hike near the trees since the beach would soon be under water.

A couple of raindrops hit her nose. "Uh-oh." She pulled up the hood on her jacket.

Judah zipped his coat. "We better hurry." He pointed toward the western sky where dark gray clouds piled up over the Pacific.

Ever since Blaine, she didn't care to see an approaching storm. "Maybe we should head back."

"We're almost there. Come on."

It was difficult to resist his grin. "Okay."

"Unless the weather report is wrong, the squall will head out to sea quickly."

"That's good to hear."

He knew this beach as well as she did, maybe better since he worked the coastline for eleven years. He knew where to hunker down to wait out a storm, if it came to that.

He led her past the clump of rocks where she and Peter built a fort when they were kids. Past a pile of driftwood they called their pirate ship. How many times did she walk the gangplank there? They trudged over the C-MER dock where part of it sat on dry ground. With Judah's workplace so close, she wanted to mention his employment again, but she refrained since it seemed like he didn't want to discuss it.

Farther down the beach, the lighthouse, a broken-down relic of yesteryear, sat as a testament to the town's history with water safety. Many times, her parents had warned her and Peter to stay away from the crumbling monument. Only once did they dare to hike that far. Their secret.

"Here it is." Judah turned to the right, guiding her up the rocks that made a natural barrier between the ocean and the land.

She noticed some giant boulders where cracks between the rocks made cool hiding places. She remembered that from childhood excursions with Peter. Judah stopped in front of a large rock that was as tall as him and had branches leaning against it. He grabbed several limbs and tossed them aside.

"My coworkers found this after Blaine." He yanked a few more branches away, exposing a cave-like opening within the formation.

She bent over and saw all the way through the rock to the other side. "Oh. That's awesome."

"The waves during Addy and Blaine must have crashed against the weakened stone. Then chunks washed away under the pressure of the storm surge. Only the outer layer remained." Judah rested his hand on the stone roof. "Should be stable. My guys checked it out."

The rain suddenly fell hard as if the clouds were wringing themselves out overhead. They laughed and lifted their faces into the moisture. She opened her mouth, catching some drops. He did too. It reminded her of other times they played on the beach in the rain when they were dating, then later in the early days of their marriage. Happy memories.

If they didn't take shelter, they'd soon be soaked. She ducked down and settled into the hollow place in the rock. On her bottom, with knees bent, she wrapped her arms around her legs. Judah squeezed in beside her, snuggling his right arm around her shoulders. His closeness, his warmth, made it easy to relax despite the rain and wind just beyond their hiding place.

"The rain can't reach us here."

She wiggled her shoes. "Maybe just our feet."

He gave her a wry grin. "My shoes are already soaked."

"The price of hero-hood." She snickered as she thought of him wading into the surf and scooping her off the boulder.

"I don't feel very heroic." He sighed, staring toward the ocean with a troubled look.

"Why do you say that?"

Raindrops dripped from his hair down his cheek. Reaching up and snagging them with her fingers was tempting. But she didn't want to disrupt his thoughts or whatever he was about to tell her.

"The job. How I got it." He gulped. "It bothers me that my coworkers blame me for getting promoted and Craig getting demoted. Although, they don't know the whole story. I'm not going to explain it to them, either."

"Is he causing trouble?"

"According to Mia."

Paisley grumbled at hearing the woman's name. "What will you do?"

"I haven't decided. Still praying about it."

He wiped a wet strand of hair off her cheek, their gazes getting lost in each other's. His cool fingers skidded over her facial skin. She caught her breath, surprised by the strong reaction every time he touched her.

He drew in a sharp breath too. Did he feel the same way? But then he glanced away, sighing. "Mind if I ask you something?"

"Go ahead."

"Have you thought any more about us saying our vows?"

"Thought about it?"

He nodded. "Other than the renovation of your dad's house and the cottage, is there something hindering us from moving forward?" His expression was vulnerable yet cautious.

She gulped. "When we're together, like this, there's nothing I want more than to be with you. Married. Life partners. Crazy in love."

"Me too." He grinned.

"But when I think about the wifely stuff, I get a thick lump in my throat. Sort of emotional heartburn."

"Wifely stuff, huh?"

"Not the intimate stuff," she clarified, and her cheeks burned.

"Oh?" He tipped his head, staring at her.

"It's the what-if-I-fail-as-a-wife stuff."

"Pais." The sweetest smile crossed his lips.

She'd better glance away. Because if she didn't—

His cool mouth fell across hers with the most delicate, delicious caress. Heavens. How could he do that, make her feel like the 4th of July fireworks exploded around her, in the middle of a fall storm? Especially when she felt windblown and frumpy.

He touched the tips of their noses together, Eskimo kissing her. She opened her eyelids that she didn't even mean to close and stared into his blue eyes. Her heart pounded out a vigorous beat.

"Our love is going to get us through everything. Wifely stuff. Husbandly stuff." He pointed at the massive rock structure above them. "Just like this shelter covers us from bad conditions. Protects us. That's what our love will do, too, if we'll let it. What God's love will be for us. The best refuge imaginable."

If only she grasped what seemed to come so easily, so naturally, for him. Grace. Trust. Belief. Even love. "I failed before."

"So did I." His knuckles smoothed over her cheeks. "All I want is to be with you. To be there for you in good times and in bad. In hurricanes and in balmy seas. For us to love each other for the rest of our lives—warts and all."

"You think I have warts?" She snorted.

"I have some." He snickered. "But your warts are cuter."

"Right."

His lips caressed hers again, feather soft. Sweeter than before. Longer than before. His kisses deepened, becoming more passionate. She didn't pull away. Wouldn't have stopped. But he did. He pulled back a couple of inches, his dazed gaze dancing with hers. *Deep blue sea in the morning!* The deep emotion she felt for those few moments sent shockwaves through her system. She gazed into his eyes, trying to convey that she wanted more of what they just experienced. Apparently, he was choosing to exercise restraint. Still being a gentleman. She sighed.

"I will fail you, at some point, I'm sorry to say."

His words cooled her right down.

"And you will fail me."

His admission, while unsettling, touched her heart. Moisture filled her eyes. Was rain getting into her face again?

"We're both human and flawed. But this life—"

She took his hand in hers, listening, wanting to hear every word.

He swallowed. "This life can be hard. We found that out before. But, together"—he gripped her hands—"you and me together, we're stronger, better, more vibrant, more alive, and we'll make it. Not just barely, either. Our love is going to thrive." His voice rose. "Grow stronger. I can't wait to get started on our forever."

"Me, either."

A calm she hadn't felt in years filled her soul. But would it last?

Thirty-five

For three years, Paisley dreaded this day. Her limbs shook. Her heart thudded in her temples. Her hands clutched two clusters of flowers she bought at the grocery store tight enough to break the stems.

Judah trudged beside her across the expanse of grass that had been cleaned of debris since the hurricane, probably by one of the brigade groups. He told her he came to the cemetery a few times over the last couple of years. A comforting thought. Still, the ache that had been building within her throbbed with each beat of her heart, with each footstep bringing her closer to her baby's gravesite.

I can do this.

If she hyperventilated and fainted, at least the grass would soften her fall.

Judah led them beyond the tall headstones, past the rows of inground grave markers of previous residents, past the crematorium. With each step, she felt herself slowing down. Taking more breaths. Compensating for her anxiety.

At the far side of the lawn, a white picket fence that encircled a cluster of tiny grave markers came into view. One step through the gate, she froze. Several days had passed since her last full-on panic attack. *God, help me,* she prayed even though she still hated desperate prayers.

"Paisley? You okay?"

"I n-need a m-minute."

He took one of the clusters of flowers. "Here, sweetheart. Hold my hand. Lean on me."

She inhaled, then exhaled, and gripped his hand. Should she search for five things to distract herself? After a couple of deep cleansing breaths, she breathed easier and was able to move forward again.

Judah stopped and knelt beside a tiny marker. She dropped to her knees beside him. Leaning into him, she let him be the strength she lacked. She laid the yellow and orange cluster of flowers next to the words forever ingrained in her heart.

Misty Gale, daughter of Paisley and Judah Grant

Trembling, she laid her hand on the damp grass. "I love you, Misty Gale. Will always love you. I've never forgotten you. Never will." She sniffed, fighting tears.

"Me too," Judah added. "Daddy loves you."

Daddy. Hearing that tender endearment unraveled her emotionally. It seemed her soul cracked open and wretched tears cascaded down her face. She collapsed into Judah's arms, crumpling onto his lap. He held her and rocked her. He sniffled then whispered something about God's love pouring over them. He didn't rush her. They kept their arms wrapped around each other for a few minutes, sharing in their grief.

After a while, he stood and assisted her to her feet. "Can

you handle seeing the other one?" His understanding and kindness meant a lot to her.

"I'm going to try." She scrubbed away the last vestiges of tears and what little makeup she put on this morning.

As they strolled through the gate, she glanced back. She'd return another day. Maybe then she wouldn't feel so broken. Or maybe that gripping emotion never went away.

They walked between the rows of inground markers. Judah stopped at another grave but didn't kneel. She stood beside him and read the engraving.

Penny Cedars, beloved wife and mom

Due to her previous emotional outburst, Paisley felt weepy again. She dropped to her knees and Judah didn't miss a beat. He knelt beside her, supporting her. She set the flowers next to a cluster that was wilted. Who had been here recently? Dad?

"I'm a terrible daughter. I'm sorry that I missed her funeral." She drew in a tattered breath. "My dad might never forgive me."

"I'm sure he will. And you have a beautiful heart, Pais." Judah held her, leaning his head against hers. "God's grace heals things. He's got this too."

"I told my dad I'm sorry."

"I'm sure he understands."

"I hope so." She stood, staring at her mom's name. Then, as they strode down the grassy slope toward the truck, she sighed in relief. "That was tough."

"It'll get easier."

"You're saying I should come back to Mom's grave?"

He gave her a sad smile. "It's up to you."

"Then I won't."

He chuckled lightly.

"Why are you laughing?"

"I'm sorry. You are just so stubborn sometimes."

"What? That's not nice." But, at least, his comment made her feel more combatant, instead of emotional.

"Don't get me wrong. I love your stubbornness."

She stopped walking. "*My* stubbornness?"

He linked their pinkies. "It's your Cedars' stubbornness that will help you remember that you want to marry me again. And it's your stubbornness that will prove to you and me and this whole town that you love me with all your heart."

"My stubbornness is going to do all that?"

"Yep. Just watch and see."

Hmm. She'd have to think about that.

Thirty-six

On Monday afternoon, Paisley tackled the walls of the cottage while Judah was at work. Being here gave her a sense of what it might be like to live in this house again. It already felt homey, so she didn't have to worry about feeling like a stranger.

When Judah got home, they tossed frozen prepackaged meals into the microwave the way they used to do, ate quickly, then kept pounding away on the renovation. He explained C-MER's plans to restore the peninsula and how signs were posted for people to stay off the dangerous rocks.

"That means you too." He squinted at her.

"You know me. I always obey signs on the beach."

He guffawed. "I don't want to drag you out of the drink again."

"But you would, right?"

He stared at her a good thirty seconds. "But I would." He stood close enough that his breath touched her cheek. Clearing his throat, he stepped back. "We should talk."

His abrupt change in tone sent up a mental alarm. "About?"

"Just stuff. Want to walk down to the beach?"

"I always want to walk to the beach, but we have all this work to do." She lifted her mud spreading tool.

He held out his hand toward her. "Please, come with me?"

"Of course." She set down the tool then clasped his hand.

Isn't this what she hoped for, that they would walk on the beach and talk when he came home from work? Why would she even delay exchanging vows with this man, living with him—eating with him, watching the stars together, and sharing a bedroom—when being this close to him stirred her heart to such a frenzy?

They stopped by the outside spigot to wash their hands, then trudged over the slight rise in the sand toward the seashore. When they reached the place where the waves rolled up to the highest point on the sand, they stopped and faced the water. The ocean's rhythmic melody soared in her mind like a symphony reaching a powerful crescendo.

"I was thinking—"

"You need to—"

They spoke at the same time.

"You first."

"I'd rather kiss you than talk." He brushed loose strands of hair from her face yet didn't bridge the gap between them. "Before you set the date for our vow renewal, there are things we promised we'd talk about."

"Oh, um, don't forget about going on some dates." She grasped for something to keep things light.

"More mud flinging?" He grinned.

"Might be nice to get dressed up and go somewhere fancy."

"I agree."

They stood silently for several minutes.

Then Judah sighed. "The day I came to Chicago, based on the detective's information about you, I waited outside your apartment in a rental car, watching your door."

Her body reacted to his words before her mind did. Her heart hammered faster. Her skin became clammy. He went to her apartment and sat in a car watching her door? Why?

He covered his face with both palms and groaned.

That freaked her out. "What is it, Judah?"

He lowered his hands. "What's in the past is in the past. Whatever happened, I already forgave you." He met her gaze with a tortured look. "I want a future with you, no matter what we talk about today. Is there even any reason to rehash our old stuff?"

Was he letting her opt out of a difficult discussion? "Only if it still hurts you."

His face crumpled as if her words stabbed him.

"Tell me."

"You were with another man." Tension strained his voice. "I waited forty-five minutes. A guy went into your apartment. Didn't come out. So I waited."

She swallowed with difficulty. During her three years away, she went on a couple of outings with coworkers. Two dates. Times when she wanted to forget Basalt. Bury her past. But this—

"Why come all the way to Chicago and not talk to me?" She stuffed down her apprehension and fear and went for gut honesty. "I was lonely. Grieving. Felt abandoned. By you. My dad. God. Even Misty Gale. I-I would have wanted to see you." Even in her darkest time, she would have wanted to know he came looking for her.

He groaned again. "When you came outside dressed up, your arm linked with some guy's, I froze." He stared hard at her. "He kissed you. Maybe on your cheek, I don't know, but I saw red. You giggled and touched his arm the way you used to do with me. I'd heard rumors. Tried not to listen. Even when my dad—" He bit his lower lip. "But there you were. There he was."

Her heart pounded frantically. She inhaled and exhaled, controlling her breathing. "Was it in December?"

"Yes."

"Must have been Glen, a guy I met at the diner."

What were the chances of Judah crossing two-thirds of the country on the same day she had a date? And waiting forty-five minutes? Did he assume they were doing something that would make reconciling even more difficult? Oh, Judah. That agonized look in his eyes hurt her heart.

"Why didn't you just get out of the car and say something?" Thinking of how he must have felt angry and betrayed gnawed on her emotions.

"The kiss. The laughter. I hated to imagine how far you may have strayed from our marriage." He lifted his hands in a helpless gesture. "For my own mental health, I had to get out of there. Even your note spoke of someone else."

Her note. A Dear John letter tucked under his pillow. What a terrible way to have told him she was leaving.

"I wanted to belt the guy in the face, so I left." He stared at the sand.

"We went out around Christmastime." She rubbed her forehead. "Judah"—she made herself say his name softly—"is this a deal breaker?"

"What? No. Absolutely not." He huffed. "I thought we should talk about it, that's all. Be honest with each other."

"Okay." She didn't want to drive another wedge between them, but he brought this up. "What if I did more in that forty-five minutes?" She felt raw and vulnerable even asking.

He made a moaning sound. Gazed up at the sky.

"We were separated." She took a step back, her boots settling in the sand. "Minus the divorce papers, our marriage had ended. I'm sorry, but if I did cross that line, would you still want to renew our vows?"

"Yes, of course!"

If eyes were windows to the soul, she searched his for truth. What if she did the worst thing imaginable? She'd thought of doing it. Of forgetting every promise she ever made.

She was thankful that she hadn't. Judah was hurt enough by her actions and the lies swirling around town about her. But she needed to know where his heart was in this matter. He talked about grace, said he forgave her, but how far did that grace stretch?

"Judah?"

He drew in a long breath. "I didn't want to bring up this stuff. I've avoided it. But I want us to talk about everything—even the difficult things. I want a clean slate when we make new promises to each other." He stared out toward the bay, then faced her again. "Even a messy chalkboard can be wiped clean. That's what I'm hoping for us, no matter what happened in the past."

She kicked at a mound of sand. "All this time that we've been getting closer, talking about renewing our wedding vows, you thought I may have been intimate with someone else. How could you do that?" She couldn't fathom what struggles he went through. Even though he thought she might have been unfaithful, beyond the unfaithfulness of leaving him, he didn't condemn her. Instead, he wooed her, kept saying he loved her, showed her such beautiful grace. What kind of man did that? She didn't deserve such a man. Such love.

"Don't get me wrong." He blew out a breath. "I prayed it hadn't come to that."

She nodded, holding her tears and emotions in check.

For several heartbeats they stared at each other. Then he spread out his hands toward her, a tender, inviting expression on his face. She didn't hesitate to step into his embrace. She wrapped her arms around him, clinging to him. He held her, his chin resting against her head. His heart beat strong beneath her ear. She sighed.

Needing to say one more thing, she leaned back. "I told you before that I'm sorry for hurting you."

"You did."

"I'm sorry about this too. For the way I hurt you when you saw me with someone else." She imagined Mia flirting with him and how that drove her crazy. "Nothing else happened with Glen. I want you to know that."

His eyelids closed for a moment. Then he smiled at her. "That's good to hear. Thank you for telling me." He stroked his thumb down her cheek. "I can't wait to marry you."

She watched his gaze land on her lips, the question in his eyes. She didn't close the gap. Didn't flirt with him—yet.

"Is there anything else about my leaving that you want to ask me?" They talked about it when she was locked in the bathroom during the hurricane. But she wanted a clean slate, too.

"Maybe just one thing." He led her back along the beach. By his silence, he still wrestled with something. Then, "How did you and Craig meet?"

****

Maybe Judah should have left well enough alone. Paisley's question about whether he'd still want to get back together if she had been with someone else momentarily stunned him. But he came to terms with that a couple of years ago. Forgiveness was forgiveness. Still, he felt relieved by what she told him. And he was curious about—

"Mia introduced us."

"Mia?"

"At Hardy's Gill and Grill, she joked about us being a C-MER family. Then she disappeared, leaving Craig and me alone."

A kick in his gut.

"I've resented her for three years. Hated that you work with such a flirt. Then, the other day, Craig started to tell me something about your dad's involvement in what happened that night." She grimaced like she was afraid of what his reaction might be. "I shouldn't have mentioned it. Sorry. I just—" She groaned and took off walking fast.

"Wait!" He jogged to catch up with her, his shoes sliding in the sand. "I want to hear what you have to say. Please, tell me."

"I don't want it to cause more trouble between us. More hurt."

"It won't. I promise." He clasped her hands.

A seagull squawked overhead. The sea roared alongside them, but he zeroed in on his wife's voice and her lovely dark eyes staring into his gaze.

"Craig didn't get the chance to finish explaining." She adjusted their hands so their pinkies linked. "But I must find out if Edward was involved in that fiasco, even if it means talking to Craig again. Even if it means unearthing something hurtful in the past."

Was his father embroiled in that incident? Or was Craig just trying to make himself sound less offensive?

"How about if we find out together?" Judah wanted answers too.

"That would be great." She smiled, looking relieved. "Thank you."

She stepped closer to him and smoothed her palms over the upper part of his jacket the way she did sometimes when they were about to kiss. He slid his arms around her, his hands coming to rest against her back. He liked this—holding her in his arms and her gazing up warmly at him.

"You know how you asked me to marry you?"

The atmosphere shifted and felt charged with electrical currents.

"Yes?" His heart did triple beats.

"And I won the dare, so I get to choose a date ..."

"I remember." He was thankful they faced some difficult things and were still clinging to each other. "If it were up to me, I'd marry you right now."

"That might be a little tricky to arrange."

A surge of hope rushed through him. "Want to go over to City Hall and check?"

Her jaw dropped. "You want *the mayor* to marry us?"

"Not really. We can ask Pastor Sagle." Their elopement pulsed through his thoughts. "Although, he turned us down last time."

"True. He may want to offer us marital counseling first." She lifted an eyebrow. "We might need it, too."

He groaned. "That could take weeks. City Hall it is."

"Didn't you say I'm worth the wait?" She winked at him.

"I did. And you are."

She tipped her head and gave him a flirty grin, even licking her lips as if anticipating a kiss. *Ah, Pais.* She was reeling him in with her soft gaze, her moist lips, her smile. He chuckled and succumbed, kissing her like a starving man. A man who loved his wife with all of his heart and wanted her to come home with him.

"How about one week?" She spoke softly against his mouth. "Then you and I will be Mr. and Mrs. Judah Grant again."

"One day?"

She giggled and leaned her cheek against his chest. Did she hear his heart galloping? With each beat he said her name, said he would always love her. And he thanked God for bringing them back together.

"Judah?" Her lilting voice was music to his soul. "I wish I never left you."

His heart nearly stopped. What could he even say to that? "I'm so glad you're with me now."

"Me too."

Holding her in his arms for the rest of his life would be a dream come true. One week? What was seven days compared to waiting three years? It would give them time to finish the cottage. Time to pass out invitations. Have that marriage counseling session.

Then let the romancing of a lifetime begin.

Nothing was going to stop them from being together.

I hope you enjoyed *Bay of Refuge* and are rooting for Judah and Paisley's journey together. Please write a review wherever you purchased this book. They say reviews are the lifeblood for authors, and I would consider it a personal favor if you wrote one. Even one line telling what you liked or thought about the book is helpful. Thank you!

I took many creative liberties with Basalt Bay, my imaginary town on the Oregon Coast. To all those who live nearby, please forgive my embellishments. I enjoy the Pacific Ocean and the Oregon Coast so much that I wanted to create my own little world there

If you would like to be one of the first to hear about Mary's new releases and upcoming projects, sign up for her newsletter— and receive the free pdf "Rekindle Your Romance! 50+ Date Night Ideas for Married Couples." Check it out here:

www.maryehanks.com

Thank you to everyone who helped make this story a reality!

Paula McGrew . . . You are a gem for walking this journey with me. Thank you for fine-tuning my words and ideas. I appreciate you so much!

Suzanne Williams . . . I love your creative designs. Thanks for bringing these covers to life!

Jason Hanks . . . Thanks for always supporting me and reminding me that I am a writer. I love your encouraging texts!

Kathy Vancil, Kellie Wanke, Mary Acuff, Beth McDonald, Joanna Brown, and Jason Hanks . . . Thank you so much for being willing to read this installment, even though it was during the holidays, and being excited to do so. That cheered my heart! I appreciate all of you giving your time to this project. Thanks for finding things I overlooked and helping me dig deeper into Judah's and Paisley's hearts.

(This story is a work of fiction. Any mistakes are my very own! ~meh)

Daniel, Philip, Deborah, & Shem . . . You always and forever have this mama's love.

Readers … I'm humbled and thrilled that you are reading my work and following this series. Thanks so much for your kindness and support!

www.maryehanks.com

Books by Mary Hanks

Restored Series

Ocean of Regret

Sea of Rescue

Bay of Refuge

Tide of Resolve

Waves of Reason (2021)

Second Chance Series

Winter's Past

April's Storm

Summer's Dream

Autumn's Break

Season's Flame

Marriage Encouragement

Thoughts of You (A Marriage Journal)

Youth Theater Adventures

Stage Wars

About the Author

Mary Hanks loves stories about marriage restoration. She believes there's something inspiring about couples clinging to each other, working through their problems, and depending on God for a beautiful rest of their lives together—and those are the types of stories she likes to write. Mary and Jason have been married for forty-plus years, and they know firsthand what it means to get a second chance with each other, and with God. That has been her inspiration in writing the Second Chance series, and now in the Restored series.

Besides writing, Mary likes to read, do artsy stuff, go on adventures with Jason, and meet her four adult kids for coffee or breakfast.

Connect with Mary by signing up for her newsletter on her website.

"Like" her Facebook Author page:

www.facebook.com/MaryEHanksAuthor

www.maryehanks.com

Made in the USA
Columbia, SC
16 May 2021